Chasing Hartes

MADYN ROSE

Pencil & Page

To all the single moms, thank you.
Here's to finding your happily ever after, the one you were or weren't looking for.

Chapter One

Millie

It was officially my birthday, and my best girlfriends Lisa, Sam, and Gia insisted on doing something big for my thirtieth, despite my protests. Since my birthday fell at the end of frigid January, they chose a weekend cruise to the Bahamas that included the promise of endless beaches, sun, and an all-inclusive drink package.

I hadn't been on vacation for a long time. As a single mother, I spent my money on living expenses and savings for my daughter's future. Aubree's now four, and it was her weekend with her dad. I had no reason to turn down the trip. It was only when I stood on the deck of the cruise ship, staring at the crystal blue waters, that I realized how much I missed *me* time. It had been so long that I almost didn't remember what it was like to be out of mom mode.

While we walked near the bar, Lime and Coconut, I

noticed the abundant number of shirtless men on the deck. I swear they weren't here earlier when we walked through.

"Have I been under a rock? All I see are abs," I whispered to Lisa as nothing but beautiful people surrounded us. It felt like I was standing in the middle of a swimsuit photo shoot. Jesus, what have I been missing? I felt overdressed in my denim shorts and purple t-shirt.

"Isn't it wonderful?" Lisa laughed. "Four glorious days of this view." She looked like a kid in a candy store as she shamelessly eye-fucked anyone who even glanced at her. "This may have been my best idea yet."

"Like anything? You could have your pick. Did you not see how many of them have been checking you out?" Gia nudged me.

"Guys, I told you, it's not happening. I'm not on this trip to bang some random guy."

"I disagree. That's exactly what you should do," Gia said.

I shook my head. I knew the girls would push some muscle-bound moron in my direction, hoping I'd throw caution to the wind, and let loose for once. They had been pointing out every man who didn't have a ring since we left Toronto.

"Yeah Mils, when was the last time you got some?" Sam asked.

I stayed silent. They all knew the last time I had sex was with my ex, Nick. Five long years ago. Nick was the only guy I had ever been with, and he was nothing but heartbreak. I guess I should have known better than to fall for a musician.

"Alright, people. It's time for the Mr. Caribbean contest," a thunderous voice came over the speakers. A group of women standing next to us started to cheer and whistle and, to no surprise, Lisa joined them, pushing us toward the edge of the rail for a better view down to the stage.

"Time to start the party," she hollered.

"I think it's already started," I mumbled while a large group of women in matching shirts rushed around us, trying to get a peek. *Jeez, girls, it's only shirtless guys.*

I was pushed to the side when it felt like I hit a brick wall. My hands flew up as a reflex, landing against a perfectly sculpted chest. I looked up into a deep-tinted pair of sunglasses and a faint five o'clock shadow across a strong jawline. He flashed me a brilliant smile, showing off two spectacular deep dimples. "Hey."

He bounced his pecs, my hands still on them. And for the love of God, I squeezed them. I could see him struggling to keep his face straight. Mortified, I withdrew my hands like they had caught on fire. My face burned in embarrassment. Holy Shit, I wanted to fling myself off the ship to escape. I stepped sideways, stumbling over someone's foot, but he put his arms around me, stopping my impending face-plant. My nose landed right in his chest, and damn, he smelled good. *Don't sniff.* I warned myself before I pushed away from him and disappeared into the crowd. The sound of his chuckle hung in my ears.

"You squeezed his pecs. Hilarious." Lisa snorted behind me. "Were they as fabulous as they looked? All hard and manly? Shit, Mils, let's go back. Take him. Did you see how he grinned at you?"

Of course, I saw. His dimples were like a flashing beckon to my lady bits. But there was no way I admitted that to Lisa. Instead, I muttered for her to drop it.

When we got back to the room, I noticed they decorated our door with happy birthday signs and the number thirty cut out. I turned to Lisa.

"What, did you think we wouldn't make a spectacle of it?" She wrapped her arms around me and squeezed. Oh, I knew they would. They always did. Birthdays were big with these girls and I was forever grateful, even when they embarrassed me.

"Now hurry and shower. We've got shit to do." She smacked my butt and waved me off, disappearing down the hall.

I stood in the shower, my mind relentlessly replaying what had just happened. *I squeezed his pecs.* They were perfect, too. Like freaking *Thor,* or whichever god gave him a body like that. My brain went to how his thick arms wrapped around me like I was nothing. And damn, his smile was even better. Pearly whites flanked by deep dimples. I was a sucker for dimples. The thought of him sent a flash of heat through my body. What is wrong with me? I swallowed hard and turned the water to cold.

I had finished my shower when Lisa came into our room with drinks in hand. We were sharing a cabin while Sam and Gia, who were a couple, were a few doors down. Lisa set my frozen drink down and picked up one of the sports bras I had left out, holding it like it was a bomb.

"Seriously? Is this what you brought? This wouldn't attract a man who just got out of prison. It looks like it would give you a uni-boob."

I rolled my eyes. "I have no need for anything else."

"We're on a cruise in the Bahamas. There's bound to be some hot single guy out for a weekend fling. Hell, I'd like to have a no strings attached romp, too."

"Lis, all you ever have are no strings attached romps."

She shrugged, not denying it. "You know, a fling might be what you need to get out of this, uh, dry spell."

"I love you to death, but you know I have a no dating rule. I have enough issues right now. I don't need to add playing the love game again." It was bad enough that my one and only relationship blew up and left a shattered heart and a cave-sized hole of self-doubt. The thought of adding anyone else to my

4

bizarre co-parenting hell was more than I could take. I shuddered at the mere thought.

"I never said you had to date. Have a good old-fashioned one-night stand. This is the perfect time to indulge. Love him, and leave him, literally. When you get off the cruise, go your separate ways. No harm, no foul."

"Oy. It's not so easy," I groaned.

"Actually, it is. It's not like you'll have to run into whoever it is again. That's the beauty of a vacation fling. What happens on vacation stays on vacation."

My face fell flat. "That's Vegas."

"Same thing." She waved her hand in the air. "Besides, if you're not sure, give him a fake name and number. He won't know until you're long gone."

"That's so wrong," I admonished.

Lisa winked. "Don't knock it until you try it." She was the queen of casual, and never being stressed over a guy was one thing I admired most about her. "By the way, those beach chairs by the main pool are already filled with towels. So, we should hurry," she said, digging into her closet. "It's hot as hell and I need to work on my tan." She grabbed her bathing suit and ducked into the bathroom.

We were already halfway through our first full day at sea thanks to sleeping in and a late brunch. The girls warned me that our afternoon was for lounging by the pool, drinking our asses off between trivia, food, and people-watching. And by people-watching, Lisa meant looking for men.

Taking some of Lisa's advice, I pulled out my skimpy red bikini. I've had it forever and yet it still had the tags on it because my ex threw a fit the last time I tried it on. Tired of fighting, I'd tucked it away meaning to return it, but then forgot it, until this trip. If I was ever going to wear it, now was the time.

I quickly put it on before Lisa came out of the bathroom.

When I looked in the mirror, I noticed I'd filled it out a bit more since having Aubree. It felt tighter in the hips, and I tried to spread out the triangle tops so that my side boob wasn't as prominent.

"Ready?" Lisa called from the bathroom, not giving me time to change my mind. When she stepped out of the bathroom, she gave me an approving once-over.

"Now that's what I'm talking about, Millie. Damn, that suit gives you ass and class!" She smirked.

I felt like I blushed to my toes. Feeling self-conscious, I pulled my white beach cover-up over me and twisted my hair up into a messy bun, before I grabbed my book as we headed out. I wanted nothing more than to relax and get lost in the book, at least for a little while, before I got dragged into something one of the girls had planned.

We walked through the expansive promenade area, set in the center of the ship, creating a mall-type feeling, rather than a boat. The shops and boutiques were luxury brands that I would never shop in. I'd never been one for big names when I could find something similar for a quarter of the price.

Sam and Gia were waiting for us on the pool deck, where they had snagged some chairs in the far back corner.

"These were the only two available. We have to share them." Sam shrugged.

"I plan on being in the hot tub," Lisa said, glancing at a couple of guys sitting on the edge.

I spread out my towel and plunked into a chair. "I'm good here."

I settled in and opened my book, eager to get into it, when I heard kids running around, squealing in the splash pad, on the other side of the deck. I turned to watch them for a minute, thinking about Aubree and how much she would love this. I missed her already. This was my first real trip away from her. It was hitting me harder than I expected. I put in my earphones to drown out the noise and focused on my book.

It was a good hour before the heat was getting to me. I was certain I was the perfect shade of piggy pink, and I should've followed Sam and Gia into the pool.

"Drink?" Sam called to me while getting out. I nodded in agreement and slipped on my wrap.

Lisa joined us as I slipped into my wrap, glancing one last time at the chairs to make sure we'd taken everything.

"You sure you're not interested? There's someone eyeing you pretty hard at the end of the bar." Gia nodded to the right. She nudged me in the ribs until I peeked at the other end, spotting a group of guys. One winked at me, and then flashed Gia a grin.

I looked up to the end of the bar where a group of guys stood, one of them with a big scruffy beard winked at me then looked towards Gia.

"Uh, they're checking out everyone. Look how many heads have turned for you, too," I argued. Gia always attracted attention with her petite frame, platinum blond pixie haircut, and her sleeve of tattoos often brought an opening line from some guy. Sam, her girlfriend, was the opposite with curves, long dark hair and light brown eyes. She attracted attention for the one reason she both loved and hated: her natural DDD boobs.

"Sure, but we're taken and you're not." Sam leaned into Gia for a kiss.

The bartender handed us our drinks. I was thankful for the change in the conversation.

"To your dirty thirty," Lisa shouted. A bunch of people cheered with us and started wishing me a happy birthday.

Oomph, they did not hold back on the alcohol on this one. My lips puckered, taking in the sweet and sour flavor of the drink of the day.

"A few more of these, and I'll be on my ass," I declared.

"Perfect. Keep them coming." Sam and Gia shouted in unison over the loud deck music that started. We finished our drinks and headed to trivia.

Two rounds of trivia later and I was ready for my nap. It was a luxury that I never got aside from the few weekends Nick started taking Aubree, and that was more out of boredom. I glanced around the lounge, where Sam and Gia were talking intimately to each other, and Lisa had gone to get a drink and looked like she found something more when a guy chatted her up. Cue for my exit without feeling guilty. I still had some time before dinner.

"Nap time." I whispered to Sam.

"Us too."

I shook my head, knowing full well they had no intentions of napping. We waved to Lisa, who looked more than comfortable where she was.

I was barely in the room when my phone rang. I turned it over to see Nick was video-calling me. I answered on the fourth ring.

"Is that what you're wearing?" he barked when I came into view.

"What a nice greeting, Nick," I retorted dryly. "Why are you calling? Where's Aubree?"

"Aubree wanted to say happy birthday, but you took so long, she went to play with Gracie. Hold on," he huffed.

I'm surprised you remembered this year. I wanted to snap into the phone, but I knew it wouldn't do much good. And the girls wondered why my dating life was nonexistent. Look at who I thought was it for me. *What an ass.*

No way was I eager to jump into a relationship. Being a single mom was hard enough, especially after I moved out of Lisa's and back to my small town, Beachers Bay. The town I once again shared with Nick and Misha, my ex-bestie and now *his wife*.

It was bad enough everyone knew everything. I had fought moving back for as long as I could, but I did it because Aubree needed a better relationship with him. The truth was, I was wrecked. A hot mess on the best of days, barely holding it together for my daughter. So, even though I missed sex and intimacy. I wasn't interested in the shit that came along with it. Sure, a one-night stand sounded appealing, but since I'd only been with one guy, I wasn't about to just bang my way around either.

"Aubree, Mom finally answered," Nick shouted, making me turn the phone away from my face. The thumping of footsteps and Aubree's squeal stopped me from telling him off.

"Hiiiiiii, Mama," she said, yanking the phone from him and sticking her face into the camera.

"Hi, Princess." I smiled. Her voice made me happy enough to move past Nick's crappy attitude.

"Mama, where are you?" she asked, moving the phone around, trying to peek past me.

"I'm on a ship with your aunties." Her eyes grew wide.

"I wanna come, Mommy."

"I wish, baby girl, but you're too little right now."

"I'm almost five," she said, pouting her pink puffy lip out. *Almost five*. She turned four a couple of months ago. *Her flair for dramatics comes from her dad*.

Thankfully, she moved on, eager to tell me all about her adventures with her half-sister, Gracie. Being the same age, they loved hanging out. They went tobogganing and built a snowman today. As much as it hurt me to hear that she had a great family life with them and not me, the girls had grown close since we moved back and that was at least something positive out of this train wreck of a life I was stuck in.

I gave her a big air kiss and told her how much I missed

her. And did I ever. I'd never been away this long. After I hung up, Nick's comment about my outfit stuck in my head. I glanced at the mirror and saw that my wrap was wide open, leaving the perfect view of my little red bikini. *Was it open the entire time? Oops. Oh, well. Screw you, Nick. It's my birthday, and I'll show it off if I want to.*

I walked to Sam and Gia's room two doors over. One look at my face and none of them bothered to ask how the conversation went. They already knew.

Chapter Two

Millie

It was hot and crowded in the nightclub. We were having fun on the dance floor, which brought back memories of my days working in the bar. The DJ called out a dance contest, and I found myself on top of the stage, shaking my ass while I belted out the tunes, way off-key.

Sam's mouth hung open in shock, and Lisa seemed proud. The song ended, and some guy who looked like he could have been a movie star came over to help me off the stage. He was cute enough to capture my attention. Plus, he smelled delicious. *What the hell is in men's cologne these days? An extra shot of pheromones?* I'd never go for this guy. He had playboy written all over him. I knew better about guys like him, but I was on vacation. A little flirting couldn't hurt.

"You're so pretty."

"You think I am pretty?" He grinned cockily.

"Shit. Was that an outside thought?"

He nodded as he pulled me slightly closer, away from the crowd. "I'm Jax. Want to have a drink?"

"I, ah, think I might," I hiccupped, "be at my limit." He pursed his lips together to stifle a laugh. Embarrassment hit me. *Jeez Millie, one weekend away, you think you're auditioning for moms gone wild.* I shook my head at myself.

"Damn, Millie. You haven't let loose like this in years," Sam said as she tucked a one-dollar bill into my cleavage as a joke. Maybe it was good to let loose. I can't even remember the last time I had this much fun. Nick hated when I got drunk. He hated me working in a bar. Heck, he hated everything I did. He was jealous, the stupid hypocrite he was. I waved my hands around my head as if I could banish my thoughts of him.

"You okay?" Jax asked.

"Mm-hmm." I nodded, flushing at how strange I must seem.

Jax introduced himself to Sam and Gia, and then he waved over some of his buddies. He told us they were here for someone's bachelor party, but not all fifteen of them were at the club.

It didn't take long for our groups to blend. Lisa had found an interest in one guy who looked like a model. He had the whole tall, dark, and chiseled thing going. I thought I'd seriously pushed my limit when I saw two of Jax standing against the bar when he went for drinks. It took a minute to register that there *were* two of them.

All the guys seemed nice, and there was a bromance factor as they teased and joked with each other. A couple of guys showed some interest in me and asked me to dance. I didn't hesitate for once.

As cute as I thought the twins were, Reid stood out the

most. He was handsome with his golden hair and light brown eyes. He couldn't dance for crap, but he didn't seem to care. He looked like he was genuinely having a good time. Although, he was subtle about flirting with me, unlike Jax, who just wanted some action, and it didn't seem to matter who it was from.

"You're missing a genuine opportunity. This boat is loaded with hot single guys. Shit, half of these guys want to hook up with you. What the hell are you waiting for?" Gia asked, coming to me when the song was over.

Why wasn't I taking advantage of a fling? A battery-operated toy could only do so much. Were the girls right? Maybe I should bang my way out of a dry spell. I have options, so why am I holding back? It's not like I was waiting for a sign or connection. *It would be only one night. We leave tomorrow.* The girls' voices rang in my ears.

Gia must have sensed my thought. "Take the one to the left. He looks like he'd be good for the night," she nodded to the twins.

I ran my hand down my face in horror, worried that he heard her, even though I'm sure he couldn't hear us over the loud music.

"Wanna get out of here?" Jax came up and slung his arm over my shoulders, shooting Reid a cocky smirk. *Yeah, as if that's going to work, Romeo.*

"Sure. Just not with you," I said loud enough that a couple of the guys around us howled. Gia nearly choked on her drink.

"Damn... Millie."

"Ow! Shot down," Jax's twin said, smacking him playfully on the cheek. Reid's face lit up, and that was admittedly adorable.

Jax brushed it off and turned to Gia. "How about you, sweetheart?"

"Sorry, you're not my type."

"Pfft, I'm everyone's type," he rebuked.

Sam grabbed Gia's ass and whispered something in her ear. The timing was impeccable. Jax's face fell flat, and I couldn't help but smirk. Serves him right.

Gia and Sam shared a knowing glance before letting me know they were going back to their room.

"Be like her." Gia thumbed at Lisa dry-humping on the dance floor, trying once more to convince me to take one guy back to the room.

I gave her a playful push to the door. I didn't stay much longer, as I felt odd with Lisa occupied and the group breaking off. The music suddenly sounded too loud, and it was giving me a headache. It was probably best if I went back to my room. Reid wanted to walk me back, but I saw a pretty brunette in the corner trying to get his attention. Not wanting to ruin his chances, I led him towards her on the dance floor. I complimented her outfit, then said I needed the bathroom, leaving the two of them there. When I looked back, she was making eyes at him. *Nice play, matchmaker.* I smiled.

I said goodnight to Lisa, who also offered to come back with me, but to be honest, she looked like she was having a wonderful time and I didn't need a babysitter. I could manage my drunken self.

Once I left the club, I changed my mind and thought it would be nice to walk across the lido deck for air. The night was warm. The sky was lit with stars. Another ship's lights in the distance drew my eye across the small waves. It was quiet compared to the disco, where the only sounds were of some chatter on the sports deck above me.

I stood for a few minutes, trying not to think about how right the girls were. Jealousy hit me when a happy couple strolled by. I'm not blind to the attention some guys have given me. Maybe a fling isn't a bad idea.

I shook my head at myself. *Yeah, right, Millie, like you're going to jump into bed with some random guy after only being with one person in your life.* I sighed. The problem was, I wasn't interested in any of them. *Shouldn't I at least want to jump someone's bones?* I laughed to myself. *Is that even what people say anymore? Shit, I'm so out of the loop.*

For a split second, my mind wandered back to the guy by the pool. For the love of God, I can't stop wondering how his arms would feel around me... Now, *he* would be dangerous. Something about him made my spine tingle. The good tingle, the kind you only read about in books or fantasize about in the shower.

A voice boomed from the other end of the deck, pulling my attention from my dirty thoughts. Unsure if they were serious or joking around, I looked. The voices got louder and angrier the closer they got. I had a feeling it wasn't going to go well.

"What the fuck? What was that?" a big guy shouted over his buddy's shoulders.

"What? What's your problem, man?" a skinny guy with bleached hair yelled back at him. I looked between them. *Brave move for someone two inches shorter and twenty pounds lighter.* This could get interesting. His friends seem to agree with my thoughts, telling him to shut up and chill out. Not that he did. As if his friends sensed something, they started walking backward, blocking him.

"My problem is you, yah fucker." His face was red, and his neck veins looked like they were about to pop. He'd puffed up his arms, ready to charge. "Keep your fucking hands to yourself next time."

"Don't do it," I mumbled, as if he could hear me.

I watched him bawl his fists and grin before he shouted, "My hands were minding their own business when her ass landed in them."

I cringed. *You drunk moron.* And suddenly it looked like a classic movie fight scene. Fists flew, people were being shoved to the side. I stood planted in place, too engrossed to move or think about any danger.

The scuffle was getting out of hand. These guys were all over the place. One big shove, and someone was going overboard. Quicker than I realized, they were in front of me.

My brain's danger warning finally kicked on. I tried to move back, but I was trapped between the railing and one of the big guys. Someone had shoved him at me. I stumbled sideways, barely able to regain my balance, when a fist rushed toward me.

I yelled, bracing for impact, but warm arms wrapped around me and hoisted me out of the way, saving me from being pummeled.

My back was pressed to his chest, and his stubble tickled against my jaw as he asked if I was okay. It sent a shiver down my spine. Lost for words, I could only nod. He gently spun me around, and my breath hitched at the same blue eyes from earlier. He cupped my chin with his hand, tilting my head up to inspect my cheek. The touch sent goosebumps across my skin.

"You sure you're okay?" His voice was low and slightly shaky.

"Mm-hmm." I nodded.

"You should have moved."

"And miss the action? No way."

"Tough girl, huh?" I swear my stomach lurched at how deeply smooth his voice was. Never had I felt such a draw to someone. We couldn't seem to break our gaze and, for some reason, I was still in his arms. A hum between my legs I hadn't felt in years brought me back to reality. Clearly, it had been that long since I had some, that the simple touch of a man had me wet and ready to go. *I was pathetic.*

"I should go," I whispered softly.

"Sure." I felt cold and strangely missed his warmth when he shifted from me.

What the hell is wrong with you? I scolded myself to get a grip.

"I'll walk you to your room."

"That's not necessary."

"The hell it isn't. I want to make sure you get back safely," he said, his voice softened. Something in his eyes had me give in faster than I'd care to admit.

He took my hand and led me away from the lingering people, trying to see what happened. Holding hands felt strangely natural, throwing me off. It wasn't something I was used to. We passed some women, who talked about the incident as if they had just seen a live *UFC* match.

We walked to the elevator bank when he let go of my hand and leaned against the wall. "What brings you on vacation?"

"Girls' trip."

"Nice. Special occasion?"

"Not really. It's cold back home." *Part of the truth.* He didn't need to know it was my birthday. I didn't want any extra attention from him. He seemed satisfied with the answer as he let it go. He tilted his head up, opened his mouth, and closed it. He looked at the number on the elevator, which seemed to take longer than usual.

He stuffed his hand in his pocket and then looked at me. "Drink?"

"What?"

"Want to grab a drink?"

"Oh, I... Um..." I shifted on my feet and then stared at the ground. Unsure of what to say until the girls' voices repeated in my head to let loose and have fun. Flirt, keep it casual. I glanced back up at him. The way he watched me was sexy as hell.

"Sure." His face lit up with a grin that unleashed a set of dimples that made my panties wet. My knees locked together, not quite trusting myself. A few more grins like that, and my panties might throw themselves at him. What was it about him that had me coming undone?

Chapter Three

Jake

Something about her rattled me. Every nerve jumped alive the second she slammed into me on the lido deck. I noticed her everywhere on the ship like I was a magnet, drawn to her. Last night, she was at mini golf and then the late-night comedy show. I saw her at the promenade this morning, getting coffee, with her nose in a book and, for the love of Christ, I couldn't take my eyes off of her in that tiny string bikini that left nothing to the imagination. Then, there was tonight. The minute I saw her cross the deck, my eyes tracked her, and thank God they did. I could see the danger she was in, so I sprinted as fast as I could. It took every ounce of strength I had not to deck the fucker who almost hit her.

Save the damsel in distress and walk away. Easy. Except it wasn't. The minute my arms wrapped around her, I didn't want to let go. I invited her for drinks, knowing it wasn't a good idea, but my big fucking mouth went rogue.

I could tell she was nervous as we walked towards the schooner bar. She wouldn't stop fidgeting. The way she tucked away a stray hair did things to me. She swayed next to me when the boat rocked to the side. Our bodies brushed, and my dick pushed against my pants. *Not happening.*

Keep within the lines, I told myself when my brain replayed the effect she had on me after grabbing my pecs and how my dick moved in response. Blurred lines ended in a lot of trouble. Although she looked like she'd never been in trouble a day in her life. She had that innocent good girl thing with her big ocean-colored eyes and a wide, bright smile. I had to tear my gaze from her and direct it to the ground as we walked into the bar.

Only a few people were still sitting around the club chairs in the bar. We sat on one of the high stools. The bartender was washing some shakers at the other end. He nodded toward us to say he would be over in a minute.

I glanced at her, but she shifted in her seat, looking anywhere but at me. *Why is she so nervous?*

"Have you checked out the shows? Or the flow-rider?" I asked, hoping to get her to relax.

She finally turned to me, her eyes locking on mine and, *Christ*, I had to grip the counter.

"Last night's comedy show was way better than I thought it'd be, and I watched a few people try the flow-rider but haven't done it. You?"

"The flow-rider? Yup, I lasted a whopping eight seconds," I chuckled as I remembered the not-so-graceful face plant I'm sure had gone viral, thanks to Carlos. You couldn't get away with anything with him around.

"What would you like? It's just about the last call," the bartender startled us.

Clearing my throat, I said, "I'll take a Corona."

"Double rum and coke."

My head snapped over to her. "Wow, bringing out the guns." She nervously smiled. "I'd have figured you for a wine girl. Maybe something fruity, like a piña colada."

"I can handle my liquor."

I tipped my glass to hers. When she tilted her head up, laying those ocean blues on me, I nearly forgot what I was saying. *Yeah, I'm in serious fucking trouble.*

The boat was rockier compared to last night. I inched closer, *not on purpose*. My body temperature rose, and I felt like a fucking teenager with his first hot girl.

"Sorry, motion of the ocean." I shook my head immediately after I said it. "Fuck, did I really just say that?"

Her laughter floated straight south. "Yeah, you did." *Back up right now,* before she gets a feel of a full sail. It was hard enough not to peek down her tight gray maxi dress with a wide scoop neck and the perfect amount of cleavage.

What is wrong with you? I scolded myself. Normally, I can hold my own around women, but this one? Nope, she has me saying some dumb shit.

* * *

Millie

I ordered a second round for no other reason than nerves. Whatever buzz I'd had before left the minute I was nearly knocked out. Not that I needed to be drunk, but it certainly was helping me. I felt like my nerves were on fire around this guy.

The bartender let us know it was the last one because he was closing. I felt disappointed I'd be leaving him after this. I shouldn't though, right?

It's clearly been too long since I've had a man. *This poor guy is just being nice and cordial, saving my dumbass, and here I am thinking he wants to jump me.* I placed my drink on the bar and stood up and wobbled to the side, right into him. *Again.*

"Ship's really rocking tonight," I muttered without realizing what I'd said. His responding laugh was deep and sexy. *I'm in trouble.*

We left the bar and paused in the hall, neither of us really knowing where to go. We slowly walked to the elevators and waited in line until it arrived. His hand grazed my lower back as he guided me inside.

"What floor?"

"Ten," I squeaked.

"Me too," he said with a hint of amusement in his voice. I was surprised to see no one else was around. I checked my phone to see if any messages had come through from Lisa. Nothing. The way she was on the dance floor, there was no way she'd go back to the room *yet.*

"Boyfriend?"

"No." I shook my head, and he shifted closer to me, reaching for the button to our floor. He seemed to be in no rush to move away from me as we stood closer than we should have. Our eyes locked, and everything went silent, except for our breath picking up in pace. I licked my lips when his gaze dipped down and snuck a peek at my cleavage. The light in his eyes was enough to turn me on like a damn switch. His Adam's apple bobbed up and down with his hard swallow. The sexual tension between us was stifling as we stood chest to chest. The elevator ding snapped us apart.

It felt like I swallowed a bag of cotton balls when I tried to speak. He stepped aside and guided me out of the doors, both of us turning to the right, down the corridor. Coincidence?

I jutted my chin. "Near the end."

He paused, making us both stop. "Wanna have another drink?"

"Aren't the bars closed?"

He raised a brow, nodding towards a room up ahead. "I have a stocked cabinet."

"Oh... I..." I froze. *I want to, but should I?* The whole thing seemed dangerous. The kind that makes you forget things like not having sex with a random stranger. *Which I'd consider with him.* Wait, what? No. No.

"It's late." I shifted on my feet, nervously.

Disappointment swept across his face. It was more than I could take. He lingered before I turned away.

Keep walking. At least that's what I told myself, but the other voice in my head was telling me to do something for myself, *for once.*

Something about him drew me back, and for the first time in five years, I wanted a man. Him. To hell with the consequences. There's no reason I couldn't love him and leave him. Like Lisa said. But could I really sleep with someone I just met? Would I regret not knowing? I tried to walk forward, but hearing his long strides stopped me.

My heart hammered in my chest, knowing that when I turned around, he'd be there, and my control wouldn't be. Every part of me *wanted* this, him. It didn't even have to make sense. I needed him.

His fingers grazed the back of my arm and the sound of the sharp inhale of his breath was everything I needed. Slowly I turned and, with nothing said, our lips found each other. It was hot and needy, awaking every one of my senses. Our mouths tangled hungrily, as if they were starved. Every thought after that went out the window.

"When's the last time you watched the sunrise?" he asked, out of breath.

"Too long ago." We bumped along the wall thanks to the

waves, and he dug his keycard out of a pocket before kicking open the door. I pulled my dress up to wrap my legs around him once he lifted me into his arms. We fumbled through the large space until he dropped me on the bed, softly landing on top of me. He gently kissed the top of my breasts as I ran my hands through his hair.

"Are you sure about this? Now is the time to pull the brakes," he hoarsely whispered between kisses.

"Absolutely." *One night. For me. I deserved it.* I was drenched already with just the touch of his hands creeping up my thigh. The sound of his husky voice drove me crazy. He yanked his shirt off, exposing a set of abs I haven't seen outside of a calendar. *Damn.*

"Lift your ass," he commanded, pulling my dress up over me. Mortification hit when I remembered the cotton underwear with pink fucking glitter hearts on the ass. He didn't seem to care as he chucked them on the floor, spreading my legs further apart and teasing me with his fingers.

"Fuck, you are so ready." *No kidding.* The sound of my electric toothbrush vibrating could get me going, let alone a super-hot fucking guy between my legs. He lowered his head, and he pressed his fingers into my thighs as his hot breath warmed my center. The anticipation of his tongue on me had my stomach twisted in knots. Slowly, he worked his fingers down until he found my folds. The rough pad of his finger sent a flood of wetness.

"You like that, huh?" He was watching me unfold around him.

I moaned, my hips twirling as he circled around. I was about to come already. *Fight it.* His tongue swiped across me, causing a surge of heat. I clutched the sheets as he teased and licked my clit before sucking on it.

"Mm, you taste sweet," he hummed into me, and the vibration of his voice against me made me buck toward him.

He pushed his tongue harder into a spot that made my legs quake. My orgasm hit me in the most delicious way.

"You, okay?"

"Mm...hmm. Yup." That's new. *I guess I could come from oral.* Clearly, I wasn't the problem. He peppered kisses up my body, bringing his lips to mine. The taste of me was still on him, and, surprisingly, it turned me on. I wanted more. I pushed him onto his back. It was my turn to return the favor. I let my gaze linger to appreciate his cock. Long, thick, and built for a damn good time.

I lowered my mouth and licked from his balls to the tip, slowly gripping the shaft. He groaned, and his head fell back.

"Shit, woman." His response made me want to give him more. I moved my hands to the base, and I lowered my mouth inch by inch, taking all of him in. His leg quivered. Slowly, I worked around him, stroking him with my tongue until he clutched onto me.

"No. I need to be in you." He sat up and pulled me onto him, roughly kissing me before he flipped me onto my back. He shifted to the edge of the bed when I heard a package being torn. He was back between my legs, fast. His hand cupped my breasts before he lowered his mouth to my nipple. Biting and teasing me, like nothing I'd ever felt.

"You ready?"

"Yes." He entered slowly, giving me a chance to adjust. "Fuck you're tight," he said, moving in deeper. I sucked in a breath of air.

"You all right?"

I moaned my reply. He had me spread wide and filled up more than I'd ever been, and it felt incredible. He gently thrusted back and forth, until I moved with him, our rhythm perfect together.

"Fuck, you feel good." He pulled out, leaving in the tip before he slammed into me roughly, and I didn't care. It was incredible, and I was about to lose my mind again. I should have been embarrassed about how fast he could make me come, but I wanted to feel it again.

"Please don't stop, I'm almost there."

He pushed harder, faster, slamming into my wetness over and over again. With one last thrust, the explosion of our orgasms hit. He stopped to steady himself. He was out of breath and glistening with sweat. It was hot as hell. We were motionless; only the sound of our breath echoed off the walls.

He rolled over to kiss me one last time before he got up and tossed the condom into the garbage. Lying there naked, the reality of what just happened hit me. I flung my arm over my eyes. I slept with him. *Now what*? I've never had a one-night stand. I thought about Lisa saying, "love, then leave."

"Need anything?" he called out from somewhere around the corner. I sat up and looked around, finally noticing how massive the suite was.

"Actually... I should go," I said, looking for my clothes.

"Seriously? You're leaving now?"

"It's late. I should get back in case my friend is waiting for me."

"Shit. I can't say I have ever been humped and dumped before." He sat on the edge of the bed and handed me a bottle of water. "Hell, I don't even know your name."

I covered my mouth. "Oh, God. We didn't exchange names." *Nice, Millie.*

"I'm—" I put my hand over his mouth to silence him.

"Stop. Don't make more of this than it is, a one-night stand, no strings. Let's keep it a night of mystery."

"You're kidding?"

"Why? What difference does it make? The cruise ends tomorrow. You'll go one way and I'll go another."

He raised his brows. "That's crap. Give me a name... Any

name… Make it up. I don't care, but give me something," he urged, closing in on me.

He moved his mouth down my neck until I was on my back, and he was on me. I could feel him harden again. He was very persuasive.

My brain stopped working. "Mi… A-melia." I caved.

"Amelia," he repeated with a grin. The way it rolled off his tongue was seriously sexy, and I hated being called Amelia. "Don't leave. Sunrise, remember?" he whispered in my ear.

"You were serious?"

"Damn right. One night." His lips swiped across mine, and he settled himself between my thighs, his cock pushing against me. The thin fabric of the sheet was a pointless barrier. "We're going to make the most of it."

* * *

Quietly, I shifted out from underneath his tree trunk of an arm, careful not to wake him. I pulled my dress back on and stood for a moment, burning the image of his naked body in my mind. He was going to live in it for a while.

Happy birthday to me. I smiled before I tiptoed out the door, careful not to let it slam.

Chapter Four

Millie
5 months later

Lisa, Sam, and Gia had just pulled into the driveway. They missed Aubree and had been giving me a hard time. Sam said she and Gia had news to share *in person*. I had one guess what it was, and I hoped I was right.

Mickey, my six-year-old lab, sat on the floor while Aubree put bows on him. She insisted on dressing him up for her aunties' visit. Poor dog.

I squealed when Gia came inside with a giant glittering rock on her finger. "Holy crap, Gia, it's stunning."

"I know. Sam did good." Gia replied as I hugged her.

I turned to Sam and hugged her next. "It's about damn time!" I smiled, having wondered when she was going to propose, after she asked for my advice on the cruise.

We celebrated their engagement by ordering Chinese food and playing in the yard with Aubree until she was exhausted.

They helped me tuck in Aubree like old times. *Damn, I missed this.* Missed having companionship, missed having someone around. Without being able to stop the flood of emotions rushing at me, I cried.

"Oh, Mils," Gia murmured, wrapping her arms around me.

They followed me to the kitchen, where we picked at our leftovers.

"You'll have this, too." Sam softly assured me.

"Yeah, Mils, get back out there. Look how many guys threw themselves at you on vacation." Gia stepped away to reach for a plate.

I bit the inside of my cheek. "No one needs my level of complication."

"What makes you so complicated? Aubree?" Lisa asked.

"It's Nick, and the damn town. No one wants to even come near me."

"Fuck Nick. The longer you stay single, the longer he wins," Lisa snapped, as she stabbed the chicken ball with her chopstick.

"No, he doesn't."

"Yeah, he does. Nick's getting the best of both worlds. He has his wife, his store, his family, his perfect life, and he never had to give you up," Sam argued. "Having Aubree made sure of that."

I sighed and stuffed half of an egg roll into my mouth. I was at a loss. We'd been through this speech a dozen times already.

"Stop hiding behind the 'no one wants to date a single mom' speech." Gia turned to me as if she could read my mind.

With my mouth still full of half chewed food, I said, "I'm not hiding."

"Oh, really? When was the last date you had? Or even considered one?" I paused, thinking back to the cruise and the mystery man, who still lingered in my head. *Me*, the over-thinker, the one who weighed all options, threw caution to the wind for one perfect night with an incredible man. A man who made me feel desired and sexy. What that man could do with a flick of his finger was enough to finish me without warning. It was embarrassing how quickly my orgasms came, but he made Nick look like a one-trick pony. Either sex had evolved, or Nick was a shit over. I learned toward the latter. My lips curved into a smile.

"What are you smirking about?" Lisa asked.

It was time to fess up to the girls. I had kept my secret long enough. It wouldn't matter now, it's not like I expected to see him again. I took a long pause.

"Um, so about the guy on the ship," I began, but Sam interrupted.

"The ship? Dimples? The guy who rescued you?"

"Yeah," I replied. My throat dried as I recalled my perfect hot and heavy night. "I may have held some information back."

"Like what? You had that happy birthday I suggested?" Sam laughed. I let silence fill the air while their jaws hung open.

"No way?" Lisa shook her head.

"Holy shit, why didn't you say anything?" Gia asked.

"Didn't come up?"

Sam snorted. "Bullshit. Sex can always come up in a conversation."

"Have you talked to him since?" Gia asked.

"No."

Lisa threw her hand up. "Why the hell not?"

"Wait, did his ass hit it and ditch it?" Sam smacked her hand down on the counter.

I shook my head and shrugged. "All of you told me to have

a simple fling, no strings. I didn't want any information, so I didn't give any."

"So, let me get this straight." Gia held up her hand. "You meet this stellar guy, slept with him, then just walked away without even a name?"

I teetered my hand back and forth. "He asked for my name. I fibbed and told him it was Amelia."

"Amelia?" Lisa echoed.

"It's not technically a lie... I couldn't think fast enough on my feet."

"Or back," Gia laughed.

"Funny." I deadpanned.

Lisa mumbled, "There goes the no one-night stands, rule..."

Gia swatted Lisa and turned back to me. "Weren't you the least bit curious about the possibility of afterwards?"

I pursed my lips and shrugged. "No. That's the point of it all."

"I'm kind of proud," Sam chuckled.

I could see the wheels in Lisa's head turning. I was about to ask something when Sam interjected.

"Wait, back to the sex. Did he have to brush off cobwebs?"

"You're such an ass." I tossed a chicken ball at her. Lisa's phone rang. A giant smile spread across her face as she tucked in her hand and left the kitchen. It must be Mitch, the guy she met on vacation. We all exchanged glances at how giddy she got when he called, especially for the queen of no strings.

* * *

I hated the weekends when Aubree was with Nick. Sure, I caught up on cleaning and mom stuff, but after a while, it got to me. The house was too quiet, and I felt lonely and bored. The weekend was Toronto's annual Rib Fest. It was tradition for us all to go, but Sam and Gia couldn't make it this year, and Lisa was bringing Mitch. At first, I wasn't going because being the third wheel was not exactly my cup of tea. But Lisa did her usual sweet talking and, after Nick and I had a heated exchange at drop off, I couldn't wait to get out of town, even if Lisa was pushing one of Mitch's buddies on me. *Again.*

Ever since I admitted to my one-night stand, she'd been pushier than ever, but I wasn't ready to date. The girls disagreed and attempted to push me toward anyone who seemed like he was the opposite of Nick, but I'd somehow narrowly avoided their setups already.

Lisa nudged my elbow just as I was about to take the last bite of my food, nodding at some guy dressed as a cowboy.

She wiggled her brows at me. "How about him?"

I rolled my eyes. "A cowboy? Sheesh, Lisa."

"Look at his ass in those tight jeans." Mitch looked at Lisa and shook his head at her. He was way more patient with her than she deserved.

"What? It's for Mils." She grinned.

He bent over and kissed her. It was so much PDA that I felt like a child watching their parents make out. I looked for our next snack as a distraction. A sign advertising fried Thanksgiving dinner and beer caught my attention. *Who the hell fries beer, and how?*

"What is it about deep-fried food that makes everything so damn delicious? Hell, you can deep fry a finger and people will eat it up."

Mitch chuckled. "You're not wrong."

"I swear I could bathe in this barbeque sauce," I said, dipping the last mac and cheese ball before shoveling the remaining piece into my mouth. Lisa tried to snag a bite, but I snapped my teeth playfully.

As I threw out my container, a tall guy with broad shoulders and a backward hat caught the corner of my eye. Something about him was familiar. Really familiar. A wave of goosebumps crossed my skin. My neck craned to the side in the hope of a better view. He was walking next to a woman a lot shorter than him, with light red hair.

"They're here," Mitch said, tucking his phone back into his pocket.

"Hmm. Okay." I said absently before turning to Mitch, who was looking ahead of me. "Wait, who's here?"

Lisa wrapped her arm tightly around me to keep me from escaping. Oh crap, what have they done? I took a deep breath and looked at Lisa, who had a shit-eating grin.

"So, funny story... Mitch's friends are here."

"Seriously?" I huffed. "I'm knee-deep in barbeque sauce." I waved my hand around my face, knowing it was covered. She laughed. *I should have known they would ambush me.*

"C'mon, they're waiting." Lisa dragged me behind her.

"Lisa, I'm not interested."

"Wait until you meet him. You might change your mind. Actually, I'm surprised you didn't meet him on the cruise. He was with Mitch and the gang."

She tugged my hand like a small child. I felt nervous. "Is it Reid?" I asked, praying it was. At least I sort of knew him.

"Nope." *Crap.* We approached a small group of people standing by the ring toss. *Oh, God, what is this?* There were at least three guys there.

"Sup, Lisa?" A guy with a sandy blond mohawk smiled at us. He looked me over. "Josh."

The other guy, with dark hair and a thick beard, wearing a Toronto Twisters baseball hat, nodded. *Man, they look familiar. Where have I seen them?*

"Kev," he grunted. A petite woman introduced herself as Denise while gripping the hand of the man next to her, Mikey.

Mitch turned to Josh and Kev. "Shit game on Wednesday."

"Could have been better if your boy actually hit the ball," Josh muttered. And now I know where they're from. *They play for the Toronto Twisters baseball team. I am going to kill her.* I should have known Lisa would hook me up with one of Mitch's sports buddies. What is she thinking of, me with a sports guy? Sure, I liked sports, but I couldn't make things work with a regular guy, let alone some high-profile athlete.

I shifted in place while they started sports talk already. Mitch was an agent, and a damn good one from what I'd heard. He had a solid roster of players from all kinds of teams. Including Josh.

I wanted to crawl under one of the food trucks. *Did they know this was a setup? Wait, who was she setting me up with?* There were two of them. I looked between them. The dark hair with the beard was cute in a rugged way. Mohawk came across as temporary. With Lisa, it could go either way.

The rich scent of coffee distracted me from my wayward thoughts. A coffee truck was across the field. *Perfect.*

"Be right back." I ducked away, not waiting for a response.

The line of people for the coffee truck was long, and I didn't mind, not that I could avoid whatever Lisa had planned, but at least I could get my head around it. My phone rang. I groaned, knowing it was Lisa.

"Where the hell did you disappear?" she asked.

"Coffee truck."

"Stay put. We'll find you. Oh, order me one, too."

I blew out a long breath when she hung up. The mom voice in my head told me not to reward her for causing trouble. I stood in line, trying to think rationally. Aside from being baseball players, was there anything wrong with hanging out with them? No, it's kind of cool. Kev has one hell of a record for amazing catches. And Josh has one of the team's best batting averages.

When I got to the front of the line, I ordered two of their

biggest iced coffees. I rolled my eyes at myself, annoyed that I was a sucker for my friend.

Hastily, I grabbed the coffee as the barista passed them to me through the window, making the lid pop off one of them. I fumbled trying to get it back on, but the coffee was sloshing, and I slammed into the woman behind me, dropping them on our feet.

"Seriously?" she snapped at me.

"So sorry," I grumbled, feeling shittier.

"Great. My fucking toes are going to be stuck together."

I crouched down to clean my toes with napkins. She lowered beside me, wiping her feet as she angrily muttered under her breath. I rolled my eyes, more annoyed I'd have to stand in line again. When I looked at her, I realized it was the woman with the red hair I'd seen earlier, when my face was covered with sauce and Mitch's friends showed up.

"Here," a man said from above us.

Every hair on my neck stood up. I knew that voice. It lived in my core memory for the past five months. *It can't be.* Slowly, I looked up to see the most spectacular set of deep denim blue eyes peeking out from under the brim of a baseball cap. My breath hitched. Holy shit. "Dimples" was standing right in front of me. I froze.

He blinked at me like I was an enigma. "Amelia?" His voice shook.

Good lord, the way he said my name made every moment of that night come flooding back in waves. My entire body felt like it was on fire. I couldn't move or think right.

"Hey, we found you," Mitch announced, coming over and talking to Dimples as if they were best friends. Neither he nor I broke eye contact.

"Jake, I see you met... Millie," Mitch said, looking between us. Lisa cleared her throat to get our attention. When I finally peeled my eyes away. Lisa's eyebrow was raised, and her smug smirk told me she knew something.

"Do you know each other?" Mitch hesitated.

"Yes," he admitted.

"No," I lied at the same time.

Jake scrunched his face, his lips parting, but then stopped when he looked at me. Mitch glanced at us, not knowing what to do.

"Right..." Mitch finally uttered. I was grateful Kev approached, breaking the tension.

"Jake, April, you guys made it." Kev playfully punched Jake in the arm.

April's eyebrow arched up. "Why wouldn't we?"

Kev shrugged and his lip twitched, but as he looked at April and me, he stopped and tucked his hands in his pockets. He tried changing the subject. "Ferris wheel?"

Not entirely sure who he was asking, I nodded anyway. April shot me a warning look that I was in her territory and not to mess with it. *Lady, I never planned to. In fact, I had nothing to do with any of this.* I never got the chance to actually say that, because she pulled Jake away by the forearm. Kev and Josh both snickered behind them.

Oh, fucking fantastic. I found the one guy I never thought I'd see again, only to meet him with his girlfriend. Not freaking awkward at all. How can I escape?

Lisa pushed me forward to follow the group. "Nuh-uh, don't even think about it."

My mouth gaped as I froze, wondering aloud. "But... How?"

Lisa stopped and lowered her sunglasses. "When you told us your little story about the fabulous one-night stand you had on our trip, you let it slip that you gave him your real name. What a coincidence that Mitch's friend, *Jake*," she paused for effect, "spent a random night with a perfect stranger that same weekend on that same cruise. She disappeared before he woke. She gave him a fake name but, lucky for Jake, I have a friend with that same name... *Amelia*," she explained, with a pointed look.

"Jesus, Lisa," I huffed. "This is not the plan. Isn't this shit supposed to stay on vacation?"

"Clearly not." She pointed to Mitch. They went from a vacation fling to a full-fledged long-distance relationship, which is still weird to me since Lisa didn't do relationships, ever.

I rubbed the sides of my head. *Now what?* My mystery man was no longer a mystery and what's even worse, he came with someone else.

"Are you seriously trying to set me up with him?"

"Abso-fucking-lutely."

"Are you out of your mind? After everything I went through with Nick, you think I want to get involved with someone who's taken?"

Lisa shook her head. "She's a physiotherapist on the team. They're not dating. She just tagged along tonight. A bunch of people are here."

"Lisa. I'm going to murder you. You better have had the best sex of your life last night. You're never having it again," I whisper-yelled.

"Oh, puh-lease." She rolled her eyes. "Did you see how he looked at you? If he's dumb enough to walk away again... Josh looked interested. Either way, you'll have a date from one of them. I'll bet my pay on it."

Chapter Five

Jake

Against all odds, I found her again. At some random Rib Fest in Toronto, of all places. I wasn't even going to go, but Mikey and Kev were trying to get me out of the funk I'd been in. Adjusting to the new team hadn't gone smoothly so far. Mitch was also in town, finalizing a deal for Jacobson, a player with the Toronto hockey team. He was going to the Rib Fest with Lisa and, since I hadn't officially met her yet, the shit head guilt tripped me.

April heard some of us talking and asked if she could tag along. She spotted the coffee cart, and I followed her while I texted Mitch to tell him we'd arrived. I had just tucked my phone back in my pocket when I noticed the woman in front of me. She typed furiously into her phone while sighing heavily. I guessed she was having a hard day. Something about her was familiar. It wasn't until she dropped her coffee that I saw who it was.

She looked amazing. She had on a simple blush pink tank top with jean shorts, her blonde hair piled on top of her head, and barely a stitch of makeup. My mind went blank. I thought it was a hallucination.

After I recovered from the pure shock, she took off with Lisa. I wanted to kick myself. For months, Mitch tried to set me up with her, but I was adamant I wasn't ready to meet anyone. I was dealing with enough shit but, if I'd known her name, things would be different. *I think.*

"I have to chat with Mitch for a minute," I told April, and quickly jogged over to him before she had a chance to come with me.

When I caught up to him, my look said to hang back for a second. I had questions, and I didn't want an audience. As casually as I could, I leaned into him. "So, that's Millie? The one you have been trying to set me up with? Lisa's friend?"

"Yeah, man. Could you eye fuck her any harder?" he snickered.

I grunted, wondering if I'd been that obvious or if Mitch was exaggerating.

"You must have seen her around the ship? Half the guys were trying to hook up with her."

My jaw clenched at the vision of my cousin Jax with her at the bar. "She's familiar alright."

"You just needed to put a face to the name." He smacked my shoulder.

Except her name was Amelia to me, not Millie. It would have been useful to know that tidbit. *Why did she lie about her name?*

I moved my stare to her, where she stood in line with Josh, who was awfully fucking friendly with her. They were in deep conversation with Denise and Mikey when Josh glanced back and smirked at me. The shit. I wanted to punch him. Something in his attitude was cockier than usual. It was almost like he knew there was something between Millie and me. I didn't have a chance to dwell on it because April planted herself next to me. I inwardly groaned. The girl couldn't take a hint, despite my attempts to thwart her advances.

I had no choice but to ride with her. She inched closer to me as I kept watching Millie from above. I slid to the side of our seat, pretending I was looking over the edge, focusing on Millie next to Josh.

"Fucker."

"Hmm, what?" April asked, leaning against me.

"Nothing."

"The view is nice up here."

"Not really," I mumbled. My eyes drifted below again. *Was he getting closer to her?* April made a few more comments to which I grunted or nodded, but the girl could have asked me to swan dive off the ride and I wouldn't have known. The ride felt like it was never-ending, with the constant stopping as people got off and on. I closed my eyes, hating every minute.

"Are you afraid of heights?" April touched my thigh.

I shifted my leg. "No." Even though I told myself not to, I looked down. Josh was staring up at me, chuckling before he said something to Millie and he dropped his arm behind her, blowing a kiss at me. *I swear, the ass whooping I was about to unleash on him.*

After the ride, April suggested beer tents. The beer garden was enormous, with several large outdoor canopies full of picnic tables. The shade helped with relief from the sweltering summer heat. Lisa and Mitch had already found a table in the far back corner, which gave me the chance to break away from April and attempt to get closer to Millie.

"Who wants what?" I asked, taking the orders like I was a server.

"Millie? Want to help a guy out?" Lisa encouraged.

Shit, her face nearly turned almost purple in embarrassment. I could see she wanted to say no, but Lisa didn't give her the option. She shoved Millie off the bench, shooing her with her hand. It would have been funny if Millie didn't look mortified. *Why was she trying to avoid me?*

Mitch gave me a thumbs up. My turn to be embarrassed. Fucking guy. We walked in silence almost an arm's length apart, while Millie fidgeted with her small cross-body purse. Not even a glance from her. *Why was this so awkward? Grow a pair and talk to her.*

I cleared my throat. "Millie... Huh? Not sure I've been fake named before."

Her gaze flicked to mine. "You said any name would do."

I hung my head. "Yes, I did. I don't think I've ever regretted those words more."

"Amelia isn't a fake name. Millie is my nickname," she said so softly I almost missed it.

"How come you didn't want me to know your name?"

"Why did you need it? Isn't that the point of a one-night stand? The ability to walk away with no expectations."

Fair point and yet here we were. "Did you know about today? Being set up?"

We took a place at the end of the line.

"Nope. I should have, though. Lisa's been pushing me about Mitch's *friend* for a while now."

"Me too." I looked up and caught her gaze. Damn, just as beautiful as I remembered. It took me a second to think about what I was saying. "If I knew Millie was short for Amelia, I would have come with him the first trip he took." I closed the gap between us. It was adorable, the way she blushed.

Finally, it was our turn to order. She reached for her wallet, and I held up my hand.

"Don't even think about it." I dropped some cash on the bar.

The bartender's face lit up. "Thanks, man."

"No problem, you're earning it. Good luck." I nodded back at the never-ending line behind us.

Josh noticed us first when we came back, piping up about saving a seat for Millie. He patted the bench space. My patience was running thin with him. Millie let out a small nervous giggle, staring at us.

He moved a little closer to her once she sat down. He was all over her, whispering, and acting all cozy. Jealousy coursed through me every time she laughed. She seemed a lot more comfortable with him than she was with me. *What the hell is his game? Is he interested in her? Do they know each other?*

Mitch and Lisa seemed as confused as I was. I fought for her to speak to me, and yet they were in a full-blown conversation. April was talking my ear off. I tried my best to be polite because she worked with us. If I was a dick, she would make my life harder. I nodded, but I hadn't heard a word she said. Angry and frustrated, I walked away from April and went to the sledgehammer game. My caveman mentality said to hit something other than Josh. If that meant smacking a giant sledgehammer to hit a tiny bell, so be it. Before I took the first swing, Josh joined me, pushing up his sleeves to show off his muscles, like I didn't already bench way more than him, and we both knew it.

We went swing for swing, trying to win a stupid oversized bear, but it was harder than it looked. The bell was weighted or something. *Figures.*

Neither of us backed down, especially after crowd formed to cheer us on. This was going to end up on Sports News. I huffed out a breath, wound up, and swung hard. I watched the bell climb the tower until it dinged. The tower lit up as people screamed and cheered. Hell, I even jumped around like a fool until the guy handed me a stuffed animal the size of a toddler. Josh rolled his eyes when I walked over to Millie and handed it to her. She turned bright red all the way to her bright pink toes. Sure, it was nothing but some macho bull-shit, yet I'd do it again.

"We're being set up. It's going to be hard to explain if you continue to pretend I don't exist." I couldn't stop the jealousy coursing through me. "Unless you wanted Josh to win it instead."

"Thank you," she whispered, lowering her eyes.

"Come on. Let's play some games." I tugged her hand, surprised she didn't resist. God, the simplicity of taking her hand and my heart raced. *Shit, Jake, calm down.*

We played ring toss first. Lisa won. She spent the next ten minutes gloating. After that, we found some arcade-style basketball. *I'll be damned. Millie won.* She beat me with a three-pointer.

"Rematch?"

"Sour sport, huh? Sure, I'll beat you again if you want to add to your misery? I won twice now?" She grinned in a way that made more than my dick jump.

After beating me for two more games, I gave up. The girl had some skills. There wasn't a damn thing I could do about it besides stand there with a giant bear and a goofy grin.

"Dude, she beat you. For real." Mitch laughed. "You met your match."

"Shut up." I shoved him playfully.

"Your competition is thicker than I thought. You might have to fight off Josh," he added, watching Josh jog up to Lisa and Millie. He threw his arm over both of their shoulders.

I rubbed my jaw. Josh was making heavy competition for her attention. I was hoping it was a ruse to piss me off. We have a playful rivalry, but he was pushing it too far.

"Are they always this way?" I wondered, turning to Mitch.

Mitch looked confused. "Tonight was the first time they met. Millie never comes out to the games when Lisa comes."

He turned to watch Josh and Millie. "I can't tell if he's making a play or busting your balls."

I grunted, gluing my stare on him. If his hand moved down any further, I was going to sock him. Mitch noticed the tension rolling off me.

"Look man, I don't know what's happening, but do you?"

"What do you mean?"

He stopped mid-stride. His eyebrow arched up. "I've known you since sophomore year in college. I've never seen you so worked up about someone you *just* met."

Fuck. I forgot he didn't know about the ship. Time to come clean with Mitch.

I cleared my throat. "Did you know Millie is short for Amelia?" He stopped and clutched my shoulder before he bent over and howled with laughter.

"Holy fuck. It's her? Mystery girl?" he finally choked out. "You know, if you weren't such a stubborn ass, you would have met her months ago. Lisa and I have been trying to push you two together."

I rubbed my face, thinking back to the times Mitch had pushed for me to meet her. *Thanks, Captain Obvious.*

"No wonder you're pissed about Josh." He stood up, hand to his chest, attempting to control his laughter. "Alright, alright. Look, man. You're going to have to either take out the competition or let her choose."

"Choose?"

"Like it or not, buddy, you might have missed your chance."

Millie's laugh at something Josh said caught my attention.

"Oh, for fuck's sake," I groaned.

"Man up and go get your girl." He then shouted at our friends and pointed toward another ride. "How about that next?"

Mitch tipped his head at Lisa, who moved to stand between Josh and Millie until I got there.

"Josh, you're with me this time. Mils, you can go with Jake," Lisa explained, pushing Millie toward me. Josh opened his mouth, about to say something, but snapped it shut instead.

Millie smirked. "Can you handle this ride?"

I bent over and whispered in her ear, "I can handle it fine. Can you?" Millie cocked her head at me.

"Don't you have motion sickness?" I said, low enough so only she could hear me.

"How did you know?"

"You were wearing a sickness patch that night." I brought my finger up, grazing behind her ear. Her skin erupted into goosebumps and, fuck, it was sexy.

"I do, but I'll be okay. I took some meds earlier, just in case." We buckled into our seats inside the sizzler ride, with Millie on the inside of the cart. When the ride whipped us around in every direction, she slid into me, which caused a familiar heat-seeking feeling for her. My arm wrapped around her as the cart lurched side to side and back and forth. She laughed with each spin. It was infectious and I couldn't help but laugh with her.

She wobbled at my side when we got off. I held onto her to make sure she didn't stumble from the cart. Her eyes turned up to me and I swear I lost my mind. The urge to kiss her was hard to fight. She raised up her arms and fixed her hair, which had fallen from her bun. The smell of her shampoo crashed into my senses. That sweet smell lived in my memory.

April was waiting by the ride when we climbed off, pissed at Millie. I knew she had been flirting with me, but I was never interested. Besides, the minute I saw Millie again, no one else existed.

Chapter Six

Millie

I was glad when April left; she was snide to me most of the day. I apologized for the coffee. If she was still going to act bitchy to me, tough luck with her. Josh snuck up behind me while I stood in line for the washroom and slung his arm over me.

"Hey, thanks for the fun today. Tormenting Jake turned out way better than I hoped for."

"You're evil." I shook my head.

"Damn right, and it was so worth it. I've never seen Jake so worked up over someone before. Whatever history exists between you two won't stay a secret for long."

"How did you know?"

"Thought so." Josh grinned. *Crap, how did I fall for that?* "Have a good night, Millie." He winked as he looked and caught Jake staring at us. He leaned over and kissed me on the cheek, lingering longer than necessary. Jake frowned. He couldn't even hide it if he tried. The way Jake would blow out a frustrated breath, or rub his head, when Josh was close to me, was a little sexy. Not at all like how Nick was in his jealousy.

I shook my head as I finally walked into the bathroom. Jake had been on my mind since the cruise, and I was doing everything I could to avoid him. All because he made me nervous. A feeling I had never had before, not even with Nick.

I was running hot and cold, flirting, and then pulling away. It was wrong and yet, I couldn't stop. I didn't have a clue what to do around him.

Take a breath. You already slept with him. Now stop hiding and put on your big girl panties. I splashed some water on my face and walked back out to the group, where everyone was standing around outside the bathroom, except Denise and Mikey, because they'd already left.

Lisa was checking out a group of guys dressed like cowboys. As I stood next to her, she nodded to one of them with jeans so tight I could have painted them on.

"Oooh, look at his ass," she tried to whisper, but she was shouting, thanks to the beer she was downing all day. I had to give it to Mitch. He was a good sport about it all, even her wild antics. If I had even looked in the direction of a guy, Nick would have flipped out at me. His jealousy was over-the-top.

Another cowboy walked by, and Lisa poked me. "Ow... Jesus, Lis... My boob. I need those." I rubbed where she practically bruised me.

"Why? It's not like you let anyone play with them, which is such a shame. They are great boobs. Don't you think so, Jake?" She honked my boob, mortifying me.

"Jesus, Lisa." Jake put his head down, shoving his hand in his pockets.

Lisa feigned innocence. "What? Someone should get to

play with them. I bet Jake will... Right?" She wiggled her brows.

He did play with them. The memory of his hands on them made me flush. I wanted to run and hide in a bush. I mouthed to her. "I'm going to kill you."

"Subtle, babe," Mitch whispered to her.

Lisa shrugged before noticing a group of young cowboys looking like they were auditioning for the next Stetson ad. By the tenth time she jabbed me, I lost it.

"Now we're back to cowboys? I thought you wanted me to take Jake home. Why are you pointing out cowboys?" The minute it left my lips, I went ten shades of red. Lisa, Mitch, and Jake stood there blinking at me. "Not how it sounded."

Lisa smirked smugly.

"I think we've meddled enough." Mitch glanced at me remorsefully.

"Mitch, can I have a minute with her?" I asked, but Mitch hesitated to leave her.

Thankfully, Jake pulled him away, saying they would go get us some water.

I planted my feet in front of hers and crossed my arms. "Lis, I get you want me to hook up with him, but you're embarrassing me."

"Oh, relax," she whined, gripping my arm. "First off, you already gave him the goods. Second, Jake is so bloody into you, it doesn't matter what I say."

"You don't know that."

"Pfft, sure I don't." She rolled her eyes.

"Lisa, it's complicated."

"All good things are, Mils. Tell me right now that you're not the least bit attracted to him, and I'll leave you two alone." I wanted to deny it, but the words didn't come. "That's what I thought."

The band changed behind us, catching Lisa's attention.

"Oh, my God, there's line dancing." She screamed as people formed the lines and started to boot and scoot. I pinched the bridge of my nose.

Lisa was like a squirrel when she was drunk. She couldn't focus, and she had to take part in everything. I should have known better. She tugged my arm, pulling me through the crowd, and lined us up.

"Okay, and we're line dancing," I muttered under my breath.

Never in my life had I line-danced. Being in the heat all day and the six ciders I drank to tame my nerves had given me a pretty good buzz. It wasn't going to take a genius to see how terrible of an idea this was. We tried to keep up with the moves, but my alcohol consumption mixed with my inability to group dance combined in the worst way. I went in all the wrong directions. I kicked when I was supposed to slide and clapped when I was supposed to turn. Lisa's was just as horrible, except she thought she was great. It was comical how delusional she was.

"We're an embarrassment to line dancing." I laughed. Uncontrollably. "Jesus, I suck," I said, giving a little boot kick seconds after everyone else.

A little old lady pointed to her feet, telling me to follow her. *Wow! Now I really know how bad I am.* It was the longest four minutes of my life. *Why are country songs so damn long?* I was huffing and puffing out of breath from both the dance and my fit of laughter.

A young cowboy who looked like he was auditioning for the cover of a cowboy magazine came to us just as Jake and Mitch returned.

"Would you like to dance?" the cowboy asked, looking at us.

"She's taken." Mitch tossed his arm over Lisa, pulling her into the crowd as they danced to a slow song.

Jake passed me a bottle of water, not taking his eyes off of me. "Here, *hon.* Sorry it took so long."

"Thanks." My voice had gotten stuck somewhere in my throat.

"Holy shit. You're Jake Parsons," the cowboy realized.

"That's me," Jake replied with an edge to his voice.

"Can I have your autograph?"

Jake relaxed. "Sure, what have you got for me to sign?"

The guy patted himself down, coming up empty until he felt the top of his head. "My hat. Can you sign it?"

Jake whipped out a marker from his pocket and signed the guy's hat.

"Thanks." He waved the hat and walked away.

Jake turned to me. "So... Um... That was some interesting dancing."

I let out a tiny snort. "Pffft, you should have seen me in Zumba."

"What the ever-loving fuck is Zumba?"

And just like that, I went into a fit of giggles, barely able to speak. "An. Exercise. Class. Spanish. Dancing," I said, adding an awkward hip swing.

He coughed, trying to stifle his chuckle. "Ohhh... And... Um... How often do you Zumba?"

My eyes watered, and my shoulders bounced. "Only a few times, but I was so bad, they politely asked me not to return."

Jake put his hand over his chest while a deep, rumbly laugh slipped out. It felt like the vibrations went right to my core, and for the first time since the coffee truck, I stared up at his perfect face, showing off his deep dimples. My knees just about buckled.

Jake took my hand, and I nearly melted. His eyes met mine. Neither of us spoke. He tugged me closer to him. My heart pounded with anxiety. He lowered his face, hovering his mouth above mine. *Is he going to kiss me right here in front of everyone*? His lips brushed past my cheek.

"Why didn't I see you with Lisa on the ship?"

My whole body felt like it was lit on fire. "I just usually stay in the background," I uttered.

"I doubt that. You're the only one I noticed." I blushed but couldn't say anything. "Can I drive you back to your place?"

"No."

"No?"

"I'm not going home. Lisa and I are at a hotel a few blocks from here. Well, not Lisa and I as in sharing a room, cause she's with Mitch... I have my own room." I ramble, a habit I had when I was uncomfortable.

He scratched his jaw. "Can I at least drop you there?"

"Um."

He sucked in a large breath. "Amelia, I... I never thought I would see you again."

Christ, I knew it. He was just playing nice for Lisa and Mitch. "Jake, I don't want to complicate things for you."

"Too late," he muttered.

What was that supposed to mean? Did he have a thing with April? I wouldn't get in the way. I knew firsthand what it was like to be rejected. Besides, I didn't even want a relationship after what Nick and Misha did to me. And once he found out I had a kid, he would run anyway. I should just walk away. Out of the corner of my eye, I saw Mitch moving through the crowd.

"It's okay. No one needs to know about us." I pulled away from him. "It was supposed to be one night with no strings. You don't have to pretend for the sake of them."

Jake scrunched his face and pursed his lips tight enough that the edge turned white. He looked angry, but I didn't ask why, because Lisa suddenly folded over and puked. I hung my head and went over to help Mitch with her, leaving Jake behind.

Mitch fished his keys out of his pocket and guided us to where they parked. I climbed in with Lisa, not giving Jake the chance to change my mind. Besides, Mitch might need help with her. He couldn't drive and hold her hair if she threw up.

The only sound on the way back was Lisa talking in her drunken state. She was muttering about cowboys and boobs. Mitch tried making sense of it, but it seemed to frustrate her. At least she didn't get sick.

Jake pulled up next to where we parked. "Need help to get her to the room?"

"Yeah," he said as he wrapped his arm around Lisa, half lifting her.

"Such a good man," Lisa slurred, tapping his cheek. I trailed behind them, saying a quick good night, before escaping to my room.

Jake looked over his shoulder at me as I retreated. He seemed even angrier. *Why was he mad?* I gave him an out. Even though I'd never had a one-night stand before, I'm sure I got the principle of it right. No promises, sneak out in the middle of the night, do an uncomfortable walk of shame, and never see them again.

Once I was in my room, I flopped on the bed, throwing my arms over my eyes. The problem was, I was drawn to Jake. He made me nervous in a way that only existed in movies. Jake made me think about wanting more, and that was terrifying. I reminded myself that he was an American ball player. Only here temporarily. Long distance would never work out and I had more than myself to think about.

Besides, I didn't need more problems with men. What I did need was a shower. My hair smelled like I was in a vat of grease, and I had been sweating all day, making me feel like I had swamp-boob. I rolled off the bed and walked into my swanky hotel bathroom. Normally, I would never have picked a suite, but Mitch booked the room and refused to let me pay. Resigned to let it go, the room was actually beautiful, and the bathroom was spacious, with a walk-in shower that had an oversized rain head shower. The water reached the perfect temperature, and I just stood there for a few minutes, letting my mixed thoughts swirl around. Logically, my brain warned me to stay away, but physically, I wanted to jump every inch of him from the moment our eyes made contact at the coffee truck.

Chapter Seven

Jake

We barely made it back to the hotel, and Millie bolted. What a confusing night. What the hell kind of bullshit was she spouting about pretending? Did I come off that way? She had been on my mind for months. I wasn't fucking pretending anything with her. We had this unbelievable night together, and then she acts like it never happened. I was about to tell her how happy I was to have found her again, but it was difficult to find the right wording, so it didn't come off heavy. She was already nervous around me. Right when I found the moment, it got all twisted, and she instead apologized for running into me again, making some comment about how it was supposed to be only one night. To be honest, it stunned me. That night changed everything for me.

Does she regret it? Regret me? Fuck, I hope not.

I couldn't let it go. I needed to talk to her and sort it all out.

We finally got Lisa into the room, and Mitch helped her into the bathroom as I stood in their doorway, debating on asking him for Millie's room number. *Why the hell am I taking my time?* I damn well knew I wasn't about to leave without sorting this out.

"Okay, smartass, you win. Help me out. I need Millie's room number."

"You gotta say it," he sang.

Oh, I'm so tempted to punch him. "Fine, you were right. Give me the damn number."

Lisa came to the door, and she smiled at me. "Three-twelve. Go get them boobies."

I fucking love Lisa. Millie would probably kill her in the morning, but I was incredibly thankful. I kissed her on the cheek and practically sprinted to Millie's room, not having a clue what to say, but I wasn't leaving tonight without her knowing my only regret was being stupid enough not to push for her number. I sure as fuck wasn't about to do it twice.

"I'm not in the mood, Lis." She called through the door when I knocked, looking shocked when she swung the door open she saw me.

Damn, she had clearly just showered, as her hair was still damp and hung loosely around her shoulders. She looked fresh and flawless in her little, short pajamas that showed off every inch of perfection. The light top was doing nothing to hide her bountiful breasts as she wasn't wearing a bra and they were still perfectly perky with her nipples showing through.

"What was that bullshit about pretending for one night only?" I asked, pushing us into her room and kicking the door closed, not wanting our conversation to filter into the hall.

She blew out a breath, backing away from me. "C'mon Jake. Be real. It was vacation, and neither of us expected shit to go the way it did. I threw myself at you. You don't owe me anything."

I was offended. "That's ridiculous." She straightened her back, about to snap at me, before I softened. "Amelia, I looked for you the next day. You were nowhere to be found. I've spent months kicking myself for allowing you to escape without a trace."

She stared at me wide-eyed. "What? Why?"

"Why? Cause you're incredible. There was something about you I couldn't forget." She stood motionless. *Did I read our night completely wrong?* "Was it a mistake? Is that why you have been hot and cold today?"

She shook her head. "No, that's not it at all."

"Then why would you think I didn't want to see you again?"

She threw her hands in the air. "Isn't that the point of it?"

That I couldn't deny, and I hated that she wasn't wrong. In normal circumstances, a one-night stand with a beautiful woman who wanted nothing in return was a dream night. I've had my fair share of them once upon a time, but none of them affected me the way she did. None of those women left me wondering about the what ifs afterward.

"Things could have been different. If you'd given me a chance."

"Sorry, I didn't know how to act. I felt embarrassed. I've never had a vacation fling or a one-night stand."

"For someone who has never done it before, you sure pulled off a spectacular stunt. Not even a name, or at least the right one." She turned a beautiful shade of crimson. Although it made my chest swell to know that I was worthy of her first one-nighter, I wanted to make sure I was her last. I inched closer, closing the gap. Her head tilted down as her chest rose and fell with her shallow breaths.

How can she deny this when I can see how I affect her?

With each step I took forward, she took one back until she was against the wall. I place my arms up to cage her in.

Mesmerized by her, only one thing came to my mind. The one thing I had wanted to do all night. I tilted my head down, and she lifted hers, her pink lips daring to be kissed. My hands trembled slightly against the wall. *What the hell?* We stood there, neither of us willing to break the tension or make the first move. I wanted to make sure she wanted this. When she cast her eyes down and bite the inside of her lip, I broke. I pressed my lips against hers and it was like a lightning bolt struck my body. She surprised me when she kissed back. Her lips were sweet and minty. *So delicious.* When I pulled away, her smile was enough to bring me to my knees. She was something else. It was impossible to keep my eyes off her.

"I have wanted to do that all night."

She bit the inside of her lip. "Me too."

Hearing that was a turn-on. I was a lucky bastard, but I had to show her how wrong she was about this lasting only one night.

"This time, I'm not leaving without knowing who you are."

"Knowing me?"

"Yeah, you know, a full name and address... This way you can't escape me again."

"Nosy, aren't we?"

I rolled my eyes. "Yeah, going for a real invasion of privacy wanting to know something about the woman I've already had sex with."

She pursed her lips adorably. She plunked into one of the plush chairs and folded her legs.

"Amelia Harte, or Millie, Mils, I'll answer to them all, although everyone uses Mils or Millie. Except you." She shot me a small smirk. "I'm thirty. I live in a small town about an hour and a half away from Toronto, called Beachers Bay."

"Wait, Amelia Harte? Like the pilot?"

"Pretty much. My parents thought it would be inspiring.

Personally, I think it's setting the bar awfully high for a baby. Plus, they aren't the ones who have to live with the puns every time someone says my name."

I chuckled. Clearly, people must say it all the time to her. "My friend Mikey's parents thought it was brilliant to name him Michael Jackson. His entire life, people ask him to do the moonwalk."

"Oh God, that's way worse," she laughed. "Your turn."

"I'm Jacob Jensen Parsons, thirty-one and from Florida originally... but a recent Toronto transplant, thanks to the trade."

Her face went solemn. "Jake, I had no idea who you were that night. In fact, it wasn't until tonight when Josh said something, I clued into who you really were."

"I figured. That's one of the things I liked about you."

"I felt like an idiot."

I grabbed her hand. "Don't. You not knowing me was way sexier and endearing because it meant you liked me for me." Being in the spotlight brought out all kinds of people. It was rare to find anyone who knew nothing about you.

We spent the next hour trading stats like a speed dating game. I learned she had an addiction to iced coffee. Her sweet tooth was butter tarts that she ate like a kid, and she hated mushrooms. She had two brothers and a yellow Lab named Mickey. She had a thing for shark movies. Her three girlfriends from the cruise were everything to her. During college, she worked with Lisa in a bar, and that's how they met. She'd earned her business degree and manages her family's construction company, which is why she moved back to her small hometown last year. I had to say I didn't foresee her in construction, and I liked it.

I told her about the trade. How it threw me off, I was still adjusting to the team. We talked about my younger sister, Jenna, who was probably just as close to me as Mitch. She had always been my biggest champion. She was the one who told me it was okay to pursue baseball instead of following in the family investment business.

She yawned. "Now that we have covered the basics, are we done?"

"Nah, we have barely scratched the surface. Any weird arrests? Embarrassing drunk stories? Messy exes?"

Her smile fell, and she straightened in her seat. *Uh-oh. Clearly, hit a nerve.* My gut said it was the ex. I couldn't see her getting into trouble, let alone being arrested. Heavy, thick silence filled the room. I ran my hands down my thighs, wiping the sweat away. *Don't overreact.*

"It's okay, don't worry about it." I tried to change the mood.

She twisted a strand of hair tightly, looking at her lap instead of me. "Jake, before this goes anywhere... I have to tell you something."

Alright, freaking out a little. What could be so big that I needed a warning? I scooted forward and clasped my hands together, waiting for her to say something. She bit the inside of her lip, keeping her gaze on her lap instead of me. I didn't have a good feeling about this.

"I have a daughter," she said in a shaky voice.

I was absolutely stunned. That was not at all what I thought she was going to say. It took a second to collect my thoughts that were spiraling into questions faster than I could process.

"So, I probably should have asked this before, but are you married? Boyfriend? Divorced?" *Please be divorced and not this 'it's complicated' bullshit.*

She sighed. "I'm single and, before you ask, yes, her dad is in the picture. We broke up before I found out was pregnant. We co-parent."

It was impossible not to notice her hesitation and unease

as mentioned her ex. It made me wonder how long that arrangement had been in place and why she cringed as she said it. I folded my hands in my lap to calm my nerves.

"How old is your daughter?"

"Aubree is four." Millie's blue gaze finally lifted to mine. It crushed me how much they filled with worry and sadness. *Shit.*

Not knowing what else to do, but seeing how much this was tearing her up, I leaned in and cupped her face. The urge to kiss her was stronger than anything I'd felt. I kissed her forehead, then her nose, and landed on her lips. It was gentle, but meaningful. I trailed my hands to her waist, taking every ounce of preservation I had to not move them to her breasts, which teased me through her pajama top.

Moving swiftly, I pulled Millie over my shoulder when I stood, carrying her to the bed, where I climbed in next to her.

"You make a terrible pillow," she murmured, resting her head on my shoulder. "You're too hard."

"Too hard? Can't say that's ever been an issue."

She smacked me on the arm. "Not like that."

We laid in silence. "Why do I always smell maple around you? I mean, I know you're Canadian, but..."

She laughed. "You can smell that? It's my shampoo. Maple something. All I know is that it's good for my hair."

"No wonder I crave pancakes around you," I teased, settling at her side.

She yawned. Her head felt heavier on my shoulder. "It's almost morning. I think we can sleep now." Her eyes closed and her breathing slowed, leaving me to think about what she said.

She had a kid. *Why the fuck didn't Mitch say anything? What about her ex? Does she date? How many guys has the kid met? Am I ready to take on a kid? Things just got way more serious than I expected.*

Glancing at the clock next to Millie's bed, I realized it was after three in the morning. There was no time to sort it out, because I had a flight in a few hours. I hadn't planned on being out so late, but I didn't want to leave once I saw her. The thought of having to go on the road for a back-to-back series made my stomach churn.

She was sound asleep in my arms, and I had brought nothing with me. How many times had I told myself to leave a spare bag in the car? Far too many. How many times did I take my advice? None. I squeezed my eyes, hating what I was about to do. But I stupidly left myself no choice. I kissed the top of her head and pulled away from her and left.

The entire ride home, all I could think about was Millie. Her sweet scent of maple lingered in my senses. It left me craving pancakes, *and Millie*, and kicking myself for not staying. I could have been with her instead of alone in a cold bed.

Man, I am a dick.

Chapter Eight

Millie

Jake was gone when I woke up. It hurt. Sadly, I expected this. At least it happened before things got real, not that I even knew where things were headed. My sadness turned to anger while I showered. *Determined to get to know me, my ass.* What a crock of shit. He only wanted to know fluff and bullshit. The minute something real came up, he bolted.

To hell with him, I thought, as I went and got ready for breakfast with Mitch and Lisa. I threw on my navy floral cropped leggings with a simple white scoop shirt knotted on the side and added a touch of mascara and lip gloss. Humidity was in the forecast, so I put up my hair, twisting it into a messy bun so it wouldn't stick to my neck. I was about to reach for my sandals when my phone pinged.

Lisa: Meet us down in the restaurant in five, or we're coming up. Should give you enough time to get a little morning action LOL.

Me: Yeah, yeah, I'll be there.

If only there was morning action. What if Jake stayed? Would I have kept my hands to myself? Because they wanted to do nothing but to run over his abs and down to that deep V that lingered in my mind.

Stop it. I sighed, my brain turning to the other side of things. How would I feel waking up next to him? It had been a long time since I woke up next to anyone. Even when Nick and I lived together, as shitty as he was, there was still some comfort in knowing I wasn't alone.

Maybe Nick was right; I was damaged goods. No one wanted the complications of someone else's kid. Jake proved it. A single tear fell for Aubree. Jake rejected her without even knowing her, and here I thought he meant what he said. I swiped away the tear and shook my head. I refused to cry over him. I grabbed my room key and headed downstairs.

When the elevator doors opened, it dumbfounded me to see Jake leaning against the opposite wall with his gaze fixed on his phone. Damn, he looked good, in a simple white dress shirt that showed off his defined bicep muscles, with his sleeves rolled up, showing off his muscular forearms. A few buttons were undone on the top, and he had that freshly showered look that made me stop dead in my tracks. *Pretend he isn't there.*

When I stepped out, his eyes caught mine, and he flashed a knee-weakening smile that made me glance over my shoulder to see if someone else was behind me.

"Hey." His voice was low and grumbly and, damn it, it made me want to drop my panties right there in the lobby.

If only I wasn't piping hot mad at him. *Jesus Millie, clearly, it's been far too long since you had sex if you would have even considered it.* He'd been my last time.

Shaking off the memory, I brushed past him and walked

toward the restaurant. He jogged up to me and pulled my elbow, so I had to stop.

"I get it. I'm sorry. I should have stayed," he stressed.

I glared at him. It was a look that warned him he was about to get launched across the lobby, via my foot, to his nut sack. He blew out a breath, about to say something, when Lisa came off the elevators.

"Hey, lovers." She winked at us.

I gave her a huge eye roll. "Where's Mitch?"

"He got a call. He'll be down by the time the coffee hits the table. Jake, glad you're joining us this morning." Lisa grinned.

"No, he's busy," I snapped.

"Millie, can we talk?" Jake interrupted, reaching for my arm again.

"Nope." I cut him off and followed Lisa.

The restaurant was busy. It was bright with giant wrap-around windows overlooking beautifully landscaped gardens. The host showed us to a corner table near the back.

"How did he know my room?" I blurted.

Lisa gave a small snort. "I told him." Well, at least she's not going to deny it. "How was last night?"

"Not even close to the same as yours."

She huffed, just as Jake and Mitch came in together. My guess was Jake waited, afraid to face the firing squad. Smart man, not that Mitch would save him from Lisa if he knew what had happened.

"What did I miss?"

Lisa was the first to speak, after sensing the tension. "Something is going on between these two and neither of them will say it."

Jake inhaled sharply, pinching the bridge of his nose. A look of remorse crossed his face. His saving grace was the server asking for our orders. When she brought her head up from her pad of paper, she stopped mid-sentence to eye Jake. She wasn't even shy about it.

"Coffee?"

"What?" she asked, turning her head toward me.

"Coffee," Lisa repeated, more annoyed than I was.

"How about you just leave the pot?"

"Funny," the server retorted. Her expression resembled a dead fish. She flipped over the cups that would have suited Aubree's dolls, and filled them with coffee. I lifted mine and scoffed. It was the size of an espresso cup, without being espresso. It was adding to my already shitty mood.

"You're serious about your coffee in the morning," Jake observed.

"I bet if it was you, she would have poured it on herself just to have you drink it off." I snapped. *That didn't even make sense. What is wrong with me?*

Mitch almost spit out his coffee. The server came back, minus a few buttons on her shirt. *Christ help me.* I wanted to smack her. *Mine or not, we're on a double date. Or whatever. Read the table and grow a brain.* Jake squeezed my knee under the table. I pushed it off, despite the warm sensation it caused.

"What'll it be?" She leaned so close to him that her nipple could have stirred his coffee. He shifted closer to me, but I refused to look at him and buried my head in the menu.

"Pancakes," he said. The memory of last night's conversation about him craving pancakes floated to my mind, sending an unwanted wave of heat between my thighs. "All I want is pancakes with extra syrup." I bit my lip, pretending not to get his reference.

"It's game day. You don't eat that crap," Mitch said.

"Today I do. In fact, I'd eat them every day." He held zero hesitation, like it was a promise. I locked my knees together. Despite being angry with him, my body responded to his words and the memory of him buried between my legs. The server rolled her eyes before taking the rest of our orders.

"You two need us to leave you alone?" Lisa chirped.

"No," I replied and kicked Lisa under the table. "What are you guys doing today?" I asked, trying to change the subject.

Mitch twirled his cup, shifting in his seat. "Uh, babe. I should let you know... Plans changed."

"What do you mean?" Lisa's eyebrow arched as she put her elbows on the table, facing Mitch.

"One of my guys is going into free-trade and flipping out. I have to leave with Jake."

Jake and I looked at Lisa and Mitch, focusing on Lisa's furious expression as she angrily flipped her napkin onto her lap. *Ouch*. She was about as happy with him as I was with Jake. Breakfast became quite frosty after that. The table was awkwardly silent while we ate. I rolled my neck and shoulders around, feeling a headache coming on. Jake softly rubbed his fingers in circles over the back of my neck. It felt good. Too good.

"Have you packed?" he whispered.

I shook my head. There were a few things from the morning that I still needed to toss in my bag. I excused myself, leaving Lisa and Mitch alone as Jake followed me.

We rode upstairs in silence. I kept my distance in the elevator. I didn't trust myself.

"Give me a chance to apologize, Amelia. Please," he begged as we reached my room. "Bailing this morning was wrong. I was an idiot. I should have left a note, but I wasn't expecting to be out for so long yesterday. I'm going on the road for the next few days, and I didn't have any of my things with me."

He almost looked sincere enough to believe it, but having to go get your shit doesn't excuse leaving after I mentioned my daughter. I jutted out my chin. "The only reason you left was because you weren't prepared?"

He ran his hands through his hair, groaning.

And that was everything I needed to know. I pushed past him.

"Fuck. I screwed up. I'm sorry. I freaked out for a minute, but I like kids. *A lot.* Let me fix this."

"Would have been better to know last night."

He continued his case, begging for a chance to prove he was honest. He grabbed my hand, slipping in a piece of folded up paper. "Here's my number. Use it. Please."

"We'll see."

"Amelia... I really want a chance." He looked disappointed. "I hoped this could be more."

"Me too, until you left."

Regret was visible in his expression. He leaned forward, hovering for a second. The scent of his light cologne was enough to make me forget I was mad. He brought his eyes to mine, making me look at him.

"I'll make it up to you. Any and every chance you give me," he assured me.

Everything on his face told me he meant what he said. I wished I didn't care, but I did. Even with him that close, it was my body closing the distance between us like a traitor. He pushed me against the door frame, his eyes never leaving mine. My heart rate picked up in anticipation of a kiss I shouldn't have craved. The truth was, I had given in before our lips even touched and when he let go, instantly I missed them. He gave me one last pleading look for a chance I couldn't commit to.

* * *

Lisa and I were both in foul moods. She's constantly pestered me about Jake. My emotions were all over the place, battling between confusion and anger. It was a flood I wasn't expecting. My life wasn't simple. Nick and I could barely co-parent, let alone add in someone new.

My past weighed heavily on me every day. It might be too much for Jake. Sure, he said he was okay with it, but he doesn't know what that even means.

Lisa was silent, stewing in the car on the drive back to her place. Maybe it was time I opened up to her. She had always helped me get to the bottom of things. If not, at least it might get her mind off Mitch.

As if she read my mind, she turned to me and stared. "What?"

"What's going on between you guys? He was grinning when he went to your room last night, but this morning, he looked like you kicked him in the balls."

"I told him about Aubree. He looked damn near terrified. And he left when I was sleeping. I can handle rejection, but I won't put Aubree through it. She deals with enough shit from Nick."

Lisa's jaw dropped. "You should have kicked him in the balls."

"I know."

"Wait, why did he come back? That was ballsy."

"Really? A ball pun?" She snorted. Waving her hand so I'd continue. "He said he was sorry. He freaked out, and he wants to prove that he *likes kids*," I said, using air quotes.

"He does like kids. I've seen them on kids' day. He goes out of his way to spend time with them."

"This isn't the same. It's not some kid you spend a minute with. She's *my* kid. All the time, not part-time."

Lisa sighed. "Hear me out. Maybe give it a minute before you snap off the idea of dating him. Let him digest it. She's a great kid. I hate seeing you use the excuse of being a *mom* to not date. You need to get back out there. Mom's date. Not everybody gets it right the first time."

"I'm not even sure about dating again, especially him. He's Jake freaking Parsons." I looked at her as she rolled her eyes, giving me an annoyed huff.

"Yeah, and? He's just a boy who likes a girl."

"For now..."

"No. Millie," she disagreed. "This is where you're wrong."

I scrunched my face. "What?"

"A couple months ago, I suggested to Mitch that we hook you guys up. He said he wasn't sure. Jake's last relationship hadn't ended that long ago, and he'd met some mystery woman on the cruise. She slipped away, and he regretted it. Then I found out it was you."

"It was a harmless fling."

"Maybe not." Lisa shrugged. "Look, I don't agree with what he did last night. And I get it. Jake is the only other guy you've been with. It's a big deal. Don't hide behind the fling. You're drawn to him, and you can deny it all you want, but we both know you're lying. I see it on your face."

"See what?"

"Happiness."

I bit the inside of my cheek. That I couldn't argue with. Around him, I felt like I had a perm-a-grin, which left me with a bigger question. *Why him?* Was it simply the thrill of a vacation fling, or something more? Until he came along, I had forgotten what it felt like to be desired. Actually, I don't think I ever felt like Nick desired me. I was simply something he had. Jake, for the love of God, already made me feel so much more. He made me wonder about the possibilities of a future, but my situation was difficult. If things didn't work out, it would devastate my kid. There was no way I could risk her getting attached to him. What if he decided a kid was too much? Cramped his lifestyle?

He had no obligation to stay with us. One thing I learned from Nick and Misha was that there was always someone else smarter, prettier, and willing to do whatever it takes to win.

Jake wasn't even a regular guy. Women threw themselves at him. I could only imagine the dating pool for celebrities and rich people. Besides, athletes were notorious for scandals. Like Nick used to say, "Just cause there's a goalie in the net doesn't mean you can't score." *What an asshole.* How I stayed with him for so long is beyond me. I blame it on stupidity or stubbornness.

"What about Nick?" I sighed. I'd never dated. Would be he okay with it?

"What about him?"

"Lis, come on. You know how things are."

"Honestly, Millie, who gives a fuck what he thinks? He's married. To your ex-bestie. Nick has no say over your dating life." Her voice hit an octave that was reserved for Nick.

When she put it like that, it made it hard to argue with her. Nick had moved on long before our relationship was even done. Hell, I don't even know if he was ever truly in it. Apparently, I sucked as a goalie.

Chapter Nine

Jake

"How are things with Lisa?" I asked on the drive to the airport. Mitch's look said it all. He ran his hand through his hair. Not sure if I should add more shit to his plate, but I had a few questions I needed answers to.

"Why didn't you tell me she had a kid?" I demanded.

Mitch rubbed his jaw, working it back and forth. "Didn't need to. I know you, man. It's not a deal breaker. The way you looked at her yesterday at the fair, it never crossed my mind."

I squeezed my eyes. "Yeah, well, I screwed up."

"Shit, what could you possibly have done already?"

"When she told me about her daughter, I freaked out. Don't even know why, but I left before she woke up. I told myself it was because I needed my shit for the road games." The minute it left my lips, I felt awful. Mitch turned to face me, his mouth agape. He took a second to collect himself.

"Shit, that was bad. Here I thought I had it rough with

Lisa this morning. You're screwed." *Yeah, thanks, buddy.* "I'm surprised you're walking without a limp. What made you come back to the hotel?"

"Did you not hear me? I left before she woke up!" I huffed in frustration, making Mitch chuckle. "Seriously, all I did last night was think about what an idiot I am. There was no way I could leave it like that."

"You never were one to walk away," he agreed. "Last night you had your moron hat on, but aside from that, you can make it work." He punched me in the leg.

Fuck. This is the first time I messed things up with a woman before it even got started. Mitch's phone rang again, after already going off the entire time to the airport. I felt sorry for the bastard.

I needed to fix this. There was something between us, even more than I could've imagined. Will she give me a chance to apologize? *I hope so.* My thoughts went to her ex.

"What do you know about her ex?" I inquired, remembering what little details she shared.

"Not much. She and Lisa never bring him up. I tried to get some facts from Lisa when she brought up the idea of hooking you two up, but all she says is Millie's the only reason Lisa doesn't have an arrest record against him."

"He's involved? I mean, he must be right? Cause I didn't even know about the kid."

Mitch shrugged. "You'll have to ask her."

Our conversation left me with more questions only Millie could answer, if she would just open up to me. Heck, I might even prove she could trust me.

"I left her my number," I continued, hopeful.

"There's not a chance in hell she's gonna use it."

I slumped in my seat and ducked my head, knowing he was right. Leaving without telling her might have sealed my fate. What the hell was I thinking?

This stretch of games was going to suck while I played the "will she or won't she" game *and* baseball. Why did I have to fuck it up and not leave myself enough time to fix it?

* * *

The away games felt like they stretched out forever. We were in Seattle for a triple series, then Chicago, before finally back to Toronto. Being the only Canadian team, we were on the road twice as much.

Exhausted, I plunked on the sofa, turning on the sports highlights. The one good thing that came out of being in Atlanta was I found a new PA, Brody. Turns out Kev knew a guy looking for a job. So far, he seemed alright. Brody could predict what I needed, fixing some messes in my schedule the other two idiot temps I used made.

Mitch was right about Millie not making the first move. I hadn't heard from her.

Lost in deep thought, I jumped when my phone chimed with a message from my sister.

Jenna: You suck lately.

Me: Wow, don't hold back.

Jenna: Never do.

Me: So, you wanted to bust my balls about the game?

Jenna: A little, but what's new?

Loaded question. I hadn't told Jenna about finding my mystery girl. Mostly because I wasn't sure what was happening. Frustrated, I felt like I wanted to vent, and I doubted Mitch would be any help at this point.

Me: I found Amelia...

Jenna: Amelia? Ship girl?

Me: Turns out she was right under my nose.

Jenna: Don't tell me... Groupie? Flight attendant? OMG, one of Jax's exes?

Me: Ha-ha, you're so funny.

Jenna: Who is she? Don't leave a girl hanging...

Me: I told you about Mitch and his girl Lisa? Lisa is her BFF.

Jenna: SHUT UP!

Me: She was at Ribfest with them... She lives an hour from me.

Jenna: Of course, you find the one girl you know nothing about. I hope you can see my eye roll from there.

Me: Yeah, I sensed it. Maybe it was just meant to be.

Jenna: *Emoji of someone throwing up*

Jenna: JK. Was she thrilled to see you?

Me: Well...

Jenna: OMG, she didn't remember you? Hilarious. I love her already.

Me: You're an ass.

Jenna: Ya, tell me something I don't know. What are you going to do about it?

Me: That's the million-dollar question. I am waiting for her to make a move.

Jenna: Hahaha! Let me guess, she wants nothing to do with you? Serves you right. Bighead. Hold on, I need to catch my breath from laughing...

Argh. I pinched the bridge of my nose and cursing under my breath before I tossed the phone on the other side of the couch. A bottle of scotch sitting on the counter was calling me. Was my sister right? Maybe Millie wasn't interested in me. Was I imagining things with us? Is she hesitating because of her kid? Not knowing was killing me. Just when I think I make progress, I lose her again.

* * *

"What a shit game," I said, slamming my locker door hard enough that it bounced back at me.

"It was something. How did you miss that fly ball, by the way?" Kev asked.

Because I can't stop thinking about Millie. I was so distracted that I made a mistake and cost us the game, but I couldn't tell him *that*.

I dropped my head in my hands. "I don't know. I thought I had it."

"Maybe use a net next time. You might actually catch the ball." Josh teased and smacked me on the shoulder.

"Fuck off." I wasn't in the mood for his shit. He'd been riding my ass since Ribfest about Millie, and I was over it.

Josh chuckled. "I'm just busting your balls. Are you in for Arcane tonight?" He whipped off his towel, tossing it on the floor before grabbing his pants from his locker.

"Don't you wear underwear?"

"Nah. I like the free swing."

"Free swing? Dude, your pants are tighter than my sister's."

"You have a sister?"

"Not on your life, pal.

Josh mocked disappointment for about a second before his phone rang. "Hey, baby," he answered, tossing up his middle finger at me before leaving the room.

I sat on the bench and laced up my shoes, half listening to the locker room chatter. Most of the guys on both teams were planning on hitting up Arcane. I resisted the urge to check my phone again.

Kev came over and kicked my foot. "Let's go, pretty boy. Looks like you need a night out."

For once, he was right. I grabbed my bag and trailed behind him, wondering what shenanigans they were up to for tonight.

* * *

Arcane was packed. It was a typical post-game spot in the heart of the club district. A perfect distraction from my shitty performance, both on and off the field. Seven fucking days. How could Millie not call or text?

"What are you drinking?" Kev asked, pointing to the table lined with bottles.

"Bourbon." Kev signaled to the host for another round.

Josh was sitting across from me with some woman in his lap. He took his eyes off of her chest long enough to tilt his head over to me. "No girl tonight?"

I didn't want to get into it with him, especially with how freaking cozy he and Millie were. The thought alone sent a spike of jealousy through me. My fists instinctively balled.

"I need to piss." I stumbled out of our restricted area before I punched him. His look said he was just being a shit, but the other part of me wondered if she would have called him by now.

Walking toward the bathroom, a pretty brunette stopped me with a tiny fucking red dress. *Seriously, a napkin covered more skin.*

"Jake Parsons?" she asked in a ridiculously nasally voice.

I stared blankly at her. "I think you forgot half your dress," I said, looking her over. She was trying too hard to show off her body.

"No, silly. It's designer."

"Then you got ripped off." She shot me an evil look, then she smiled. *What the hell?*

"Wanna dance?" She grabbed hold of my hand, yanking me onto the dance floor. *How the fuck is she so strong?*

"Not really. I have a girl," I said, hoping she would back off.

"I didn't see you with anyone." She glanced over my shoulder. "Don't worry, I won't tell. Besides, if you were mine, I'd never let you out alone." She flashed a creepy smile, pushing herself against me. I shuddered. *Not happening.*

I looked around for an escape. Josh caught my eye, flirting with some blond by the bar. *Ha. Payback's a bitch.* Gently, I pulled my arm back and nodded toward the guys.

"He's very single." I winked, pushing her into Josh. She broke out into a huge grin. Josh looked confused at first, then his face dropped once he realized what I was doing. I flipped him off, laughing. That girl was a straight-up clinger. *He's going to have to Houdini himself to escape her.*

That should teach him a lesson about messing with me. I had no interest in staying any longer, so I hailed a ride. As much fun as the guys were, the distraction was minimal. My mind was stuck on Millie.

Chapter Ten

Millie

A week had passed, and I still hadn't called Jake. Should I have? According to the girls, yes. My confusion was clouding my head. He apologized, but he left.

My fear of rejection for Aubree ran deep. Nick was never around much when she was born. It already felt like I was his second choice. A mistake. He spent a lot of time telling me how much of an inconvenience it was for him to have to drive all the way to the city to come to visit when he was balancing Misha and their baby, plus he was opening a store.

The number of times I cried over him could fill a lake. Last year, I made the gut-wrenching decision to go back home to our small town, Beachers Bay, so that he could be more involved in Aubree's life. I was sick of hearing his bullshit excuses and being an afterthought. He was going to treat us the way he should have been, and if that meant I needed to sacrifice myself, I would. At least I had my family back home.

Already I felt guilty for staying away for so long, even though they understood why.

Being back in this God-forsaken town, could I even handle dating? Everyone was in everyone's business. The town nearly imploded when I came back. The scandal Nick, Misha, and I caused was front and center all over again.

Christ, I must be out of my mind to think about bringing someone else into my life. Jake's deep eyes, pleading for a chance, tore me up. He wanted more, but I was nervous. What was more? The only love I had ever known was Nick. *See how it turned out?* There was no comparison between the two, but I had a nagging feeling it wouldn't be simple. I was a single mom, with a dick of an ex in a small town and meddling friends. The poor guy should run like hell.

* * *

"Aubree, go wash up for dinner," I called into the living room. "Uncle Avery and Uncle Alex will be here in a few minutes."

"Yay!"

My brothers had been bugging me to visit Aubree. They bribed me with pizza and butter tarts. Bastards knew my weakness.

"Pizza's here." Alex announced, coming through the door. Aubree screeched and ran out from the powder room, launching herself at Alex.

"Woah, Kiddo. You're lucky Uncle Avery is holding the pizza," he chuckled.

"No pep-or-oni, right?" She furrowed her brows, wagging her finger at him.

He straightened up and, in his most serious tone, he said, "No, ma'am. Cheese for the princess."

"Yummy." She rubbed her stomach, coming to the table and plopping into her seat. One might think I never fed her with the way she acted when it was pizza night. Aubree bombarded her uncles with her silly stories that didn't seem to make any sense, but made us all laugh, until I put on her favorite movie.

"Still into that movie, huh?" Avery asked, watching Aubree sing and dance along with the movie.

"Yup," I chuckled. "I can recite the movie in my sleep at this point."

Alex snorted and hung his head. "So can I."

Avery stuffed another bite of pizza in his mouth before asking, "How's Lisa? You guys went out last weekend?"

"How did you know?"

"Mom mentioned it. Plus, I think Lisa posted something on her socials," Avery said, taking a big bite of his pizza.

"Stalking Lisa now?" I teased. He guffawed, but the sudden shade of pink he turned said something different. "She has a boyfriend."

"What?" Alex sputtered as he choked on his soda. "Boyfriend? Miss One-night Stand?"

It seemed strange to me also, but seeing them together last weekend, I got why. "She met him on the cruise. They've been together since."

Avery snorted in disbelief, causing Alex and I to turn toward him. His face scrunched up and his mouth opened and closed. "Never mind." He had a soft spot for her. They had spent a lot of time together through my pregnancy. I was sure he had a crush on her for a while, but he never made anything of it.

"Expecting someone?" Alex inquired as the doorbell rang, causing us to look at each other.

"No."

"I get it." Aubree bolted from the floor to the door. I followed behind her as she flung the door open. "Woah," she said, looking at a bouquet of red roses.

"Amelia Harte?" the person asked from behind the bouquet.

"Yeah," I answered, confused. I had never been sent flowers. Ever. "Thanks." I said, taking them from him.

"I wanna see, Mama." Aubree tugged at my arm as I closed the door.

"Hold on. I'm not done yet," he said, grabbing another bouquet of all white flowers from the porch. My mouth went slack when he went back to his truck and unloaded dozens of bouquets.

"Holy shit," Alex said when he stepped into the hallway.

I smacked him. "Language." He winced.

Just when I thought it was done, the man handed me one last bunch with purple and white flowers. A tiny card was tucked onto the top. "For Princess Aubree." Christ, I melted right there.

"Anything you want to tell us?" Avery asked with a small smile tugging at the corners of his mouth, despite standing with his arms crossed.

Aubree tugged my arm again, pulling at the last bouquet. "Who is it from, Mama?"

"Yeah, Mama, who's it from?" Alex mimicked. My face could have matched the color of the roses, or at least that's how it felt when I flushed. They could only be from one person, but how? It only took a second for it to click. *Lisa*.

"Where are all of these going?" Alex asked as he glanced around at the seemingly endless amount of flowers.

"Anywhere there's space."

My brothers grabbed the flowers and placed a bouquet in each room of the house.

Avery put his arm over my shoulder when he came back. "Whoever he is, he's already better than Nick."

He is. I feel like a jerk. Jake didn't even compare to Nick.

Alex and Avery insisted on putting Aubree to bed and

helping me clean up. As much as they denied it, I knew they just wanted me to open the card that I'd tucked away before they could snatch it. Once they left, I held it in my trembling hands, nervous to open it. I doubted I would have any strength to resist Jake after this. I opened it after counting to three.

A flower for each day that I've thought of you.
Jake

One scribbled sentence was enough to break all of my willpower. I'd been making excuses not to call him, but he deserved that call. With the card clutched in my hand, I pulled out the folded piece of paper with his number from my wallet.

I'd dialed twice, never completing the call. *You're being ridiculous.* Taking a shaky breath, I paced, finally dialing the full number. *Please go to voicemail.*

It barely rang. "Hey, beautiful." The sound of his voice was instantly calming my nervous energy.

"I got your delivery."

"I'd hoped the flowers would work."

"Work?" I paused in awe, looking around the living room. "Jake, you didn't need to buy out an entire florist to get my attention."

He chuckled. "I didn't buy them out."

"There are hundreds of flowers!"

"Nah. One for each day I've thought of you since you captivated me on the lido deck of a cruise. One hundred and sixty days ago."

My voice caught in my throat, and tears rolled down my face. It was the sweetest thing anyone had ever said to me. He had me without the flowers.

"Jake, it's... It's so much. You're, hell, I don't even know..." I stammered, not making any sense.

"Amelia, I want you to know I'm dead serious. I'm sorry about leaving. I'll wait until you're ready, but we have something here. I want to see what it is." He paused, waiting for my response.

I sniffled, uttering his name.

"I hate to go, but I'm about to head onto the field."

"You have a game? Why did you answer?"

"I'd hoped it was you."

I sighed, his words twisting in my heart. "Thank you."

"Don't thank me yet. It's only the beginning, Amelia." He hung up, and every part of me shivered with what he said. I buried my face in the soft velvety flowers and took a deep inhale of the floral scent. It was everything. Damn, he really is dangerous.

A smile crept across my face and my heart wanted to explode out of my chest, overwhelmed with emotions I'd never had. I immediately called the girls. They demanded I conference called them on video so they could see. After all of their swooning over the flowers, they scolded me, frustrated I hadn't made more of an effort with him yet.

I thought about what they said, while I took some pictures surrounded by the flowers for my socials. I didn't want anyone to know who they were from, so I simply captioned it, "A visit from the flower fairy", and settled on a pic of Aubree and me. My face was flushed, but I didn't care.

* * *

It was my weekend with Aubree, and we went down to visit the girls. They missed her and video calls would only go so far. After my run-in with Nick and Misha in the morning, I was more than happy to get us out of town.

When we pulled up, Lisa was on the porch in a Toronto Twisters jersey. I rolled my eyes at her. Could she be more obvious? I knew it wasn't just the team she was rooting for.

She swung Aubree around as I dropped our bag inside and asked Lisa why she was outside.

"Cause we're leaving," she stated matter-of-factly.

My expression fell. "Please tell me we're going to the bar to watch the game."

"Nope. Now let's go." She swooshed me back down her driveway.

Planting my feet, I turned to her. "Aubree is with me. This isn't right." Angry was an understatement. I had no interest in involving Aubree when I wasn't even sure if there was anything to be involved in.

"Mils, it's a baseball game... All of us will be there. He won't even know we're there." *Doubt it.*

Not having much choice once Aubree heard we were going to the game, I reluctantly walked toward the subway while Aubree talked animatedly about seeing an actual baseball game. I was sure she had no idea what she was in for, but Aunt Lisa was doing her best to hype it up.

We waited on the platform for the train. Aubree was so excited. She and Lisa were playing hot hands. Maybe she's right. *It's just a game. He won't know we're there.*

When we got to the stadium, I looked around for Gia and Sam. "Where are the others?"

"Gia had a late meeting and Sam is waiting for her. They should be here before the first pitch."

The dome top of the stadium was open, giving us a clear view of the blue sky and picturesque clouds. She led us down to the 100 level. Clearly, someone had done their homework to find the best section to sit in. I had zero doubt Mitch was in cahoots with this.

"We made it," Gia announced, wiping her brow. "Damn, it's packed in here."

We stood for the anthem and, while the lineup was being announced, I tried for a bathroom break.

"Trying to escape?" Lisa asked when I stood up.

"Have to pee, smart ass. But, yeah, if I didn't think you would tackle me before I got out of the stands, I would."

"Glad you know it."

"I'll come. I didn't go before I got here." Gia added, standing up next to me. She glanced at Lisa with a sly smile. *Jesus, it feels like I'm being supervised.*

When I got back to my seat, I noticed how close we were to the players. "What a view."

"And the players," Sam added. She turned back to Aubree, who was digging into a tub of popcorn.

The players ran into the dugouts. It felt like the heat rose ten degrees and I was sure I was turning red when I found Jake. And, damn, that hat did things to me. I sat on the edge of my chair, my eyes bored into him. It was hard not to notice how his biceps flexed when he threw the ball, let alone the way the uniform hugged his ass. Just watching him on the field, I couldn't remember for the life of me why I was playing so hard to get.

The sound of the crowd and the crack of the ball distracted me. The ball flew toward us. Jake sprinted across the field. He leaped in the air and crashed over the wall, landing on the guys in the front row.

Popcorn flew in the air, beers crashed down, and a string of profanities came out of the guy he landed on. Everyone held their breaths, watching the commotion. Jake freed himself from the big lug he landed on. He held his glove up, showing off the ball.

"He caught the ball!" Aubree cheered wildly.

The crowd thundered for him, except for the surly douchebag who lost his food. Lisa let out this giant whistle. Everyone turned towards us. I wanted to crawl under the seats. Jake's head snapped up, looking right at me. I swear my heart skipped a beat. I froze, and so did he.

He shoved through the crowd right to us, only a few rows from where he landed, and stopped in front of Aubree, who stood on the seat next to me. I swallowed the lump in my throat as his eyes shifted between us.

With a big grin, he asked her if she wanted a ball. She reached in and hugged him, screeching in delight when he handed her the ball. The crowd lapped it up.

Sam tapped my shoulder and nodded toward the large screen above the field, which was focused on Aubree, who jumped up and down with the ball.

Chapter Eleven

Jake

For once, I was on the right side of the press conference. The hero of the game, thanks to that catch. Except, I didn't give a damn about it. She was here. *They* were here, and Christ, Millie's daughter was an exact mini replica of her. It left me speechless.

I sent Jimmy, one of the guards, over to get them after the press left. If Millie thought she was leaving without saying anything, she was out of her mind. I had thought the flowers would help bring us together, but I'd been on the road, and she hadn't reached out since. Tonight was the first in our series against Boston. Her being there was like a breath of redemption.

When the cameras stopped clicking, they gave us the all-clear to leave. For the first time in ages, I was nervous. The guys congratulated me on my catch, and a few handshakes later, I grabbed my duffel and headed out into the tunnels. A few reporters were still clicking away when I saw Millie and Lisa standing against the wall with a couple of women I recognized from the cruise. Aubree clung to Millie's hand.

"Hi." I grinned, lowering my eyes to Aubree. "Did you like the catch?" I asked, kneeling, so I was at eye level with her.

"You fly like a superhero," she shrieked.

"I do?" I teased. "I don't know. They have capes." She cocked her head to the side. "Want me to sign it?"

"Nope." She shrugged, making us all laugh.

Ruthless. I love it. I cocked my head toward Millie, who nervously shifted on her feet. The silence was awkward. I nodded, extending my hand to the two I hadn't met yet. I introduced myself and learned they were Sam and Gia. "Nice to meet you. What brings you into my neck of the woods?"

"Meh, I thought you needed a favor." Lisa winked. *She's quickly becoming my favorite person.* Millie closed her eyes and held her breath for a second. I sensed her embarrassment. Since this seemed to be an unexpected evening for Millie, I wondered what else Lisa had up her sleeve.

"Any plans now?" I asked. Millie opened her mouth, but Lisa cut her off before she could speak.

"Actually," Lisa backed away from Millie, "we're taking Aubree for a special aunties night... Sorry, but moms and boys aren't allowed." *I thought it was a nice play by Lisa, but Millie's expression suggested otherwise.* If looks could kill, Lisa would be buried in the field.

Even though this wasn't planned, she hadn't said no. I wanted a chance to talk to her and, with how things had been, that might be it. "So, I guess it's just you and me?"

Millie wouldn't make eye contact while she was absently twirling Aubree's hair. "We don't have to. I'm sure you have plans."

"Even if I had plans, I'd cancel them to spend time with you."

"Oooh, smooth. I like it," Gia gushed, nudging Millie toward me while Lisa slipped Aubree away with the promise of pizza and a slumber party.

After a lengthy goodbye and several warnings to the girls not to spoil Aubree, we walked out to street level.

"Hungry?" I asked, taking Millie's hand once they were out of sight.

I paused, turning to look at her scrunched expression, as we waited for the light to change.

"Sure. Do you have something in mind?"

I rubbed the back of my neck. If Lisa had given me a heads up, I would have planned a proper date. Whisked her to the moon and back if I had to.

Her face softened. "I don't need plans," she reassured me after I hesitated. "Winging it is perfect."

Jesus, this girl. The way she was looking up at me with a sheepish smile was more than I could resist. I tugged her hand, pulling her closer to me, our lips a mere inch apart. Her sweet maple scent made my dick jump. I cupped her cheek with my palm, tracing her jaw with my thumb. She licked her lips in anticipation. I lowered my mouth to hers. My brain went into a state of fog. My body ached for more. If she only knew what she did to me.

"We can go wherever you want for dinner," I whispered.

"How about your place? We can order in."

My eyebrow nearly arched off my head. "If you come back to my place, I'm not sure I'll be able to restrain myself."

"I'm sure you'll do just fine, slugger." She winked, pulling away from me. My hand eased into hers, like a reflex, as we walked along King Street to my condo.

Inside, Millie wandered around while I went to see if I had anything other than water to offer her. My place was simple, with a modern box design, generic gray monotone colors, and neutral furniture. It was still staged and not very lived-in.

Angry about the trade, I never changed it. The gorgeous view of the lake from the wrap-around balcony was the selling feature. Nights like tonight, when the sun set, turning the sky pink and purple against the deep blue lake, made it feel like home.

"Nice." Her gaze circled the room, landing on the sixty-five-inch screen that consumed the only wall with no windows.

"Too big?"

"Ha. Never." Millie smirked.

"At least your neighbors can save on cable. Half of them can just watch yours," she said and walked out onto the balcony.

She stood against the railing, and her hair blew in the light breeze. Well, damn, that was the best view yet. Reminded me of the ship, that night on the deck. That night changed more stats than I care to talk about. It will all be worth it, though. She's worth it. *I'll bet my career on it.*

"That better be all they watch," I said as my arms wrapped around her waist, squishing her to me while my lips kissed her shoulder. She giggled. The sound floated right into my chest.

I rested my head on her shoulder. "I'm so glad you came to the game. All of you. Including your adorable look-a-like."

"Yeah, she's got my sassy attitude to go with it."

"I don't doubt that at all. Her eye roll is savage already," I laughed. "Was today her first game?"

"Yup. I didn't think she would be into baseball. She's in a princess stage."

"We can work on that." Her head cranked to the side, her ocean eyes piercing me. They were fierce, like she was trying to read me. Her protectiveness was utterly beautiful. The impulse to kiss her took over. She kissed back, making me want more of her, all of her, right there. It took a minute for that trigger warning to blare, to slow down. It was a marathon, not a sprint. As much as I didn't want to, I pulled away and tried to refocus my thoughts on something other than taking her into my bedroom and making sure she didn't want to leave it.

"What's wrong?" She looked confused.

"Nothing." I tucked a piece of hair behind her ear without taking my eyes off of her. "Why? Do you think I only want you for sex?"

Her cheeks turned a light pink, and she moved her gaze to the ground. I brought her chin up so she was looking at me. I needed her to know I wanted more from this than casual hookups.

"I'm in no rush."

"A little redundant?"

I moved closer to her. "Completely different pretenses. You only wanted a one-night stand then."

"Didn't you?"

"No," I said matter-of-factly.

She stared at me, a puzzled look on her face, as if she thought I was lying.

I held my ground. "I mean it. I guess fate thought it should have been more, too."

Millie laughed, placing her hand on my chest and tapping it. "It was more Lisa and Mitch's intervention."

I cocked my head. "Maybe, but fate guided them along, and now you're here, so let's accept it for whatever this is going to be."

She nodded in agreement. I suggested ordering sushi from the place around the corner and Millie suggested a movie. We settled together on the sofa, and the sight of her lounging on my couch was something. A warmth spread through me.

* * *

I woke up with Millie snuggled against my chest. We'd fallen asleep on the couch, and she felt good nestled into me. I knew she didn't want to spend the night away from Aubree, so I slowly moved to wake her.

"Mm," she moaned in the sexiest voice I've ever heard.

My dick shot straight up. Fuck, I wanted her to stay, but I *couldn't* be that guy. She stretched, her shirt lifted, showing the tiniest bit of her stomach, while she rubbed her eyes. It took every ounce of preservation not to show her how much I wanted to recreate our first night, but I was adamant to prove to her I meant what I said.

"You're beautiful."

Millie rolled her eyes. "You're one cheesy guy with the lines."

"Have you seen you? It's no line." I kissed her forehead, lowering mine against hers. "I want to tie you to the bed so you can't leave."

"Now there's an idea." I stared at her for a second in disbelief before she laughed. "Wow. Your face right now!"

"You're evil," I taunted, standing and extending my hand for hers.

When we got to the parking garage, she stopped dead and stared at the rows of luxury cars. "This isn't like one of those things where all the cars are yours, are they?"

I laughed. "I only have one," I told her, pointing to the matte black sports car.

She stood still and blinked at me. "Of course, you do."

"What? The company is a sponsor." I shrugged and folded into the front seat. Millie gave me the address to Lisa's and watched me plug the directions into the navigation system. I was not at all familiar with Toronto yet.

As we drove the fifteen minutes to Lisa's, I couldn't stop glancing at her, wondering how long it would be before I could see her again. "When can I see you again?"

She inhaled and looked out her window. It was only a few seconds, but it felt like an eternity before she answered. "I'm not sure. Send some days that work for you."

What a simple thing to say, to blow me off, and yet it felt like she didn't. *How does she do that?* She was quiet the rest of the ride and I was dying to know what she was thinking, but I didn't want to push her. I had a feeling it might be new territory for her. When we got to Lisa's, Millie was already pulling out a key before I parked.

She put her hand on the door handle and I rushed around to open the door for her, holding her hand to help her out.

She stood at the side of the car and fiddled with her hair. "Thank you for tonight."

"Next time, we will plan it," I assured her.

A mischievous look crossed her eyes. "Spontaneous seems to works for us."

I shook my head and pressed her against the car door. "Touché, but I want a proper date with you," I implored.

Her voice lowered when she replied, "Then you better find some time."

Holy hell. This woman. If she only knew how fast I was going to find time for her. My lips crushed hers until my head spun. I was reluctant to let her go, but I did. She walked to the door with one grinning glance at me. I already wanted her back.

I shook my head, not knowing what to do, because the rules were different with her. I couldn't ask her to stop doing life to wait for me or wing it as I have in the past. She was a mom first, and I respected her for that. It sucked to drive away and not have concrete plans, but she was coming around.

* * *

I was back in Florida for a three-game series. Man, I was glad to be home again. I liked my condo in Toronto, but it wasn't the same. My phone pinged as I got in the car to drive home from the stadium. It was Brody, my new PA. He was letting me know he set everything up and food was on the way. Already this guy made my last PA look like a clown. Brody was laser focused, organized, and I swear a fucking mind reader. He knew exactly what I needed and how to handle everything as I would without having to check with me. It was a relief.

I hosted a last-minute poker game with some of my team-mates and friends. I missed those fuckers. Carlos was the Bays' catcher, and Mikey was an outfielder with a mad batting aver-age. The guy was a machine. My idiot cousin Jax found out I was in town, so he invited himself, as usual, the dick. With Jax came his twin, Justin. The three of us grew up more like brothers, anyway.

They arrived as I changed after my shower, with Jax tapping my face while walking through the door.

"Jak-ie," he taunted.

"Stop that shit." I pushed his hand away.

Carlos chuckled behind him. Justin and Mikey followed in a few minutes later.

"Shit, man, your last game looked like you were playing from the parking lot," Jax teased, referring to the ball that whizzed by my head last night.

"Yeah, yeah." I knew I fucked up the play. I didn't need to relive it.

"How's Canada treating you?" Carlos asked.

"Alright. The guys have been great, welcoming really. The transition was rough at first."

"I was shocked to find out the Bays traded you. I mean sure, your last season was crappy. We've all been there."

I grunted in reflection. My personal life took a nosedive,

and it affected my game as much as I tried not to let it. "Not my finest year."

"How's Josh?" Carlos asked, chuckling. He knew the history between us.

"Still a dick."

Mikey chimed in while he dealt out the cards, sensing I was done with the conversation. The game started, and we became the poker sharks we were. After an hour, I was up ten grand from Jax. Millie was my good luck charm, since I couldn't get her off my mind. Thinking about her made the corners of my mouth turn up. I felt like a kid with a crush.

"You finally get some?" Jax asked, looking at me suspiciously. My hesitation was answer enough for them.

"It must be love. I have seen the look before," Mikey laughed.

"Woah! Slow down with the love word," I said, getting up to grab another beer. "We just met... I like her a lot, but I'm not there yet."

"That stupid shit-eating grin plastered on your face says otherwise." Carlos playfully slapped my cheek. I pushed his hand away.

"Jakie, are you falling for some hot snow bunny Canadian girl?"

Ugh, these fuckers

"Drop it," I warned, tossing some more money down for the flop. They were nosy shits. I wasn't ready to divulge about Millie just yet. I was still trying to figure things out.

"What's the matter? Is she blowing you off? Is that why you don't want to talk?" Justin pressed. I lifted my stare from my cards.

"Shit. No." Carlos said, surprised.

"Wow. A woman brought down the great Jake?" Jax mocked.

"It's not like that."

"Then what?"

"Shit, man. I don't know," I replied. "She's got a life that's busier than mine. That's all."

"Actress? Model?"

"No, you ass. She's got a job and a life that doesn't revolve around sports and special events, or charities."

"What are you saying?"

I paused. What *was* I saying? "It's complicated."

"Complicated? You looked like Cupid shot you in the ass with a fucking crossbow not too long ago." Jax teased. Was he right? Did I really have that love-struck look, or was he messing with me?

"Maybe it's not as complicated as you think." Justin said nonchalantly. I waved him off and tried to focus on the poker game, but it was a lost cause.

I hadn't heard from Millie since the game. I wanted to text her or something, but I'd hoped she'd make the first move this time.

The guys left, and I sat and thought about what they said. Was it complicated, or was I over-thinking things?

This was all so new to me. Never have I waited for a girl. *Is this what a woman feels like when a guy says he's going to call them but doesn't?*

In my drunken state, I debated whether to take the plunge and text Millie. After a twenty-minute debate with myself, and three shots of whiskey, I hit send, but not to her.

Me: Why hasn't she called me? Sent a text? Smoke signal.

Me: I am dying here.

Me: I hate the waiting game.

Me: Dude, wake the fuck up. I feel like a teenager waiting for her to call.

Mitch: Dude, it's 3 am.

Me: I don't care. What's wrong with her? Doesn't she know it's rude to leave someone hanging?

Mitch: Are you drunk?

Me: Yeah.

Mitch: Call me when you sober up.

Me: Might be awhile...

Mitch didn't reply, and I couldn't help but think he knew something I didn't...

Chapter Twelve

Millie

"Ugh," I yelled when I hung up the phone. "Fucking Nick."

Since I returned from Lisa's, he was worse than ever. If I didn't know better, I'd think he knew about Jake because he was more of an ass than usual. I wondered if he had been told about the baseball game.

Our relationship had been tumultuous since the beginning. I was used to his temper and mood swings, but his excuses not to take Aubree had me losing my shit. Even the past weekend, I had to fight with him to take her for the night. He had canceled the last two. It hurt me for her. All I wanted was for him to want to spend time with her. It was the whole reason I moved back here.

When he finally picked her up two hours later, he let me know Misha was pregnant again. All the feelings I had been suppressing bubbled up to the surface. Right back to the night

I found out about them, and just how long they had been cheating behind my back.

I shouldn't care, yet I did. I was still envious of Misha. She had everything I wanted. Including the person I spent a decade wanting it with.

Out of the whole heartbreak and scandal, it was really the loss of Misha that hurt the most. My best friend betrayed me. She stole the life I wanted and then flaunted it in my face. It broke me more than Nick. I couldn't bring myself to look at her for a long time, let alone speak to her. Hell, we joked when we were younger about how close our kids would be, like siblings. Never in a million years did I think they would be sisters.

In a world that spun out of control, the only rule I ever enforced was that Aubree would never call Misha any version of "mom". She was Misha. The other names I had chosen were unacceptable for a child.

* * *

The upside of being angry and needing a distraction was that I'd plowed through my work during the morning and now there was a lull. I thought I'd go by the house and check on the last of the renovations being done and bring the workers some treats.

I greeted Mike at the bakery the next afternoon, grateful he knew my usual order. I added on a bunch of pastries for the guys. He busied himself behind the counter. I paced, waiting for him to fill the large order.

"Are you excited?" Mike asked as he filled up the two take-home coffee packs.

"I can't wait to not be living in a construction zone."

"I bet. I heard you did some massive renovations to that old place."

I nodded, thinking back to the way it looked before. It was originally my great-grandparent's home, but my parents had kept up well enough during rentals. When the last tenant left, my parents asked me to rent it. They would let me design and renovate it myself, hoping to make it more enticing to come back. For years, they tried to get me to move home to help with Aubree, but I stayed with Lisa, mostly to avoid the drama of living near Nick and Misha.

"I'll have a party or something when it's ready." I smiled at him and grabbed the boxes of coffee, taking them to my SUV parked in front of the bakery.

I paused when I saw Misha at the kitchen store her family owned on the main strip. She was behind the counter, talking to Max and Maddison, old friends of ours. Misha rubbed her non-existent baby bump and laughed about something. I watched longer than I care to admit. The scene made me angry, her with their perfect life taunting me. It was bad enough she robbed me of my boyfriend. She took my friends with her.

I thought back to the days when Nick and Misha acted like they hated each other. Seriously, they deserved an award for their enemies-to-lovers act. Frustration hit me. All I ever did was prove to Nick that I loved him. I thought I could make us work. I bent over backward for him, losing so much of myself. Why I stayed as long as I did was beyond me. If I had to guess, it was because I was young and naïve when we met, and he was the only relationship I'd had. It scarred me for life. I realize I had no clue how to move on, or what a functional relationship should be.

Maybe the girls were right. Nick was creating a lot of doubt about moving on, but what was I waiting for? Nick and Misha were having another baby and there I was, frozen, stuck half in the past, half in the now.

I called Lisa, and she knew something was wrong before I could say anything.

"How do you always know?" I asked.

"I just do," she replied, the noise in the background muffled. I guessed she tucked the phone between her shoulder and ear. I heard her giving directions and a loud clang before she came back.

"Sorry," she said once it was quiet again. "Delivery day."

"Oh, shit. I forgot it was Thursday," I grumbled, knowing she was busy. Delivery days at the bar were a full restock of food and booze and setting up for the weekend crowd.

"Oh, whatever. What's going on?"

I let out a long huff before I dished out what happened over the past week and a half. She sighed and cursed throughout my rant.

"God, I hate him," she groaned. *Tell me about it.* "Alright, let me talk to the girls. We're due to come up for a visit."

The thought of her coming up here suddenly worried me. "I'm not bailing you out of jail," I warned.

She scoffed. "If we don't come up there and let you vent it out, we'll be bailing *you* out."

I laughed, which Lisa was always good at making me do when I was in crisis mode. I drove back to my house and placed out all the goodies, calling over the team. I glanced around at the last finished spaces. I smiled because, for once, I had something that was mine, and no one could take it from me.

* * *

A few days later, I was nervous about facing Nick again, and Aubree was due home in a little while. I had made dinner already, cleaned the house twice, read a book, and walked the dog more than he needed.

I checked the time and, with two hours before she'd be home, I stretched out on the couch and flipped on the television. I surfed a few channels when I came across the baseball game, which had me sitting on the edge of the cushion.

The Twisters were at bat, down one point in the seventh inning. I whispered to the player to hit the ball out of the park. I watched as he missed the first ball, then fouled the second. The memory of Jake as he crashed over the wall made me smile.

The camera shifted to the player edging forward on the base, as he looked like he was about to attempt a steal. It only took a split second for me to realize it was Jake.

I stood on my feet and paced, stuck between cheering and yelling for him to stay where he was. The batter punted the ball, and Jake took off the base. He sprinted hard down the line, and there was a scramble with the ball. He slid into third base just as he was tagged, and the umpire called it safe. I jumped up and down like I was there in the stands.

He popped up with a big smile as he brushed himself off. Damn, he looked hot. His hat was low down his forehead with his deep-tinted sunglasses. He looked like he hadn't shaved. The thought of him rubbing his scruff on my shoulder the morning I woke up with him on the cruise warmed my body. Why hadn't I called him? I reached for my phone when it pinged with a message from Avery. He was with Aubree, and they were sharing a giant ice cream sundae.

Avery: Look who I ran into at Scoops...

What the heck? I looked at my phone again, surprised and happy that Nick took her out for ice cream.

Me: Tell her I miss her.

It took a few minutes for him to answer, which felt like an eternity.

Avery: I can't now. Misha was on her way back from the beach with the girls.

Me: Where was Nick?

Avery: No idea. Misha said it was girls' day.

I huffed loudly. Fucking Nick. I went to his message screen.

Me: Why aren't you with Aubree?

Nick: Wow, gossip travels. Let me guess. Your nosy brother?

Me: Doesn't answer the question.

Nick: I had to run to the store. Some of us have to work for a living. She's fine. She's with her mom and sister.

She's not her MOM. He knew how I felt about that. It was like he was egging me on. My hands trembled with rage.

Me: I do work and she's not her mom. You said you were off this weekend, that's why you asked to change days.

Nick: Something came up. And I hardly call working for your parents "work". I have actual responsibilities. Relax, I'll be back with them in an hour.

I tossed down the phone, and the sound of the game turned my head. Jake was now on the bench, chatting with one of the guys. My heart sank. *This is why I haven't called him. I'm a hot mess with baby daddy issues that he doesn't need to deal with.*

Chapter Thirteen

Jake

I woke up feeling like shit. My phone rang nonstop for the last twenty minutes. I hadn't been that hungover in a long time. I knew better than to drink myself out of troubles with women, but I did it anyway. The last time I'd turned myself inside out, I had Katrina to thank. One of my exes from when I first started out in my career. Turned out she was using me to level up. She broke it off with me when she thought she found better. Until she learned who I really was. She tried to come crawling back, but fuck that shit. I saw who she really was. Women like her caused a whole different level of drinking. I've had plenty of women in my life since, but none that did that kind of damage. Wouldn't let it. Drama free was what I was after. Even with my recent ex, Haley, it was calm. No big drama, even after the break-up. Heck, she even looked relieved when we called it quits.

"What?" I grunted into the phone.

"Aw. Rough morning, princess?" Mitch chuckled.

"I hate you."

"Not after this... You still want a chance with Millie?"

Yup, I'm awake. I popped out of bed. "What's the deal?" I rubbed my palm down my face.

"Be ready in an hour and bring an overnight bag."

Overnight bag? He hung up. *That's not cryptic at all.* I was dead tired after that set, and I only had off 18 hours before the next practice. Was he serious? What did this have to do with Millie?

Mitch showed up right on time with Lisa. They grinned at my hung-over state.

"You look like shit." Lisa laughed.

"Wow, okay. Thanks Lisa." I shook my head, practically having to fold my ass into Lisa's compact car.

"What have you two gotten me into?"

"Millie's little town is having its annual summer festival. Besides, do you care what we do?" She had a point. I didn't care what they planned if it meant I got to spend time with Millie.

"Is she expecting me?" I asked, leaning forward in my seat. The look on Lisa's face was a dead giveaway. *Fuck me. Another ambush.* "I hate you guys," I grumbled and sunk down into my seat.

"You better be stopping for coffee." Mitch grinned and passed a large cup at me. "Just how you like it."

I blew on the lip of the paper cup, taking a sip. Damn, it was good. Rich and silky. I popped in my ear buds. I needed a distraction other than listening to Lisa and Mitch. My stomach knotted for the entire ride.

As we got closer, my palms began to sweat. I was nervous. No one has ever had that effect on me. I groaned to myself. *Shit, Jake, you can handle big tough crowds, angry fans, reporters, yet one woman makes you quake like a teenager about to go on the first date.*

The drive down the main street took the longest. Traffic was brutal. Apparently, the festival was a big deal. The small town had only one way in or out of it. Inching along, I gazed out the window, taking in the picturesque town with bright flowers everywhere. Storefronts gave off that small town everyone knows us, vibe. I could see why she lived there. It was perfect for raising kids.

We turned onto a street with mature trees and a mix of single-story houses that were spread out with large yards. We drove toward a newer, bright white Cape Cod-style house with the navy roof. It had a large, welcoming porch with colorful flower planters on it. It reminded me of a beautiful little garden house. I watched Millie walk out of the house, thankful for the tinted car windows. She looked amazing with her long blond hair down. She wore olive green cargo shorts and a simple white tank top. Millie looked like she had been in the sun. My chest tightened.

I hesitated before I got out of the car, unsure of how she would react. A yellow lab ran onto the porch, barking at Lisa and Mitch.

"Mickey, enough." Millie shushed him as she scratched his floppy ears. He sniffed at Mitch and Lisa. His tail wagged wildly. *Now or never, Jake.*

Millie's head jerked up when I climbed from the car. "Hey, you," I greeted her.

Her dog's fur stood as he woofed at me from behind Millie. I put my hand out for him to sniff, and he stopped barking enough for me to hear Millie.

"Hi. I wasn't expecting you."

"I figured." I squarely shot Mitch a look. "If it's a problem, I'll make Mitch drive me back. I'm sure he won't mind. Right?"

"Ah, well." He pulled at the back of his neck. Lisa opened her mouth to say something, but Millie stopped her.

"It's fine." Although she said it, she looked weary.

"Are you sure?" I asked, while Mitch unloaded the trunk. Millie swallowed hard before she nodded. When we went in, the size of her place impressed me. We stood in a T-shaped entry with a hallway down to the back of the house. There was a living room to the right, and a wide staircase to the second floor on the left before another sitting area. I noticed the archways were all oversized and curved.

"Come with me," she directed, taking us through the main hallway. The dog followed behind, sniffing our bags. There was a guest room on the right with a queen size bed and two nightstands. It was decorated in muted blues and greens with some small beach-like decor. "Lisa and Mitch, you are here."

Mitch put their bags by the closet before we continued to a small powder room. We backtracked into a formal living area, painted in a deep blue with an oversized soft gray sectional that looked like it was built for naps. It was plush, with deep cushions. It sat in front of a gigantic fireplace with a shiplap wall with a live edge wood mantle.

"Is that wood burning or gas?" I asked.

"Wood. The winters here can knock out the power. My dad was adamant wood burning was still the best fireplace money could buy." Millie smiled, and man, she was stunning.

"Smart," I agreed, already liking her dad.

"Uh, Jake, you'll be in here. The couch pulls out into a bed, and it's really comfy." She patted the back of the sofa.

"No problem." I tucked my bag into the corner so it would be out of the way. She continued the tour across the way into the den area, which had a smaller couch with a television that was open into her farmhouse-style kitchen. White cabinets with butcher block counters and stainless-steel appliances. Off to the side of the kitchen was a breakfast area surrounded by floor-to-ceiling windows and French doors leading outside.

"Was it recently remodeled?" Mitch asked.

"Yeah, it was one of my parents' old rental properties. When the tenant moved out, my parents asked me if I was interested in it. I love them to death, but living with them was never on my list. They were planning on remodeling, anyway. My dad told me I could design it."

"You did a great job," I told her, glancing around the room.

"Thanks." She blushed, and it softened my nerves.

"Where's Aubree?" Lisa asked.

"With my mom for now. She wanted to take Aubree on some errands."

"That was nice," Mitch interjected before I could.

"Let me show you the yard," Millie said, moving towards the French doors. It was a great space, fenced in with a play structure. She had a large deck with an outdoor kitchen covered by a canopy. In the center was a fire pit table surrounded by four gray wicker chairs with bright-colored fabrics. She had good taste, that's for sure.

"What do you want to do?"

"Why don't you show Jake around the rest of the place? I've seen it." Lisa wiggled her brows. A look of utter disapproval washed over Millie's face.

"Actually, I'd like to talk to you for a second," I told her. "If that's okay?"

Millie's expression softened, and I followed her inside, leaving Lisa and Mitch on the deck.

We walked upstairs, where there were two more rooms and a bathroom. A large purple bedroom with princesses and snowman decals on the wall was obviously Aubree's. The bathroom was at the end, between the rooms. Millie's room was last. She propped the door open for me. The room was big, with two huge windows facing the front yard. They painted it a soft pink with cream accents and wood-stained furniture. She had abstract pink and gold art, and one picture of palm trees in the sunset.

"Didn't see you as one for pink," I noted.

"I'm not usually, but I wanted a change, and it's surprisingly calming." She stood in the doorway, with her hands behind her back, watching me snoop around. I joined her on the other side.

"I'm sorry about another ambush." I tried to make her smile, knowing we were both surprised. "Why haven't you called me?"

"I was going to, but... Things with me are complicated. I have a kid." Millie gazed into my eyes.

"A cute kid," I clarified, warmed by her smile. "I asked you for a chance, Millie. Let me try." She studied my face. Her eyes told me she was conflicted. "Come here," I said, wrapping my arms around her waist. Her scent of maple was enough to send me over the edge. "What have you done to me?"

"What?"

"You. I can't stop thinking about you. All damn day. You consume me." The blush on her cheeks brought me to my knees. I tilted her chin up. "I'll go at your pace, but I don't want to chase you. I want a chance, and I'll use this time with you and Aubree to prove it. You can decide after that if this is something you want to pursue. If I'm someone you want."

"Jake," she whispered, but I kissed the top of her nose to interrupt her overthinking.

"Twelve hours. I don't want to know until then," I continued. She swallowed and nodded at me. I hugged her tighter to my chest and pressed my lips to the top of her head. I meant it. I was going to do everything I could to prove that this was something.

We joined Mitch and Lisa, who had broken out some cards.

"Euchre?" Lisa asked.

"Sure." Millie shrugged. We sat around the table. Lisa partnered with Mitch, leaving Millie and me together. We were losing badly after two games.

"I had no idea that having a partner could suck so much." Millie shook her head at me.

"Wow, now." I pretended to be hurt. "I told you I was rusty. I'm a poker guy."

"That's rusty? Have you ever even played?" She teased.

"Ouch. The girl is serious about cards." I chuckled at her. "Next time, I'll bring my A game."

"I'd settle for a C game at this point." I pretended to twist a knife in my chest. Lisa and Mitch both laughed at me.

Just then, we heard a woman call out for Millie. I guessed it was her mom.

She stiffened, and her face paled. We all stood up as Aubree came flying out the door, stopping in her tracks when she noticed all of us.

Millie scooped her up, giving her a kiss. "Hi, sweetie."

"Mama, look!" Aubree waved the dolls she held in front of Millie's face.

"Another doll? Wow!" Millie looked at the woman behind Aubree. "Nana must love you lots." It didn't take much to see the relationship. Millie looked just like her mom. Blonde hair, blue eyes, and wide smiles.

"Aunt Lisa!" Aubree flung herself at Lisa.

"Sup, princess? Are you keeping Nana busy?" Aubree nodded, eyeing Mitch and me. "This is my boyfriend, Mitch," Lisa introduced, linking her arm around Mitch's.

"What's a boyfriend?"

"Well, he's a boy I like. A lot," Lisa whispered loudly to Aubree. "This is our friend Jake."

"Hi. Remember me?" I knelt at her height. She furrowed her eyebrows and tapped her chin. *Jesus, she's adorable.*

"The baseball," she squealed, surprising me. A surge of pride hit me. She remembered.

"Hi there," Millie's mom interjected, looking at all of us. Her stare stopped on me. She was sizing me up. I was intimidated for once. "Rose," she said, extending her hand.

"Jake," I replied, standing from Aubree and shaking Rose's hand.

"Nice to meet you." She looked over my shoulder at Lisa and Mitch. "You staying out of trouble, Lisa?" The way she smirked at Lisa made think she knew a lot more about Lisa than we did.

"Meh," Lisa replied, her hand teetering back and forth. Rose shook her head. Lisa officially introduced Mitch to Rose, who huffed like she was Lisa's mom, too.

"Oh, Lisa." Rose smiled. "Millie says you're all in town for the festival. It's getting busy, so you better get down there." She gave a chop-chop motion, telling us politely to move our asses. I've never seen four adults move so fast. She exchanged glances with Millie in what seemed to be a secret conversation. From their looks, Millie was already flustered. Rose kissed Aubree goodbye and told us she would see us there later in the afternoon. She had some things to finish up. She didn't divulge what those things were, and no one seemed to care enough to ask.

Chapter Fourteen

Millie

I was one hundred percent freaking out. The thought of spending the day with Jake and Aubree had me upside down. It was the first time she was hanging out with my 'friend', or whatever he was. I had no idea how it would go. At least she knows him from the game, but this was different.

"Lisa, come help me," I said, yanking her away from Mitch. I needed some girl talk. I grabbed Aubree's backpack and filled it with stuff while I talked to Lisa alone.

"What were you thinking?"

"What do you mean?"

"The festival?"

"Yeah?"

"I don't think it's a good idea. Everyone in town is going to be there."

She wiggled her brows. "Oh, I know."

"You're really going to kill me, you know that, right?" I

asked, having a mini anxiety attack. Jake was going to get a crash course in my small-town drama.

Lisa grabbed some items I had out and shoved them in the bag. "Mils, the guy is into you. Personally, I don't understand why. All you've done is blow him off, even though we both know YOU LIKE HIM. You're being stubborn. Did you know he's been waiting for you to call? He was full on whining to Mitch about it. Mitch has never seen Jake this way over a woman before."

"Seriously? That's a stretch. He's Jake Parsons, for crying out loud. He has an entire fanbase trying to get to him. I doubt he's waiting for some single mom nobody to call him."

"Jeez, woman. I love you to death, but you're so dense sometimes." She shook her head at me. "The guy fawns over you. When we pulled into the driveway, I swear I heard his pulse hammering away. He was so damn nervous. It was cute. Now stop being a baby, put on your big girl panties, and make that hot guy yours."

Lisa joined Mitch and Jake. I needed a minute to collect myself before I could go back out to them. My mom left, already telling me to call her if I changed my mind and wanted her to watch Aubree for the night. Breath in and out, I told myself, nervous as hell. When I got outside, Jake looked calm, like it was no big deal. He was loading my SUV. He looked great doing it.

"Ready?" Lisa asked. I nodded, not the least bit sure I was.

My silent conversation with my mom warned me about being out with a guy. The rumors would spread like wildfire, with no way to stop it. Except she was amused that I was taking a date. *I've seen exactly how this works.* The rumor would start with the truth that I was with a group of people, and by the time it got to the end of the line, it would be twisted into a rumor about me having sex on the Ferris wheel. *Today is bound to bite me in the ass.*

The festival was in the expansive town park surrounding the waterfront area. There was a kid zone, midway, and various booths that sold local art, jewelry, and souvenirs.

We walked along the trail that ran across the length of the park, separating the festival from the beach. In the far corner, you could see a restaurant already bustling with the brunch crowd.

Aubree was in heaven; she wanted to go everywhere and do everything. She was tugging my arm towards the mini pony ride. Amanda was on ticket duty. *Crap, couldn't it be someone else?* She was a huge town gossip, like speed dial to the gossip train.

"Hey, Mils," she greeted us when we approached her to buy our tickets. "Four and a kid?"

"Yup."

"Have fun," she said smugly, her phone bouncing in her hand. *Let the games begin*, I muttered to myself when we walked away. I wondered how fast the rumor would spread.

We spent a good hour wandering around, letting Aubree play on everything she wanted. She even convinced Jake to go on the teacup ride.

"He looks like he might hurl," Mitch said, watching the little carnival ride spin in circles constantly.

"This is why I don't go on it," I agreed, feeling sorry for Jake. I watched Jake do a mini sidestep when he got off the ride. I giggled at him. "How are you doing, champ?"

"Man, I don't know how kids do this. That ride is awful." Even though it looked painful, he let Aubree drag him from ride to ride before we stopped at some bouncy castles. Jake let out a gigantic sigh of relief because he didn't have to go on another spinning ride. People were staring at us. I tried to hide my embarrassment.

Jake laughed, catching the glances. "Does everyone stare this much, or am I lucky?"

"I told you it was a small town. They have nothing better to do than make a spectacle of themselves."

Lisa and I watched Aubree wrap Jake and Mitch around her tiny fingers. They would have walked across coal if she asked. I was finding it hard to resist Jake. He was so protective and sweet with Aubree, like it was the most natural thing in the world to have her around, and I wasn't sure if that was good or bad for me.

The longer we walked around, the more people recognized him. They asked for autographs and pictures. Unfazed by the attention, he focused on the kids. He was genuine and encouraging.

Lisa nudged me, grinning. "See? I said to give him a chance."

Jake posed for several pictures and autographed hats, shirts, and paper. A flash bulb went off as someone called his name over the crowd.

"Uh, is that going to be on the news?"

"Probably. If not the news, I'm sure someone will put the video online."

"Oh," I said, taking a step away. Jake chuckled, finally able to escape the crowd.

"Can we go to the beach? I hot," Aubree asked, tugging on my leg.

"I don't have a suit. I am not sure underwear is appropriate," Jake muttered.

"Sure, it is." Lisa winked. Mitch and I shot her a look. She put her hands up. "Fine."

"There's a store on the main street with some. It's a ten to fifteen-minute walk," I suggested.

"Sure. Are you okay with going?" He glanced at Aubree.

"She sure is. We can go buy some shaved ice to cool down," Lisa chirped, a little too eagerly.

Jake flashed her a smile, mouthing thanks. I handed

Aubree's backpack to her. "Everything is in here." I slathered sunscreen on her face again, for good measure. "Floaty goes on, if you go in the water."

Aubree could swim. I had been taking her since she was a baby, but with enormous crowds, it was easy for accidents to happen.

Lisa gave me a thumbs up, taking Aubree's hand.

The festival had really filled in within the past hour. It felt like everyone in town was there. People watched as Jake and I crossed the field out to Main Street as if they were star-struck. They waved, winked, or gave me a thumbs-up as we passed. *Jesus. This town.* It had been so long since I had a date that I forgot what the attention was like. Jake seemed amused by all of it.

"Anything I need to know about the town?"

"Yeah. Avoid Mrs. Peterson. She's handsy." I laughed. We walked further up the street, keeping the conversation light.

"Does it ever get to you?" I asked.

"What?"

"The people? Cameras? The pressure?"

He slowed. "Sometimes. I'm used to it by now. I mean, I wish I had more privacy and not splashed over television or the news, but that's not the life I chose. It comes with the territory."

"What made you choose baseball?"

"As a kid, I was high energy. My stepdad put me in it, thinking it might help. Turned out, I was good at it. It gave me something to focus on. I don't think anyone ever expected me to become a pro."

"Why not?"

He shoved his hands in his pockets. "I guess they assumed I'd follow my family in investments," he hesitated, "but when I was in college, my sister, Jenna, was the one who told me to go for it. Follow my dream, because the family stuff would always be there."

"She sounds great."

"She is." I grinned.

We made it into the general store, and I showed Jake where the men's stuff was. We filtered through the racks, finding a few swimsuits. I found a decent pair of navy-blue board shorts with palm trees on the side.

"Not bad, not sure about the palm trees."

"Too bad. I love palm trees. I almost got a tattoo of one a while back."

"Oh yeah? How come you didn't?"

"A few reasons." My voice trailed off, remembering the argument I had with Nick when I mentioned I was going to get one. I thought about getting one when we broke up, but I found out I was pregnant with Aubree and never thought about it after that.

"Change room?" Jake asked, sensing my shift in behavior.

"Back corner." I nodded to the left. While I waited for him, I wandered around, checking out some of the new stuff. There was a hot pink neon flamingo sign perfect for the back-yard bar area, a cute little princess sand bucket, and a beach ball set for Aubree.

Jake came up behind me. "Find anything?"

"Yes, I did." I proudly showed him my goodies.

He snatched the items out of my hand. "I'm going to pay."

"Hey, those are mine," I said, trying to grab them, but he was too quick. He wiggled his brows and took off to the regis-ter. I went to follow him, but stopped dead when Nick entered the store. *Shit.* He waved, spotting me. *Waving? Were we friends? I don't think so.*

"Where's Aubree?" Nick demanded.

"With Lisa."

He grunted unhappily. He didn't like Lisa. His eyes shifted, taking in my outfit. "You left the house like that?"

I looked down at myself. "What's wrong with it? It's a beach outfit."

"You're half naked..." his voice trailed off.

I rolled my eyes hard enough they could have hit the ceiling. "It's a good thing I don't give a damn what you think. Did you tell your wife how to dress?" I followed his gaze outside the window where Misha stood with Gracie, talking to some blonde girl. Misha looked like her usual stylish self in a pretty floral maxi dress. She patted her stomach, which had a blip of a baby bump. One that you wouldn't even know existed if she wasn't rubbing it. Of course, she was one of those gorgeous, glowing pregnant women.

My pregnancy was awful. I puked for the entire nine months, and I was big and swollen.

"You need something, bro?" Nick snapped, looking over my shoulder.

"Yeah, my girl here," Jake said.

It felt like all the color drained from my face as the sound of my heartbeat whooshed through my ears. My eyes flicked between Jake and Nick, while Jake his eyes on Nick. Jake didn't give two shits about who Nick was to me. It was sexy, the way he gently placed his hands on my hips, pulling me closer to him, for added effect.

Nick's face flashed with anger. "I doubt that. Who's this guy?"

"Are you freaking kidding me? He's none of your business." I scoffed, feeling confident in Jake's arms. Nick sneered. It surprised me how great it felt to have someone claim me in front of Nick.

"I have a right to know."

"What do you want to know?" Jake snapped.

Nick's eyes narrowed as he was about to say something I

knew wouldn't go well. I grabbed Jake's hand and yanked him out of the store. *This is exactly what I was afraid of. Damn, Lisa.*

What was I thinking, parading around with Jake? I should have known I would run into Nick. *Them. Ugh. How dare he even ask who Jake is?*

"Hey, are you okay?" Jake squeezed my hand.

"Peachy."

"Um, I don't mind the hand holding, but you're kinda crushing mine."

"I'm so sorry." I let go, and he rubbed his hand. I ran my palm down my face. Jake's mouth opened, but immediately shut, not wanting to talk yet.

I took a sharp left into Ma's Bakery. There was a long line, but Mike looked up and saw me.

"Mils, the usual?" He looked at Jake. I could see he recognized who he was.

"Yeah, Mike, but I'll take an extra iced coffee, and a lemonade for Aubree." I turned to Jake. "Want something?"

"Water." Mike rushed around, grabbing stuff. As he piled our order on the counter, he froze and looked at Jake.

I groaned. "Jake, this is Mike. Mike, Jake."

Mike grinned and shook Jake's hand with enthusiasm as he rattled off stats from Jake's last few games. I paced the counter, waiting for our order.

Jake tossed down cash and grabbed our tray. Mike winked at me and gave me two thumbs-up. *Jesus.*

Chapter Fifteen

Jake

She was mad, the scary mad that made her silent. Silent women were fucking terrifying. I knew enough to shut up and keep walking. Millie would talk when she was ready.

It wasn't until we were halfway back that she whispered, "He's Aubree's dad."

Really? That was him? I mean, I guessed he was an ex who wasn't over her, but I never would have thought he was Aubree's dad. She looked absolutely nothing like him. Thank God she was all Millie, with her cute little blonde hair and big blue eyes. How the hell he landed Millie is beyond me.

The way she'd slumped her shoulders and kept her head down gave me more questions and concerns. I didn't like the way he spoke to her in the store or how he seemed controlling. I was concerned for her and Aubree.

I guess that's why she's so damn hesitant about starting something with me. Well, he has some thick competition now.

Lisa and Mitch found a shaded spot for us. They had laid out everything Millie had packed for a day at the beach. Aubree squealed, seeing her new sand bucket set.

"Ready to cool off?" Millie asked, standing up and dropping her romper to the ground in one fell swoop. All that was left was the tiny bikini she wore. It was doing nothing to hide her bountiful breasts, and the bottoms were showing the crests of her round ass. My throat went dry. There was no way to hide the thorough eye fuck I was giving her. God, she was trying to kill me.

"Come on, slowpoke," she teased, halfway to the water. I strategically placed the beach ball over my junk to hide my arousal, and I carefully walked to the water.

"We want to play with the ball," Mitch laughed. I'd kill him if I didn't need my hands right then. I looked around, considering how the water was probably the best place to be if I didn't want to get arrested for indecent exposure with my dick tenting my bathing suit.

I was barely one toe in the water when I jumped back. "Holy shoot, that's cold."

"No, it's not." Aubree huffed at me while the adults laughed.

"I am certain I saw a penguin go by in this arctic water you swim in."

"You're so silly. There are no penguins," she said, rolling her eyes at me, just as sassy as Millie.

"Don't be a baby," Lisa yelled from the water.

I stood at the edge before Mitch called out, "Grow a pair, would yah?"

"My pair ran back to Florida to find warmth," I called, laughing.

Out of nowhere, Millie kicked some water at me. I shot out of the water as if I was on a rocket. *That's it!*

I took a deep breath and ran after her. I held back every

one of the swear words threatening to escape my mouth as my ball sack plunged into the cold water. Tears welled in my eyes from the pure shock of the cold. I swear my dick turtled so far in to find warmth, I wouldn't be able to coax him out for a week.

Millie laughed hysterically until I grabbed hold and tackled her, so we both crashed down. We came up sputtering and laughing.

I grabbed her by the waist. "You think that was funny?"

"Heck yeah. You should have seen your face."

"There is something wrong with you, Canadians. How is the beach packed with the water so cold?"

"It's the lake, not the Ocean."

It was a few minutes before I adjusted to the cool water. We played with Aubree, making sandcastles. I even let her bury me in the sand. Then Mitch and I went and played in the water, chasing her around like sharks. She giggled in hysteria as Millie and Lisa chatted on the beach, watching us. Aubree was one cool kid. Finally, Millie called for us to dry off before we could get some lunch. We wandered around until we found a grilled cheese food truck.

We were just about to eat when Aubree looked at me.

My sandwich was halfway to my mouth when Aubree turned her head to me.

With a mouthful of food she asked, "Jake, do you kiss mommy?" I froze, along with the rest of the table. *Damn, kid. Nothing like just putting it out there.*

Millie's jaw dropped. I stammered, not knowing what to say, other than, "uh", so I looked at Millie for a sign. She was too stunned to do anything other than blink. Aubree wasn't even fazed as she munched on another fry, and kept talking. "Are you mommy's boyfriend?"

Mitch's eyebrows arched with his goofy grin, waiting for an answer. *For the love of God, help a guy out.*

Do I say she's just a friend? A special friend? I looked around for help, and everyone was wide-eyed but silent.

"I... Um... Well... She's a special friend." After hearing that out loud, I realized how creepy it sounded. "Well, not special. Just a friend?"

"Mommy's not special?" Aubree tilted her head.

"Of course she is." I rubbed my head, and I started to sweat. I could barely look at her because I felt so embarrassed. Aubree shrugged her little shoulders like she no longer cared.

Millie looked mortified and relieved. I wasn't so sure how I felt about that.

Out of nowhere, Aubree jumped up, excitedly pointing to where Millie's ex and some brunette stood, "Daddy, Daddy." My eyes darted to a little girl they were holding hands with. She was a spitting image of the woman. I snapped back to Aubree, when she was begging to go see them. From the dreaded look on Millie's face, I could tell it was the last thing she wanted to do, but she reluctantly agreed.

"Want me to come?" Lisa asked before I could.

"Nope. I do not need you getting arrested."

As Millie and Aubree approached them, the woman saw Millie and left to go talk to someone else. Obviously, there was some history between the women. I watched her chat it up with one vendor. I had to say she was pretty, with her long dark hair and blonde highlights. She had a small baby bump showing through her floral dress. *How does this guy get these women?*

"Who's the woman, his new girlfriend?" I asked.

Lisa rolled her eyes. "Misha, his wife."

I could hear the disdain in her voice. Wife? I was so confused. The little girl looked to be the same age as Aubree. Maybe it wasn't his, but the new baby was? Or maybe Millie was the mistress? It didn't make any sense to me. Between the two women, Millie was the better choice. I watched their interaction, and I could feel myself tensing. I didn't like Millie's body language. It was the same as it was in the store. *What the fuck is with this guy?*

Lisa grabbed our stuff and shoved it in the bag. "Come on, boys." I wasn't the only one who didn't like this situation.

We got there in time to hear him ask Millie, through gritted teeth, "Why didn't you just ask me if she could stay with us, so you can go play with your new *friend*?"

Calm down. I took a deep breath. My hands closed into fists. Not wanting to make a scene, I could do nothing but watch for now.

"I am not doing this with you, Nick, so back off."

Lisa took a step forward, but Mitch firmly held her hand.

Nick put his hands on his knees, making him eye level with Aubree, which made all of my hair stand up.

"Hey, Aubree. Do you want to come and have a sleepover with Gracie tonight?" Nick asked smugly. I had to turn away before I unleashed a fury on that asshole.

I couldn't believe what an epic douchebag this guy was. He pushed my last nerve. I nearly bit my tongue off, trying to hold it together. I was seconds away from going over and punching him in the face, but Mitch grabbed my arm with his free hand, reading my mind. He shook his head. As much as I hated to admit it, he was right. If I started something here, it might make things worse for her. Aubree looked at Nick, then tilted her head to the side as if she was considering her options.

"No."

I laughed out loud at him. I was so proud of Aubree as I grabbed her hand.

"Want a shoulder ride?" I scooped her up and put her on my shoulders. She squealed as we walked away, Millie right behind us. I saw tears in her eyes, and I wanted to drill the fucker right in the mouth, but his expression with me leaving with Millie and Aubree was more powerful than anything else.

"The nerve of the brick. I was going to kick him in the nuts if Mitch hadn't been holding my hand," Lisa said angrily.

"He should have let you," I muttered under my breath.

Millie said nothing, her eyes said everything. I wanted nothing more than to take her in my arms and comfort her, but I was hesitant in front of Aubree.

* * *

When we got back to Millie's, she went straight into cooking dinner. I offered to help, but she wanted to be alone. Lisa told me cooking helped her relax. Their friends Sam and Gia showed up shortly after we got back. We kept Aubree entertained while Millie busied herself. Everyone took turns offering to help but all of us got whooshed away. I didn't like it. Not one bit. But I didn't want to make a spectacle either.

After dinner, Millie put to Aubree to bed, and Lisa wasted no time filling in Sam and Gia about Nick. None of them seemed surprised at his behavior towards Millie.

"You should have seen the way he looked when he saw Aubree with Jake. I almost died from laughter. Nick looked like a cartoon with steam coming out of his ears," Lisa explained, laughing.

"Serves him right, the jealous asshole," Sam scoffed.

After listening to them bash Millie's ex, it was clear none of them liked him. It made me wonder even more what their story was. I went inside to check on Millie, leaving them to continue talking in the yard.

"Hey," I said as she came downstairs.

"Hey."

"Come here." I tugged her into the living room. I wrapped my arms around her and pulled her into me. Gently, I kissed the top of her head. She sighed, but let me hold her. Her body melted against me, and it felt really fucking great. We stood for a minute before she pulled away.

"Thanks for today."

"For what?"

"For just letting it go, not badgering me. I'm just not ready to talk yet. Okay?" The look in her eye crushed me. How could this guy inflict so much pain on her? I just want to see her smile again, and not the fake smile she had plastered on throughout dinner.

"Hey, I got you something," I said as I walked over to my duffel bag.

"Jake, you really didn't need to."

"I know, but I wanted to. I meant to give it to you when I got here, but I got distracted." I pulled out a small, gift-wrapped bag and handed it to her. She peeked in inside, her eyes lighting up. She pulled out a Toronto Twisters jersey set. One for her and one for Aubree. I'd gotten them after the game they'd come to, in hopes she'd give me a chance. Millie beamed as she held it up.

"It's even got your name on it," she cooed.

"It helps if someone other than me has one."

"I don't know, I usually wear Ronald's."

"That's not even a little funny," I said, jealousy hitting me when she referred to Josh. She gave me a lopsided grin and then leaned forward. She planted her lips against mine and, shit, I was floored. The kiss was deep and passionate, like she was claiming me, and damn if it wasn't sexy.

* * *

When everyone was tucked in for the night, I sat on the sofa, my mind stuck on Millie. *Her Ex*. None of it sat well with me. I tiptoed up the stairs. Aubree's door was open, and I peeked in. She was tucked into her blanket, fast asleep. My heart tugged. She was fucking adorable.

Millie's door was also open, so I tapped on it.

"Hey," I sputtered. She got up from her bed, revealing her cotton shorts with rainbows on them, and a little pink cami. Fuck, she looked amazing. Immediately, I went over and greedily cupped her face. She responded right back. I nudged the door closed with my foot, careful not to let it slam. Every sensible thought I had disappeared. We hit the side of the bed, and I pushed her onto it. She stared into my eyes, and I lost it.

"Oh, the things I want to do to you," I groaned into her ear. She pulled me on top and kissed me. Our tongues grazed side to side, getting lost in this feeling of euphoria. "I so want this, but you have a houseful of people and I have zero intentions of holding back when the time comes."

She bit her lip. *Oh, God.* "I shouldn't have gotten carried away."

"Trust me. Right now, I'm a fucking idiot."

I shifted off her and she scooted up on the bed, patting the space bedside her. "I want you here."

"What?"

Her voice was low and soft. "Stay. At least for a while?" There was no way I was walking away from her. I sat next to her, draping my arm around her. She pushed her ass into my cock.

"I'm trying to be a gentleman with you."

"Such a shame."

"You're killing me, you tease." I kissed the back of her neck. "You smell like paradise." I kissed her shoulders, not wanting tonight to end. Tomorrow was going to suck.

Chapter Sixteen

Millie

I woke up still tucked in beside Jake. It was early, but he had to get back for his next game.

"Morning, beautiful," he sleepily greeted me.

"How are you this morning?" I whispered, not wanting to wake everyone.

"Good." He smiled at me.

"I should go downstairs before anyone wakes and sees an empty couch," he offered.

"In a minute." I tucked in next to him and rested my hand on his chest.

We finally got out of bed. Jake went to shower, and I made coffee. My mind drifted to the possibility of a relationship. It was hard not to after waking up with him. He had asked me to let him prove himself and he did that and so much more. There was more than just my heart at stake. Were we ready for Jake? How would Aubree handle it all? I thought back to them on the rides and at the beach. How protective and sweet he was. How she already adored him. She asked me for him to tuck her in last night and I melted.

Jake came around the corner, fresh from the shower in jersey shorts that clung to him with a Twisters t-shirt. His hair was damp. Damn. He came and planted a kiss on my shoulder. A warmth spread through me as I passed him a cup of coffee, pinning my eyes to him.

"Okay."

His face scrunched up. "Okay, what?"

"This." I wagged my finger between us. He stopped mid-sip. His eyebrow arched.

"*Us?*"

He grinned so wide, leaning into me, placing his coffee on the counter, and pinning me there, nose to nose. His lips found mine, soft at first, then needy. I moved my arms behind his neck, pulling us closer together. Until we were breathless.

Someone cleared their throat. Jake slowly turned his head to the side to see Mitch. "Nice timing, dickhead."

Mitch chuckled while I buried my face in Jake's shoulder. He turned back and kissed the tip of my nose. I heard Aubree shuffle down the stairs. Jake backed up against the other counter.

Aubree rubbed her sleepy eyes. She waved to us and then sat on the couch, asking to watch a movie. It wasn't long before Lisa, Sam, and Gia woke and joined us. When Jake and Mitch left, my friends attacked me for details.

It felt like a part of me went with the girls when they left later. As much as I loved having my independence, I missed them. I thought back to the conversation and how far we all had come. Lisa was buying the bar, Sam and Gia were getting married and I had a boyfriend. *A boyfriend.* It sounded so foreign to me.

* * *

I sat on the porch with a book in my hand, basking in the warm summer sun, but my thoughts were stuck on everything that had happened over the last few days. The rumors around town had caught fire.

"Mama, can we get ice cream?" Aubree asked as she flopped down next to me, nearly knocking over Mickey, who sprawled out in the sunlight. I thought about it while Aubree continued to beg.

"Want to walk? We can take Mickey." At the sound of his name, he bolted up, one ear flopped over with a dopey look on his face.

"Can Uncle Avery and Alex come, too?"

"I'm not sure, sweetie. I'll ask," I said and fished my phone out of my pocket, shooting them a quick text. Both responded within a few minutes, saying they would meet us there.

Scoops was packed. We found a table on the patio. I sat with Aubree and waited for my brothers to arrive. Aubree had picked out a rainbow sherbet, and I ordered a praline crunch. In my periphery, I saw Nick walk around the corner with one of his old band buddies. I hadn't seen the guy in a while, so I thought they had fallen out. He turned his head and saw me. *Fuck.* He tapped his buddy on the arm and pointed him toward the shop. I groaned.

"Hey," Nick said.

Aubree jumped up and hugged him. "Daddy."

"Hi, Aubree." He leaned down to hug her. At least he was affectionate with her. "What did you get?"

"Rainbow. It's yummy," she said, then patted her tummy with her free hand. I couldn't help but smile at her.

"Where did all mommy's *friends* go?"

I rolled my eyes. *Seriously? Involving her instead of asking me.* Aubree turned up to him with a puzzled look on her face, then shrugged and went back to her ice cream. My eyes flicked to him with annoyance.

"Sweetie, stay with Daddy. Mommy needs to pee." I got up and walked around to the other side where the washrooms were. When I came out of the bathroom, Nick was standing there, waiting for me.

"What are you doing?" he snarled at me.

"Using the bathroom."

"Who's the new guy, Mils?" He snagged my elbow, stopping me from getting past him.

My eyes drifted down to where he held me. "I told you yesterday, none of your business."

"The fuck he isn't. In case you forgot, it was my kid he was parading around with. I have a right to know who my daughter was spending time with."

"Right, Nick. As if I would endanger our daughter."

"I don't know, he could be some guy preying on a desperate single mom." *Desperate?*

"He's Jake Parsons, he's not preying on anyone."

"Who the fuck is Jake Parsons?"

If he only got his head out of his 90s rock bands, he'd know something. Nick's temper started to show. Being in the middle of Scoops with Aubree, I wanted to avoid any further tension. I replied, "He's a friend."

"I'm not an idiot. He's no friend."

"What do you want from me? You want me to say he is or isn't my boyfriend? I'm not dragging this out."

"Let go now," Avery called. Nick's head whipped around, and he released my arm. I pushed past him down the hall, back to the table where Alex was sitting with Aubree as she finished her ice cream. Nick stormed out, not bothering to say bye to Aubree. I was angry at how quick he was to dismiss her.

"What was that about?" Avery asked, plunking next to me.

"Yesterday."

"The new guy?" Alex chuckled. "Figures the hypocrite would be pissed."

"Alex," I warned.

He raised his hands, "I said *missed*." I swatted him. We finished our ice cream and walked along the street. Alex took Aubree up ahead.

"Don't let him give you a hard time."

"I know."

"Do you? Nick's an asshole. I love and hate that you moved back here. He's just going to keep doing shit like this to you, make it hard for you to move on. And you deserve way more than that jerk was ever going to give you."

"Need me to take a swing?" Alex called over his shoulder.

"No," we both said. We walked over to the park to let Aubree burn off her ice cream, enjoying the last bit of the sunset.

* * *

Since the festival, Jake and I texted regularly. His schedule was busier than ever and yet he always made time for me. I felt happy for the first time in forever. I had pushed Nick's words out of my head. Maybe there was some truth to it, but I wanted to feel good, and Jake made me feel *great*.

The Toronto Twisters were back in town for a series against the Ravens. I had planned to text him after the game.

I was knee-deep in emails working out a permitting issue when Aubree came bouncing into the office, smiling at me. "Hi, mama."

What the hell? She pushed onto my lap, grabbing a pen. Nick came in the door with her bag. "Um, what are you doing here?"

"I got a last-minute gig for tonight and tomorrow. I can't take her this weekend."

"Are you freaking kidding me?"

"No, I'm not kidding. It's a big deal." He rolled his eyes. "Why? Do you have plans with your boyfriend?" His voice was icy.

"Boyfriend?"

"Yeah, Mils, don't play stupid with me."

"Sweetie, why don't you go see Nana? I'm sure she has some snacks for you," I said, plastering on a fake smile. The mention of treats had Aubree practically sprinting to the door.

The perk of the office being on the property of my parent's house is, my mom was always near when I needed her. I stood at the door of the office watching Aubree cross the driveway to my mom. My mother rolled her eyes at seeing Nick's car.

I made sure she was out of earshot. "You haven't seen her in weeks. She was excited about this."

"It's a big gig. I'm not missing it so you can go fuck your new boyfriend."

"Jesus, Nick. She is your kid *all* the time, not whenever you choose."

"Yeah, well, I have to work, too, you know. Did I ruin your plans?"

"What is your problem?"

"I don't have a problem. I'm busy this weekend. Cancel your plans."

"You know what..." I stopped to calm myself before blowing up. "Never mind. Aubree will just come with me."

"Like fuck she is. I don't know this guy. I don't know who you are allowing our kid to spend time with," he shouted at me.

"And your band buddies are any better?"

"Oh, fuck off. This is different."

"Why? Because he's my boyfriend?"

"So, he *is* your boyfriend? A baseball player? Who are you

kidding? Have you seen who professional athletes hang with?" He laughed. "These guys party with celebrities, models, and shit. You think he's going to stay with a boring single mom, nobody?"

"Guess you do know who he is..." He stared at me, anger blazing in his eyes.

"Do you ever think, maybe, I'm the one using him? For sex? Maybe I want nothing more than mind blowing sex that lasts longer than three minutes." It was a cheap blow, and he deserved it.

His smug smile fell instantly, and fury took over. His lips curled, about to retort something, when my dad came into the office.

"I think you should leave now. I believe you told Millie you had a gig, and you were pulling out of your responsibilities to your daughter, right?" he clarified, stepping between Nick and me.

Nick stormed out, slamming the door. It rattled worse than my nerves. When I turned to my dad, I saw his face was on the verge of turning purple. "Dad, I..."

My dad held up his hand. "I don't want to know anything more. I already want to burn my ears off." I bit my lower lip, trying to stifle a giggle. "Your mother is making dinner. You're staying," he demanded, looking at his feet. I nodded, because arguing was pointless.

Alex and Avery showed up shortly after. I tried to be chipper throughout dinner for Aubree, but Nick was under my skin. He had a knack for finding my insecurities. My parents were angry at him for Aubree. Nick was a sore spot. It was easy to hide how shitty Nick was when I lived with Lisa. I lied for Nick often, despite all the things he put me through. For some stupid reason, I wanted my parents to think better of him as a dad than he ever was a boyfriend, but moving back home was straining that image I'd built up. My mom offered to keep Aubree for the weekend. As much as I appreciated the offer, it wasn't fair. My heart was already breaking for her.

"I just don't understand. What does he do with Gracie? It's not like he gets to walk away. Doesn't that jackass understand he has *two* daughters?" My mom stomped around as she cleared the dinner dishes. I stayed silent, my tears on the brink of pouring out. "Honestly, Millie, I'll never understand how you put up with him. I should have let your dad pummel his ass a long time ago." She slammed the dishwasher closed.

"Or me," Avery said, overhearing us. I shot him a look that he ignored. "Still can, you know. Just give me the go-ahead." Avery winked before Aubree called for him. As much as I loved them, I knew I had spent the last decade protecting Nick. I was exhausted, and he didn't deserve it anymore. He never had, and appealing as it was to want Nick to get what he deserved, I was worried about what would happen to Avery if he did.

Chapter Seventeen

Jake

I missed Millie and Aubree. It was stupid of me to wonder if a kid was a problem. Ten seconds into meeting her, and that little girl had me wrapped around her fingers, just like her mom. It was impossible not to. Both of them were something else. Beautiful, smart, and sassy. I wanted to be a part of their lives. But I've never had to fight so hard for someone's attention, not that I don't understand her caution. Being a single mom was no easy job, especially after meeting her ex. Man, that guy was a dick.

He could complicate the shit out of things. What I don't get is why? It didn't make sense. He's married with a kid. Something in the story is missing. The way Millie and his wife act around each other, I'd stake my life that he cheated on her, probably with her mortal enemy, the douchebag. Guys like him bother the fuck out of me. He can't have her, so no one else can either. I'd like to forget him, but he's Aubree's dad. I'd

136

have to figure out a way to deal with him, other than drilling him in the face.

I'm glad we had turned a corner and even though I was nervous about ambushing her again, with me in her town. It was a game-changer. It hurt to leave them the other day. So much of me wanted to tell her to come with me, but I knew it wasn't possible. I had to do things differently with her than anyone else. That included having to pack my patience between dates.

My phone dinged. It was Millie. I grinned like a fool whenever she messaged.

Millie: Good game, slugger. ;)

Me: That's what it takes to get you to message me? Wins?

Millie: LOL... I messaged you a lot... I just never sent them.

Me: Why not?

Millie: You're busy. I don't want to bother you.

Me: You're never a bother. I've been waiting for you.

Shit, a long pause. Did I go overboard? She was skittish. Here I thought women wanted the guy with the bold, no-head-games relationship. Somehow, she's the one woman who went backward in this relationship. We started by sleeping together. Ironic, right? I scratched my jaw.

Millie: You're in Chicago?

Me: Are you following my schedule? That's damn hot.

Millie: Maybe...but, not stalker-ish or anything.

Me: I like the idea of you following me. Please stalk me!

Millie: Bet you don't say that often...

Me: Never.

After a pause longer than I liked, I thought I should change the subject.

Me: How're things? Aubree?

Millie: Boring work stuff, fighting with the city over some new permits I needed like yesterday. There was a problem with one of the code regulations.

Me: ...

Millie: I know, boring. How are you? I saw you hit a home run yesterday.

Me: I love when you tell me you watch the games.

Millie: *eye roll*

Yup, exactly the dramatic eye roll I could see her giving me. I wished I was looking at it in person, though. Nothing beats those damn eyes of hers, but the image in my head would have to do until I could see her on the weekend.

Me: Are we still on for this weekend?

Millie: The thing is...

Long pause.

What?

Millie: Nick canceled again. I'd have to bring Aubree. I don't want to leave her with my parents.

Me: Babe, that's fucking fantastic.

Millie: Really? You're not mad?

Me: Are you kidding? I can't wait to spend time with my girls. Come to the game?

Millie: Sure, Aubree would love to. Let me look for tickets.

Me: Look for tickets? No way. I'll have tickets at the box office for you.

Millie: Jake... I can buy tickets

Jake: What's the perk of dating the first baseman if I can't get you tickets?

Millie: His hot ass?

Blink. Blink. Did she just say that? I chuckled.

Me: You're killing me.

It was the truth. I missed them. And knowing that she was

comfortable enough to bring Aubree just about made my chest burst with pride.

* * *

It was Saturday, and Junior Twisters Day, which meant that families would pack the stadium. I'll admit, watching the little kids run around the bases filled with excitement was pretty darn cute. Some of us hung back to meet the little tykes and sign stuff for them. Today held extra excitement because Aubree would be one of those kids. My chest squeezed with just the thought of it.

All throughout the warm-up, I couldn't get them out of my head. I was itching to see them. Take them out for dinner, or stay in. I didn't care what we did. Millie could pick. I chuckled, rethinking that Aubree would probably pick.

I stood on the base and watched the crowd. I still hadn't seen them. I wondered if she had issues getting the tickets.

By the second inning, I tried to focus on the game and not panic that they weren't here yet. Did her ex give her a hard time? Did they get stuck in traffic? Shit, an accident? My pulse hammered with that thought as I scanned her seats again.

A thundering crack snapped my head back just in time to feel a ball whiz past my head. I spun and followed the direction to the outfield where Kev caught it. *Fuck, that was close*.

"Get your head out of your ass," Josh yelled over to me.

I shook out my nerves and rolled my head. *FOCUS*.

The inning changed, and I headed into the dugout. I sat on the bench and immediately got grilled by the coach. I rubbed my jawline, frustrated with myself, and since we had a no phone-on-bench rule, I had no way to find out where she was.

I leaned forward to watch Kev at bat when, out of the corner of my eye, there was a movement in the crowd. There they were. People shifted out of their way so they could take their seats. Aubree had a bucket of popcorn while Millie carried soda and water. Relief washed over me. Millie looked flustered.

I watched them off and on during the game. I couldn't disappoint Aubree. In the eighth inning, I got a double. It gave us a 3-2 lead. Shit, when Aubree jumped up on her seat, her little hands waving in the air. That was it, man. Best fucking feeling.

After the game, Aubree opted for pizza.

"What happened? How come you were late?"

"Ugh, my stupid truck. It was giving me a hard time. My brother Avery came over and lent me his instead. He said he'd look and take it to the mechanic if he couldn't figure it out."

"Okay." I was relieved that it was only a car problem and not her ex. But then I wondered how safe her car was.

* * *

When we got back to my place, we put on a movie as requested by Aubree, and made a little snack picnic. I had stocked up. Well, I sent Brody to get stuff, not having a clue what would be good. We all snuggled up together, and it was a whole new feeling of comfort.

Family nights, cartoons, and cuddles. This was my favorite date so far. Aubree talked me into trying to sing along with her, which I was terrible at. I didn't know any of the words. I made a mental note to watch it a few times.

Despite the sugar high and her fit of giggles, Aubree crashed out just over the halfway mark of the movie.

While Millie put her to sleep in the spare room, I cleaned up the living room. She leaned against the kitchen counter and stared at me when she came out. I just about swallowed my tongue when I realized she was wearing only my jersey.

"Damn, it was sexy to watch you."

"Cleaning is sexy?"

"Uh, yeah... If women wrote porn, it would always be the pool boy or the male nanny cleaning."

She came and stood next to me. I dried my hands and put them around her waist. I looked around nervously since we had a no-PDA rule in front of Aubree, but I couldn't keep my hands off of Millie when she was dressed like a fucking baseman's dream.

"She's asleep," she said, arching on her tiptoes before she planted her lips on mine. It was slow and passionate. Our mouths intertwined I pulled her closer to me.

"I've been waiting all night to do that."

"Me too."

Our lips crashed back onto each other, hungrier, deeper. She ran her fingers gently across my chest. It was delicate and sensual. It took all of five seconds to make me hard as a rock. I was trying not to jump her, but if she kept this up, I wasn't sure I could hold back.

The only reason I hesitated at all was Aubree.

"You keep touching me like that and I won't be able to stop."

"Maybe I don't want you to." I was stunned as I froze in place, gripping the counter. The simple flutter of her eyelashes was enough for me to forget any rules we'd created.

I grabbed her and hoisted her onto the counter. My hands ran down the fabric of the jersey and slowly I pulled the buttons open. She was bare except for the shirt. Her breath became ragged as I cupped her breast, flicking her nipple.

"You're perfect."

"Are we really going to do this... Here?" She glanced around the kitchen.

"Why not? The cleaning lady said it was clean enough to eat off." I chuckled. She swatted the top of my head.

"Do you want me to stop?" I kissed the inside of her thigh and moved closer to her center.

Millie dug her fingers into my shoulders. "Don't even think about stopping."

She clutched the counter and muffled her moans. It took no time for her to fall apart. When she caught her breath, she sat up with a wicked grin before she pushed my pants down. My cock sprung free. Her eyes lit up, and fuck if it didn't grow an extra inch. She firmly gripped my shaft.

"You like that?" she whispered in my ear.

"Fuck yeah." I hesitated, glancing toward the spare room. "Are you sure we should?" Millie followed my gaze.

"We're safe," she assured me. "If it wasn't for sleeping kids, parents wouldn't have a sex life."

I hoisted her over my shoulder, her bare ass right next to my cheek. I gave it a tender nip and a quick slap. She squeaked in surprise. I dropped her on my king-sized bed, and I grabbed a condom from the drawer. I was back on her with lightning speed.

It had been far too long since we had sex. The last thing I needed to be was a one-pump chump. *Pace yourself.* I leaned down to kiss her. She spread her legs and welcomed me in. She felt too good. I slid in and out. Her tits bounced with each thrust. I grabbed her legs and draped them over my forearms, raising her ass up. She buried her head in the pillow to muffle her screams as I slammed into her over and over. I felt her tense and tighten around me. It sent me over the edge with her. Christ, my orgasm was so intense I almost blacked out.

It took us a minute before either of us could speak. "You okay?" I asked.

"Uh, you could say that. Damn, you were better than I remembered," she murmured. We cleaned up, and she looked hesitant when I tapped on the bed for her to come back.

"Actually, I should sleep with Aubree."

"I figured."

"You don't mind?"

I got up and walked over to her, lowering my hands to her hips. I pinched my fingers together and stuck out my bottom lip. "A little, but only because I want to feel you next to me. I get it. This is new for all of us. If Aubree woke up scared and not knowing where she was, I'd feel like crap, so I promise it's all good."

She wrapped her arms around my waist and buried her head into my chest. "Thanks for understanding."

It sounded like she was near tears. I kissed her head. "Babe, I will always put Aubree's and your needs first."

She tilted her head up to me and kissed me. "Thank you."

Chapter Eighteen

Millie

Before we left Toronto, we had brunch with Lisa, Sam, and Gia.

"Hey, sunshine." Lisa grinned widely. I rolled my eyes as I sat down with Aubree at the table. Sam and Gia came in full of smiles.

"I want to hear *all* of it," Gia said, sliding in next to me.

"No." My eyes darted to Aubree.

"Aubree, did you like the baseball game?"

"Yup. I did a wave, and I runned the... Mommy, what did I do?"

"Ran the bases."

"Yeah. I did that."

"So cool."

"How did mommy like the game?" Gia asked slyly.

"Just fine, thanks. It was an amazing game." I wiggled my brow, and the squeal that came from Gia was enough to make half the restaurant turn to us. My face flamed red in embarrassment.

"Better or worse than vacation."

"What's better?" Aubree asked, looking at us.

"The food." I snapped. Sam bit her lip.

"I'm sure the sausage was fantastic compared to the little cocktail weenie you had before."

The server dropped off some menus and left Aubree some crayons. She turned to the coloring section, ignoring us.

Lisa nudged me, waiting for an answer. I thought for a moment about how I could describe just how amazing the night was, but in a kid-friendly way.

"It was, uh..." I looked at Aubree, who was laser-focused on staying in the lines. "Delicious, spicy and filling." I smirked.

Sam slapped the table. "Damn."

"Millie, I'm so stupidly happy for you," Gia said with the most genuine smile on her face.

"You're bringing him to the wedding, right?"

I froze. I hadn't thought about it. The blank stare must have registered with them. "I don't know his schedule. Is it too soon?"

"No," they said in unison. My expression fell flat.

"A wedding date is a big deal."

"And?"

"I don't want to add pressure."

Lisa clasped my hand. "It's okay to move slowly. It has been a hot minute since you had a man in your life. Not that I consider Nick much of one. But I digress. It's just dinner and dancing. Mitch is coming, so it's not like Jake will be stuck alone."

"I'll think about it."

The girls shrugged, but let it go. I had a lot to think about. Jake was proving to be something unexpected. There had to be a flaw, right? Like a super great hot, rich guy doesn't just land in your lap? Unless you're in some romance movie. But that's not real. At least not for me. Not from what happened before. I almost felt bad for Jake. Sometimes when he reaches for me, I flinch. Like when he grabs my hand. It's so casual for him, but for me, it brings back flashbacks of trying to hold Nick's hand. He would literally pout. He always said it made him feel like he was on a leash and being punished for something. A leash? Clearly, it wasn't nearly long enough for the shit he pulled off.

* * *

It had been a long weekend, and the rage texts from Nick had rolled in right on cue. I tucked Aubree into bed and went down into the kitchen, where Mickey was pawing at the back door. He scratched his ears as I flipped on the patio light before opening the door. Nick was sitting there on the deck. He scared the crap out of me.

"What the hell are you doing?" I snapped.

"What? You thought our conversation was over?"

"It is over."

"No, it's not," he snapped. "It's far from over."

"What the hell is your problem?"

"Did you stay with him? With our daughter?"

"Yes." I crossed my arms. "We're dating. It's normal for us to spend time together, and since you bailed on *our* daughter, she came with me."

"You're going to blame me for working when you could have canceled?"

"Why should I cancel? There was nothing wrong with taking her to a game. In fact, she likes baseball. Maybe you'd know that if you bothered to ask her."

"I know my kid."

"Sure you do."

His eyes narrowed. "Look at you...One guy gives you some attention, and you're acting like a whore."

I felt like someone hit me. A whore? Ironic, since I have only been with two people. It was his cheating that caused our breakup, yet he calls me a whore. I stared at him, anger blazing in my eyes.

"How dare you? What's wrong, Nick? Is it because I am with someone else, or who he is? This sure as hell isn't about our daughter."

"Sure, it is. You're tied to me for life." He pointed to his chest, and his hand shook. "Wait until he realizes it. Eventually, he will tire of all this."

It took every ounce of willpower to not punch him in the throat. "Shut up, Nick. You know nothing about me. Or him."

He snickered. "Oh, I think I do. Don't tell me you think he is in this for life? Come on, how naïve are you? Jake Parson's going to give up his big baseball career or celebrity life for what? You?" He laughed. "You're nothing but some hot piece of ass to pass his time until he gets traded again, or maybe someone better will come along. You know how it is." His words were like venom, making my blood boil.

"Go to hell. You petulant asshole." He glared at me, then stomped away. The gate slammed behind him.

I stood shaking on the deck. Completely torn. Scared and angry. Something only Nick could do to me. I locked the door. My nerves were shot. I fought the urge to throw up. I didn't want to be alone, so I called Lisa.

"That's messed up. Jealousy is one thing, but this borders on crazy," she screeched into the phone. I didn't disagree. Nick always pushed boundaries, but this was scary. As much as I wanted to block him out, I couldn't help thinking about what he said. What would happen when the season was over? Jake and I hadn't talked about it. Would he go back to Florida? What if he got traded? Was I convenient for him right now?

"What do I do?"

"Don't tell Jake."

"What?"

"Mils, he can't help you right now and he would want to. I'd bet he'd go all millionaire hero and charter a plane to get to you." I sighed, both loving and hating that she was right.

Anger took over. Nick here, unannounced like some crazed-out ex, was pushing my limits. As if he thinks he gets to dictate to me, I've learned a lot about how messed up our relationship was. The rose-colored glasses I fought to keep on came off the minute the stick turned pink.

His words sunk in. No matter what, I'd be tied to him forever. I love Aubree to death and wouldn't change anything. She was my light in life, but I was trapped.

Ten minutes after I hung up with Lisa, there was a knock on the door. I cringed, wondering if Lisa called the cops. I peeked out the window to see Avery standing on the step, and he looked pissed.

"What are you doing here?"

"Lisa called me. I came right over. What the fuck is happening with him? You should never have moved home. You were safer with Lisa," he groaned, looking around the place as if Nick was still there.

"I know, but I couldn't stay away forever." Avery shook his head and gave me a hug, telling me he was staying for the night. I didn't even try to argue.

Jake called after the game. My attempts to concentrate on our conversation were futile. The background noise made it hard to hear. Guilt hit me. He should hang out with his friends instead of being stuck on the phone with me. Nick's voice was still in my head about his lifestyle and partying. Maybe I was holding him back. My nights were filled with bedtime stories, not late-night clubbing or hobnobbing with the rich and famous.

"Babe, are you okay?" Jake asked with a touch of worry in his voice. I guessed I wasn't paying as much attention to the conversation as I'd thought.

"Yeah, tired is all," I lied. I wondered about telling him what happened with Nick, but I didn't want him to deal with my drama. I had already involved him enough. The last thing he needed in the middle of his series was to worry about me. I ended the call. He sounded disappointed, which only made me feel worse.

My head was swirling, I felt sick, and my chest ached. I liked Jake a lot, but would we really last? I had nothing to offer him. Our lives were opposites in every way. Maybe I was being selfish.

* * *

I had just woken Aubree when my phone went off. It was Jake. I checked the time.

"What are you doing up? It's so early."

"It's the first day of school. I wanted to wish Aubree a good day. Can we video chat? I want to see your faces."

"But you had a late night."

"Millie, it's a monumental day. I can't be there with you like I wanted to be. The least I could do was call."

I nodded as Aubree came into the kitchen full of energy. She was beyond excited about going to school now. I turned on the video so he could see us. I prayed I didn't look like the wreck that I felt.

"Hi Jake-e," she said, snatching the phone from my hand. I got it back, then put it on the counter while I made her breakfast. She carried on about all her new school gear. Jake smiled sweetly as she talked his ear off. He told her to

149

listen to the teacher and hoped she would make lots of new friends.

"Hey, do you have any juice?" Avery called out.

Jake's face changed. "Who's that?"

"Uncle Avery," Aubree answered, chewing a mouthful of cereal.

"In the fridge." I nodded to him. He had just come around the corner.

"Everything okay?"

"Yeah. Look, I have to go. Get Aubree to school."

"Oh, okay, sure." He didn't look happy, but I couldn't tell him what was going on. He had a game today. It wasn't fair to involve him in this. I hung up as Avery came over and ruffled Aubree's hair.

"Kiddo. First day of school."

"I know."

"Well," he scoffed, gulping down his juice.

"I gotta get to work. Are you going to be okay at drop off? Or need me to come?" He rubbed his elbow as if he was going to crack Nick in the head with it.

"I'll be fine."

* * *

I stood out at the fence with the other kindergarten parents, giving Aubree a once over to make sure I hadn't forgotten anything. I watched Nick and Misha pull up in her silver BMW. They both got out and stood next to another couple at the other end of the school driveway. Her baby bump was more noticeable. Rage, anger, and sadness flooded me. He gets to move on and I'm living in self-doubt. Misha looked over at me and nudged Nick's rib. They begrudgingly walked over to us. *Crap.*

Gracie and Aubree almost tackled each other with excitement. Nick hugged her next.

"Hey," Misha said.

I was stunned. We hadn't spoken since the night she told me she was pregnant with Nick's baby. "Hi."

"I hope they have a good day," she added, shifting on her feet, while she waved off to the side to one of the other moms. *Typical Misha, this is all for show.*

Once the bell rang, the girls were sent to their respective teachers and, just my luck, they were in the same class. *I can't wait until parent-teacher night. That will be super freaking fun.* I hung my head and walked away. The sight of Nick glowering at me had me rehashing last night's conversation.

What would happen if it ended? I mean, I'm a big girl. I can handle the heartbreak, but poor Aubree was already asking about Jake. She loved watching baseball and every time we saw him on the screen she would jump and yell for him, which melted my heart, until now. She's attached to him, and it was worrisome. Plus, I wasn't one of his exciting supermodel types he was used to hanging out with.

My head hurt from the thinking I did. Every scenario played out in my head, and nothing was coming out right anymore. I wasn't going to see Jake for another week. Maybe I'd have answers by then.

Chapter Nineteen

Jake

I kept my eye on the time, waiting for the clock to hit three-thirty so I could call them. It felt like time stood still, as if the clock mocked me. I had wondered how Aubree's day went. Did she make friends? Was she picked on? How did she like her teacher? I can't imagine how Millie must have felt. Would she do okay with Nick there? Hell, would he even show up? My jaw tensed, thinking about how angry I was that he'd be there and not me. *Stop. Aubree is his kid.* He should be there to support her, whether or not I liked it.

The minute practice was over, I called them. Instantly, I knew something was wrong. Millie's voice was tight and low, like she'd been crying.

"Hey... Why are you crying?"

Sniffling, she answered. "Today sucked."

My fists balled up. Already not what I wanted to hear.

Take a breath and listen to her. I told myself as I stood against the wall and forced myself to ask for more details.

"This morning, Nick and Misha came together for Gracie's first day. It's not like I wasn't expecting that, but they came over to us like Aubree was an afterthought. She was so excited, and it barely phased him. Misha stood there, acting fake as shit, because all the other parents watching us."

I ran my hands down my face, wanting to hit something. The problem was that I had no way of helping her at that moment. What a prick. I didn't want to overreact. It would push Millie away. "I'm sorry," was all I could muster.

"I hate this for Aubree. They placed Gracie and her in the same class. Can you imagine parent-teacher night? What a fucking joke. Hey dad, hold on, we need to switch out the moms and daughters? Ugh, I forgot how small the town is." She paused, letting out a long sigh. "Maybe moving home was a mistake. I thought I was helping their relationship, but now I don't know. I feel like the girls will be in constant competition."

I nodded as if she could see me. "I wish I could have been there today."

"Thanks, Jake, but it's not your job to be there." She sighed.

What the fuck? Not my job? It hit a nerve I wasn't expecting. "It's her douchebag father's job to be there and put in the effort, but he's busy playing head games. I *wanted* to be there." I snapped into the phone.

"I didn't mean it that way. It's just... I dunno."

"Is that Jake?" Aubree asked before I heard the phone rustling.

It broke my heart to think she didn't think I would have. "How was your day?" I asked softly.

She told me all about her class, and who she played with, and she was very excited to have her own cubby. I didn't exactly get the cubby thing until she told me she could decorate it and make a name tag and she had chosen her favorite princess sticker. Wow, something so simple had her so damn excited was just one more reason to love this kid. How could her dick of a dad not?

When Millie said goodbye, the sadness in her voice was gut-wrenching. I didn't like it. I know my schedule is less than ideal for us. The pit in my stomach wouldn't go away. She needed me and I couldn't be there. This would be harder than I thought, and I still had three days to go.

* * *

It was a great game, with a crowd to match, but I wanted Millie, and not to be alone across the continent. I wondered how she was, hoping distance hadn't made things worse, so I called her.

"Hey," she answered softly.

"I miss you," I blurted. "I'm sorry about earlier. I hate seeing you doubt yourself because of Nick, but I was angry I wasn't there with you like I wanted to be."

"It's just that—" Someone knocked on the door before she finished. "Hold on," I called out through the apartment, then telling Millie someone was at the door. They knocked again. *This better be fucking good.*

I swung the door open to see Mitch standing there, grinning.

"Miss me?" He smacked me in the chest, pushing past me. I rolled my eyes. "Who's that?"

"Amelia."

He made a kissy face like a ten-year-old before he snatched the phone. "Hey, Mils. Lisa said you guys were going dress shopping tomorrow."

How did Mitch know she was dress shopping, and I

didn't? I snatched the phone back in time to hear Millie say she had to go before she hung up.

Fucking Mitch. "Nice timing, buddy."

"What's going on, man?"

"Something is off with Millie. Our conversations are shorter and lighter. Her brothers have stayed at her place a few times. Something isn't sitting right."

"You think it's the ex? Lisa said they had a run-in recently." I gawked at him like he had three heads.

"What run-in? At the school?"

Mitch's face scrunched as he shook his head. "Like last week or something? Right after you left. I don't know exactly. I only heard Lisa's side of the conversation. It didn't sound good. If they had something else, it's separate."

What kind of shit did he do? I started pacing, not liking any of what I was hearing. She was hiding this from me.

"Dude, you have smoke coming out of your ears. What are you thinking?"

"Lots." I shrugged. "Finding time is hard because we are in games every day. I leave for a series in Boston, home for two, then off to New York."

"If it were me and this was Lis, I'd just show up. She can't dodge you if you're standing in front of her. Besides, it's what, a forty-five-minute flight from Toronto to New York? Leave first thing in the morning and you'll make it to practice."

I grunted. I'd put Brody on it. It sucked that I'd have to wait so long. It already felt too long, but it was nearing the end of the season. My schedule was shit, but I checked my calendar to see if I could head out to Millie's right after the game, stay a couple of hours, and then make it back for practice.

The days seemed longer than usual, and my temper was shorter with my mind stuck back home and on my girls. For the first time in my career, I was worried about something other than my batting average. I was worried about *them*. That afternoon was my last game in Florida, and I couldn't wait to see Millie and Aubree. I video-called a couple times, but Millie was growing distant.

* * *

My head was with Millie and Aubree all week. The countdown started the minute I landed in Toronto, when I also texted Millie. It was early, but Aubree was an early riser.

Me: On the way to the stadium.

Millie: Have a good game.

Me: What're your plans?

Millie: I'm working today.

Me: It's Sat...

Millie: We landed a massive project and there's extra work.

Me: Boo. Try not to work too hard xo.

Millie: I'll try.

I got to the front of the stadium, and I saw a familiar figure. My jaw clenched, and my shoulders tightened instinctively when I noticed Nick against the wall. What the fuck? The nerve of this guy. I was furious.

"What are you doing here?" I barked.

"Come on, man, you're a smart guy. You can put two and two together."

I wanted to take a bat to his head already. *Calm down, before you smash his teeth down his throat.* Carlos came over, asking if everything was alright.

"Yeah," I said through gritted teeth. Glaring at Nick, I warned, "I don't know what your game is here, or whatever the fuck you think you're doing, but let me tell you. It's not happening."

"The fuck it isn't." Nick snarled. "You have some big balls

for trying, but I'll never let you take them. I can't control what Millie does, but I know how she thinks."

"Too bad you don't get to choose, Nick."

"Sure, I do. You're not around much. How are you going to prove you can be a stable family guy? I was there on the first day of school. Not you. Just like you won't be there for other important stuff, or everyday moments. Think about it. You're living out of hotels for what, eight months of the year? What kind of life is it for Aubree? Nah, man, you'll ruin it soon enough. Now I'm going to pick her up to spend the weekend with her." He snickered menacingly and walked away.

I wanted to punch the little runt right in the mouth. What a vindictive prick. I ran my hands down my face. Confusion took over. How would this impact Aubree? Fuck, I really hated that guy.

My head was stuck on everything Nick said. I'd lost all concentration on the game and, to make matters worse, my temper flared when I missed the ball and took it out on the pitcher as if he had purposely aimed it at me. It got so bad that the coach benched me. I threw the bat down in frustration.

When the game was over, I sat in the locker room. Nick's words played over and over. Was he right? Would he get to her? He made a valid point, as much as I hated to admit it. How could I be all the things I promised? I kicked my bag across the floor and paced. Stuck not knowing what to do. Am I complicating things?

"You okay?" Kev asked, coming around the corner.

I shook my head. "Yeah." He stopped and waited for me to continue, but I didn't. He shrugged and pulled his phone from his pocket, walking away.

My plan to see Millie was crumbling in front of me. I picked up my bag and stalked out of the locker room. I walked back to my condo, furious at myself, the situation, and the doubts Nick left me with. He was getting under my skin, and I didn't know how to deal with this fucker.

It was silent and cold inside, and I hated that I came home instead of going to see Millie. She hadn't messaged me since the afternoon, but I didn't message her either. I checked my phone again, realizing it was after ten. *Let it go for tonight.* There wasn't much I could do. After my tantrum, the coach gave me orders to show up early for practice the next day.

I slept like shit, tossing and turning with the pit of my stomach aching. Giving up, I went for a run. Running was one of the few things that usually helped me work out whatever situation I was in. I ran harder, as if I could outrun the feeling I had of both losing Millie and dealing with Nick.

* * *

The long practice was shit. The game was worse. I couldn't get my head out of my ass. I got into a scuffle with Ben Stichlin, the second baseman for the Sox. Guys were in my space and I snapped. It was nothing, but ended up with me benched again. It was the bottom of the eighth, anyway. I took a cold shower after the game, wondering why the fuck I hadn't heard from Millie since the morning when she said she was swamped. All I could think was maybe Nick got to her. I was angrier than ever at myself for letting him create such doubt. I sent her a text.

Me: How's it going?
Millie: *emoji of fire and poop*

Panic hit me. What did he do now?

Me: What happened?
Millie: Just work stuff. It's been such a shit show today. I watched some of the game. You okay? That seemed rough.

What an understatement. I felt relieved it wasn't something Nick did.

Me: Yeah, crappy day. Are you home now?

Millie: Nope. Still here. Probably another hour, I hope.

Me: Okay. Get home safe. Message me.

Millie: Okay.

I paced in front of my car for about three minutes while I debated about going up there before I got my sanity back. I punched in the address I found for Hartes Construction. If it was the last thing I did, I'd prove that douche wrong.

I pulled off the highway and drove down Main Street. The bakery sign was still on. I ran in and grabbed a few of Millie's favorite things. I had a feeling she hadn't stopped to eat.

Her SUV was parked in front of her office. The lights were still on. My eyes flicked to the rearview mirror, and I pushed down my hair that had gone awry from the number of times I ran my hand through it on the drive-up. Damn, I was nervous.

It was silent except for my footsteps. I walked in and glanced around at the architectural drawings of houses before and after lining the walls. The work was spectacular. A sofa sat in a lounge area with a coffee machine, and a flat screen hung on the wall. I saw she had on the game highlights. My heart just about exploded. My gaze fell across the large desk in the far corner and immediately stopped on Millie with her head down on the desk. Her hair had half fallen out of the bun with a pen sticking out of it. Her arm was outstretched, and her computer was glowing in her face. Adorable. I went over and placed the coffee on the desk and stroked her arm.

"Babe..."

"Hmmm," she groaned. Her head tilted up, and she wiped a touch of drool off her chin. I chuckled. Her eyes snapped open. "Jake?"

"Hi, beautiful."

"What are you doing here? Your game? And you have another one tomorrow in New York." Her face flushed.

"I will fly out tomorrow morning." I paused, feeling silly. "I missed you."

She silenced me with a rough and demanding kiss. My body thrummed in electricity, and everything I had thought about melted. I needed this. Instinctively, my hands wandered around her waist.

"Sorry," I muttered, lowering my hand.

"Don't stop."

"Wait, what?"

"I missed you too. I don't want to stop."

She backed me up against a desk, her hand finding my zipper and slipping around my cock.

"I don't want to either, but... We're in your office, next to your parents."

"Uh-huh. There's a lock on the door, and a couch."

She brought her other hand up and undid my pants until they puddled around my ankles. She walked to the door and snapped the latch. The curtains were already closed. *Oh shit, she's serious.*

She came back, and I pulled her into me. Our kisses were heavy. Filled with want and need. My hands reached for her breast. Her nipples were popping out of her bra, hardening from my touch. Gently, I took one in my mouth and ran my teeth over the soft pink skin. She tugged my hair, shifting me backward onto the desk.

Oh, damn. Millie grabbed hold of my balls, rolling them in her palm. I swallowed hard. She moved her hand up and down the shaft, perfectly squeezing it from the base to the tip. I had to lean against the desk for balance.

She started running her tongue over my pecs, licking my nipple while she tugged my cock with one hand. My head rolled back, and my cock twitched for more. She stroked me harder and faster. At this rate, I was ready to cum.

"Holy fuck," I moaned.

She dropped to her knees and, without wasting time, she put my entire cock in her mouth. I gripped the desk as she moved her mouth up and down, palming my balls. Her thumb was running up and down the underside of my cock.

"Babe, I'm going to cum." I tried holding back, but she was relentless. "Shit, woman." I gripped the desk hard as my orgasm hit. It was powerful enough to make me see stars. I finally caught my breath and noticed Millie grinning at me.

She stood up and reached onto the desk, then popped a mint in her mouth. I pulled close to kiss her. "If this is the greeting I get on surprise visits, I'm coming home every night."

She let out a beautiful laugh. "This was a onetime special."

"I have to get back to work."

"The fuck you do," I argued. "You're kidding if you think I am letting you out of this office without returning the favor."

A knock at the door startled both of us. "Mils? Are you there?"

Her eyes widened and her mouth dropped open in horror. "It's my dad!"

"Your dad?" I jumped away from her and ran my hands down the front of me, smoothing myself out, then jumped onto the sofa, crossing my legs as if that would help. She crossed the room to unlock the door. Her face was the shade of a ripe tomato.

Her dad was tall and built. He had a tanned complexion, which told me had spent a lot of time in the sun. He had thick salt and pepper hair and a heavy beard. Millie was absolutely nothing like him. He stilled when he saw me sitting on the couch. *Not exactly how I pictured meeting him.* I inwardly groaned at myself.

"Jake Parsons?"

I stood up and walked over to shake his hand. "Yes, Sir."

"Well, I'll be damned. Shitty game, by the way."

Millie's face burned red. "Dad!"

"What? He knows... He was there. In body anyway." He chuckled.

"Yeah. Not my finest game." I scratched my jaw.

"What brings you up here?"

"Here to see Millie." I didn't falter. It was best, to be honest with him. *Especially after nearly being busted by him.*

"I heard you two were an item, but I just thought it was Mrs. Peterson and her damn town gossip, since Millie had said nothing." His gaze wandered to the desk and the tray of pastries, as he then wasted no time in scooping up a butter tart. *I see where Millie got her sweet tooth.* "Don't you have a game in New York tomorrow?"

Nodding, I shifted on my feet, slightly nervous. I had an idea, but I was banking on being denied. "Yes. I came to ask Millie if she'd come with me."

Millie's eyes widened. "What?"

I cleared my throat. "One night in New York?"

"Yeah... Come to New York?" she echoed like it was the most absurd thing she's ever heard.

"I'm serious. The flight's early, and it's an afternoon game. I'll have you home in plenty of time for Aubree."

Her dad crossed his arms over his chest. *Oh, crap.* "I think you should go," he agreed. Millie's gaze snapped to him. "Kiddo. You barely ever go anywhere. Act your age and have some fun for once, besides I already like this one."

Well, that wasn't what I expected. I made a mental note to send her dad tickets.

"Take care of my girl," he ordered, shaking my hand with a firm grasp.

"I'm trying, Sir."

He nodded. "Call me Peter," he said, before leaving us alone. A grin spread across his face.

Turning to Millie, I took her hand in mine, squeezing it as I whispered above her ear, "Tick tock, Blondie. We have a flight to catch."

Chapter Twenty

Millie

When Jake suggested New York, I thought it was a joke, yet here I was on my way to the airport. When he showed up, risking his game for me, it made me realize how selfish I was being. He was putting in all the effort, and I was doing nothing but making it harder. Plus, if I was truly honest with myself, I missed him more than I let on. I pushed my guilt aside and told myself it was ok that I wanted to spend time with him. There was nothing wrong with me taking time for *me* or *us*?

A private jet was waiting for us at Buttonville Airport, and I felt underdressed and overwhelmed. I hadn't changed from work. I was still in my jeans and a t-shirt. Jake sensed my nerves and tugged my hand. When we got on board, I noticed it was larger than it appeared. It had two designated seating areas, one with a large couch against the wall, flanked by two large wing chairs. The back had another area with four large chairs surrounding a table. The furnishing was luxurious, with soft creams, silver trim, and walnut wood tables.

"This is nicer than my living room," I muttered, afraid to touch anything.

Jake snorted and ushered me into a chair. He sat across from me with a twinkle in his eye. It was adorable. A few people hurried about after the doors closed. As we took off, Jake held my hand, rubbing his thumb across mine. My heart fluttered.

"So, Mr. Fancy Pants, do you always travel by private jet?"

He shrugged. "Not always. Time was of the essence today." He grinned, showing off his deep dimples. A young flight attendant came over and handed Jake a bottle of water and me a glass of champagne.

I thanked her and took a sip. It was cool and sweet. I wasn't a champagne girl normally, but it was delicious. The cost crossed my mind.

"You seem nervous."

"A little."

"Why?"

"I don't normally jet-set off to New York on a whim. This is new."

"Amelia... I get this will be tough sometimes and I know the risk you're taking. My life is complicated, but I love that you're willing to try."

I choked up. Not wanting him to see me, I rushed and asked for a bathroom.

He grabbed my hand and took me to the back of the plane. When he opened the door, it surprised me to see a large bedroom.

"The door on the right."

The bathroom was fancy, just like the rest of the plane. I splashed my face with water to relax. Jake was pulling out all the stops to make things work, and I was always hitting the brakes. *Maybe I should practice what I preach.* I told Nick it was just sex. I knew that would rile him up, but I wondered if a summer fling could be exactly what I needed to move on with my life. It will fizzle out on good terms, and Aubree would be none the wiser.

When I came out, Jake was still at the door, running his hands down his face.

"You want to nap?" I asked, pointing to the bed.

"It's only forty-five minutes, give or take." He shrugged.

"I can think of something else." I smiled boldly. Jake's mouth hung open.

He wiggled his brows, pushing me onto the velvety soft linens.

"I was kidding!" I burst into laughter as he tickled my sides, lifting my shirt over my head.

"Too late." He kissed me. "Besides, I still owe you from earlier." His thick arms locked me down on the bed, and the way his deep blue eyes fixed on mine was all I needed to lose my inhibition. It wasn't long before we ripped off our clothes. Lost in the moment, all of my doubts were forgotten.

Out of breath, we were nestled side-by-side, breathing erratically, when an announcement rang out over the speakers informing us we were landing. I covered my face, remembering where we were, and that everyone on board knew what we just did. I couldn't help but chuckle.

"What's so funny, Blondie?"

"We just had sex on a private jet... I couldn't be more bougie."

Jake let out a deep laugh, the vibrations of his chest making my body shake with him. "First time in the mile-high club?"

I blushed to the tip of my toes. His question made me wonder how many others were in that club with him. I wasn't naïve; I knew who he was, but...

"This was a first for me, too," he interrupted my doubt. When I brought my gaze to his, his eyes narrowed. "I don't bring women on the jet." I felt a flutter in my chest and a small smirk pulled at my lips. His face relaxed as he brushed the pads of his fingers over my shoulders and kissed the top of my head. I buried my face in the crook of his neck and ran my hands over the faintest bit of his chest hair.

"Come with me to Sam and Gia's wedding?" I whispered, afraid to ask it any louder.

"What?" He said, gazing down at me.

Chewing on my lip, I asked again, making his smile widen. He promised he'd make it work, even though it was in November.

"I'd love nothing more than to be your plus one." Jake's eyes were so bright and gleaming in a way I had never seen anyone look at me. He placed a quick kiss on my lips.

"Good timing." I laughed, hurrying to clean up and get dressed.

* * *

Even after midnight, New York was exactly as I had seen in all the movies and shows. Bustling with people, yellow cabs weaving in and out of traffic, narrowly missing pedestrians. We settled into the hotel, and it felt like home when I woke up nestled in Jake's arms. *I could get used to this.*

He pulled me closer. The scent of his woodsy soap still clung to him from his shower last night, and it was lighting up my insides all over again.

"God, I love waking up with you," he murmured. Everything about him was sexy; his tired voice, his arms tightening around me. I melted into a huge puddle of wetness.

How do you respond to that? Sex. I wanted to show him how I felt. I brushed my lips across his. He responded immediately, taking hold of me. The kiss was deeper. I moved on top, straddling him, and lowered my mouth to his again. He eagerly kissed me back, cupping my face. Our kiss morphed into something more than just passion. My heart raced.

He stilled, staring at me. There were no words. He dragged my shirt over my head and slid his hand between my breasts, down my abdomen, to my pubic bone. He trailed his fingers over my clit, making my insides clench until I was begging for more.

When I opened my eyes, Jake was staring at me with such adoration, I almost burst. I spread my palms around his shoulders, pulling him closer.

"Do it again," I demanded. "Make me come."

He rolled me onto the bed, removing his boxers, letting his thick cock tease me, then he stopped.

I quietly protested until Jake crawled on top of me. He kissed me while raising my leg and swiftly filling me up.

"Yes, babe. More." I moaned. He thrusted deeper in response. We moved into a rhythm, kissing along the way.

"Fuck, the way you say that kills me." He nipped at my ear.

"Please, babe, don't stop."

"Never. I never want to stop." He huffed. Before long, we both cried out in ecstasy, panting and sweating.

"You're going to drain all my energy for the game," Jake grunted with a smirk and tugged me off the bed. "Shower time."

Drain him was right, except I wasn't the one who instigated the shower. A bit of soap running down the swell of my breasts and Jake had me up against the wall, begging to get in. *This man is insatiable.* Since our extra romp took more time from Jake's schedule, he left the shower before me.

"Blondie, someone is calling you," he yelled while I toweled off in the bathroom.

I padded out to the room when the phone stopped vibrating. Not thinking much about it, I grabbed my bag to get dressed.

"I'm going to get us coffee." Jake kissed me on the nose before ducking out of the room. Again, my phone vibrated on the nightstand. *What the? Who is calling me?* I turned the phone over to see Nick's number. I surveyed the hotel room, as if he could see me. It was foolish because it wasn't a video call, yet he still affected me... And I hated that.

"Hey."

"Why haven't you answered?"

"I was sleeping."

"Must be nice."

"Do you actually want something or just to annoy me?"

He huffed. "Aubree got hurt."

And, in an instant, panic washed over me. "What do you mean?"

"Her and Gracie were playing this morning and I guess one of them spilled water on the floor. She slipped."

"How bad is she hurt?"

"She's been holding her arm. We're going to take her to the emergency room to see if it's broken. I've been calling you for like an hour to see if you wanted to meet us there."

My stomach dropped at hearing she needed to go to the hospital. "Yeah," I quickly replied, but then I remembered where I was. "Wait, no."

"What do you mean?"

Fuck. I grimaced. I had to tell him. "I'm not home."

"Where are you?" His seething response made me cringe.

"Does it matter? I'm not home."

He scoffed. "This is exactly my point, Mils. Aubree needs you, and you're off with him. Great fucking mom. How about you tell her why you can't be here then?"

Tears rolled down my chin as Aubree spoke into the phone. "Mommy…"

I choked down my tears and tried to steady my breath. "Hi, baby. Are you okay?"

"My arm hurts."

"I know, sweetie. Daddy told me."

"Can you come get me?" She cried.

My throat closed as I tried to answer her. "Not right now. Mommy is on her way home. Daddy will take care of you. I'll be home soon."

"Okay. I love you, Mommy." Her voice drifted off at the end, and my chest squeezed as if it was about to implode.

"I love you, Aubree." I didn't need to hang up because Nick already had.

I was sobbing on the side of the bed when Jake returned, asking me what was wrong.

Through choked breaths, I explained what happened, and that I needed to get home to Aubree. He immediately went to his phone and texted someone.

"A driver is ready downstairs and I'll have the jet take you home. It will be ready in forty-five minutes." He came and knelt in front of me.

The guilt I felt was thick. How could I be so reckless? I wasn't there for my kid for the first time because I was trying to be something I'm not. Abruptly, I got up and paced, surprising Jake.

"I never should have come here."

He reached for me. "Hey, you didn't know Aubree was going to get hurt. She's with Nick on his time. Don't blame yourself."

I shook his hand off. "I should have been there for her immediately, not having to fly home. This was a mistake."

He stepped back. "What the hell do you mean?"

I waved my hands in the air. "Come on, Jake. I can't fly to different states on a whim. This isn't me."

"You're upset, I get it... But don't say being with me is a mistake."

I hung my head while tears rolled down my cheeks. *This was all my fault.* "I'm not this girl. Maybe you should be with someone who fits your lifestyle, someone who can drop everything for you, because you are so worth it. You deserve better."

"I deserve you. I want you."

I grabbed my suitcase and threw whatever I had taken out back in. Nothing made sense anymore. All of Nick's words haunted me.

"I can't follow you around. I won't leave my kid, and Nick made it clear he would never sign off on me traveling with her."

Jake stilled, eyeing me. "What do you mean? Is that what this is all about? Is this why you have been distant? Fuck, Millie. Don't do this. He's a jealous asshole."

He came to me, pulling my hand to him. "Don't, please." He begged.

Every one of my doubts bubbled back up. "Why? We both know it's not forever... You'll leave or get traded, then what?"

"Not forever?" He echoed angrily. "You think this is some fling? Some game I'm playing with you?"

I stared at the ground, afraid to see the hurt I caused.

"How do you not realize how crazy I am about you?" He shook his head. "How could you think so little of us? Of me?"

I swiped away more tears and pulled my shoulders back, willing my next words to him, even though I hardly believed them myself.

"Jake, you need someone less complicated, with no drama. Don't make it harder on me." I grabbed my bag, hiding my shaking hands, and left without letting him try to convince me to stay, because I'm sure he could have. It was for the better, even if he didn't see it.

I was halfway down the hall when I heard him punch something and yell. My heart broke.

"I'm sorry," I whispered into the empty hall, as if it would mean anything.

As the elevator doors closed, I gripped the wall to hold myself up.

Chapter Twenty-One

Jake

We didn't make it to the playoffs, although we were close. We drowned our sorrows with a team party, when I would've been with Millie and Aubree, had it not gone to shit two weeks ago in New York. I was there to drink away more than just ending the season. Drinking was the only game I was good at these days.

Josh had picked some club off Peter Street. With too much time on my hands and nothing but trouble to get into, I joined the chaos. Why the fuck not? It wasn't like shit could get worse.

The loud thumping music was enough to void any thoughts and anything anyone was saying. Fine by me, since I wasn't there to talk. I was going to lose my shit if one more person asked where Millie was.

I drank and sulked in the corner with my face stuck in my phone. Kev hit me on the knee when Josh let in another group of women. I rolled my eyes. *Give it up, man.* I wasn't interested in anyone. Instead, I went back to my phone and onto Millie's social media *again.* I had learned she didn't really use it since some of her stuff was really old. Her only recent picture was of her and Aubree surrounded by the flowers I had given her. Her face was glowing and, even though it was causing me to feel worse, I couldn't stop staring at it.

A movement to my left caught my gaze. One woman struggled with her skimpy dress, as she moved from side to side, awkwardly tugging at it. Christ, I missed Millie in her simple joggers and no make-up. That shit was way sexier to me than some tight mini-dress. I ran my hands down my face, taking another shot.

Some blonde came over, flashing a genuine smile when she greeted me. I simply nodded. She took the seat next to me, keeping her distance.

"Are you okay?" she shouted over the noise. I waved her off and grabbed a beer. She didn't leave. Instead, she started a conversation with the woman next to her. I noticed she wasn't throwing herself at anyone. She had a drink in her hand, but hadn't touched it. Logan tried to talk to her, but she mostly ignored him. *What was her angle?*

After a minute, she looked at me. Her face scrunched up before she leaned closer. Her perfume was stronger than it needed to be. "Want to go get some air?"

As much as I didn't want to admit it, it seemed like a good idea. They had started the fog machine not long ago with an annoying sounding air horn. I staggered up and swayed, nearly falling on her. Her hands flew up to stop me from crushing her. It reminded me of Millie running into me on the cruise, the night we met, when everything started.

"Sorry," I mumbled, walking toward the exit, with the blonde behind me.

Outside, the cool air smacked me in the face. *Just what I*

need. Sucking in a huge breath, she stood across from me, lighting a smoke. She seemed to be lost in her own thoughts. Her olive-green eyes surveyed the crowd. She was different, and I was curious about her.

"What's your name?"

She took a long haul off her smoke, hesitating before she answered, "Maggie."

My voice stuck in my throat. I must have heard wrong. It sounded like she said Millie's name. "What?"

"M-A-G-G-I-E."

My muscles tightened, then relaxed. "Oh."

She shivered against the breeze that came, and goose-bumps erupted on her bare arms and shoulders. I put my jacket around her.

"Thanks."

Don't ask me why I waited for her to finish her smoke, but it felt wrong to just leave her. She reminded me of Millie in a small way, except she smelled floral, and all I craved was maple.

"You want to get out of here?" she asked.

It was a quick debate. Sure, I could take her home for empty sex, but I only wanted Millie. "I have a girl."

"Thought so." She handed my jacket back and went back to her friends.

I shook my head at myself for lying. Millie had left me, but the idea of taking anyone else home was unfathomable.

* * *

My head felt like I had used it as a ball for batting practice. Since Millie ended things, I was a miserable bastard on a drinking spree. The light that filtered through the edge of the curtain made me think it might have been late in the morning. Not that I cared much.

My schedule was temporarily blank. Since the season was

over, I was headed back to Florida, because I had no reason to stay in Canada anymore. I had packed up the last of my stuff, and I couldn't wait. The sheets still had Millie's scent on them. And like a love-sick freak, I refused to wash them.

Flashes of last night started playing in my mind when I heard someone in the living room. What the hell? I jumped out of bed, grabbed my bat from the corner, and tiptoed out of my bedroom. Mitch was sitting on the couch with a couple of coffees on the table. I breathed a sigh of relief. He stared at me and laughed.

"What the hell were you going to do with a bat and boner?"

I glanced down at my tented flannel boxers. "Shut up, man. I just woke up." I knew it was a mistake to give the fucker a key. I tossed the bat down and went to put on a shirt and pants.

Mitch yelled, "That was your best defense? I don't know what I was more scared of."

When I returned, dressed and ready to kick his ass, he held out a coffee for me. Nudging his outstretched feet off my coffee table, I flopped down next to him.

"What the fuck are you doing here?" I asked.

"Poker night."

I checked the time. "It's eleven in the morning."

"What's your point?"

"You weren't invited."

"And?"

"Don't be an ass."

He sighed. "Jax told me about it. Last weekend in Toronto? Or some bullshit?"

The need to bolt out of this city before I lost my mind is my best defense. "Yup. The lease is up. I leave for Florida tomorrow."

Mitch ran his hands over his shaved head. "It's a mistake. "

I glared at him like he grew an extra head. When shit hit the fan two weeks ago, I called him in hopes he'd give me advice on how to get Millie back. Instead, the asshole agreed with her. A kid changed the lifestyle. Talk about confusion. He introduced us, then he said it wasn't it a good idea?

"Aren't you the one who agreed with Millie? You told me to get some perspective, to understand where she was coming from." He opened and closed his mouth, then he just shrugged. "Why would I stay? Everything in here reminds me of her."

"Is this why you ignored my texts?" I grunted in response to his question. "What the fuck are you doing? I get that you two broke up, but night after night at the bar? All I see are random pictures of you posted in the tabloids or on social media."

"Who cares?"

"Dude, there's only one woman on this planet I've seen you drink yourself into oblivion over. Remember the last time?" I didn't need him to remind me. It was just adding fuel to the fire. "Are you even alone?"

"Why the hell would you ask me that?"

He rolled his eyes. "The pictures."

What pictures? Why would anyone be here? Insulted, he asked. "What the hell are you talking about?"

"No blonde with you?" he asked, peering over my shoulder at the bedroom, as if someone was about to walk out of it.

"What blonde?"

My frustration grew with his line of questioning. I went to find my phone. *Of course it's dead.* I didn't bother charging it last night since I wasn't in the mood to talk to people. He grabbed his phone, showing me a picture of me on a patio next to a pretty blonde, wearing my coat. I vaguely remembered her.

"So? If you recall, I'm single," I snapped at him.

Mitch quirked his brows and drummed his fingers, his tell-tale sign he had something on his mind. I wanted to ignore him, but I had a feeling it was about Millie.

The words fell before I could stop myself. "Spit it out."

Mitch groaned, shaking his head. "Millie saw the pic, and Lisa said she cried."

And there it was, one thing I didn't want to hear. Although we broke up, I would never have wanted to hurt her or for her to feel pain. I felt like an asshole, even though the whole thing was innocent.

"It's not what you think. She was there with friends. I was piss drunk and needed air. We went outside. She had a smoke."

"She's wearing your coat, man."

"It was cold," I said defensively. "It was for a few minutes. She asked if I wanted to leave, but I told her I had a girl."

Mitch blew out a breath. "Alright. I'll slip it into our conversation when I talk to Lisa. They should be home later tonight." His brow arched at my confusion. "Sam and Gia's Bachelorette weekend? In Niagara?"

Right. I'd forgotten all about it. It would've been my first weekend off. I wanted to spend it with her, but she was going away. "How was it?"

His phone beeped. He flipped it over and broke into a smile. He turned the phone to show me a picture of Lisa with a stripper, getting motorboated.

I chuckled. "She had a good time." I noticed Millie in the background, so I snatched his phone. "Let me see."

Mitch rolled his eyes. "Go to Lisa's Instagram. There are better pics of the weekend."

He was right. Lisa had a shit ton of pictures. Everything from group shots of them standing in front of the waterfalls, out at dinner, and a bike tour. Millie was more beautiful in each picture I swiped through. The pictures of the wine bike tour made the corners of my lips pull. The group was posing with giant smiles and various glasses of wine at the start but, by the end, you could see the effect of the wine and the cycling. They were miserable. I dropped my head. It sucked that I wasn't there to hear about it.

Something told me to keep going through the album. When I flipped to the next set, they were in a club. My chest tightened at the first closeup of Millie's big aqua eyes and her bright smile. I stared at the photo, missing the fuck out of her.

The angle of the camera showed off a sultry silk top that was nothing more than a negligee. Jealousy hit me. I wished I was with her. I locked my eyes on the photo when my stare fell on her necklace. *She found it.* It was supposed to be a surprise. I had tucked it in her bag in New York, not wanting her to see it until she was home. Mostly because I didn't want her to reject it. The thought made my chest ache for her. I'd had enough. I pinched my nose and handed Mitch his phone.

My phone pinged. It must have been charged enough. The first dozen messages I ignored. Most of them were from the guys, saying they were all in for poker later, and a few from Brody that weren't urgent.

A single text from Millie stole my breath. My heart stilled, opening it.

Millie: I found the necklace... not if I am sure still meant to have but it's beautiful thasnk so mucj love u xoxo.

Aside from it being a drunk message, I still had to re-read it ten times, not believing she signed it "love u". It left me wondering, did she mean it? Was it "I love you"? Or like a friend's "luv u"? Was it only because she was drunk? There were too many possibilities, and I wanted to believe it was more than just her being nice.

I put my head in my hands and rubbed my throbbing temples. Christ, I was too hungover to think so much.

"Thinking about winning her back?" Mitch pressed.

Clarity hit me. "I was never giving up. I was letting her breathe." *I need to work out a few things before I can get her back.*

"Are you still coming to the wedding?"

I shook my head.

"Why?"

"Dude, you know I'd love nothing more than to see Millie, but crashing her best friend's wedding? Not my style."

Mitch nodded, then his phone pinged again. "I gotta bounce. I have another client to meet."

Since he was getting serious with Lisa, he had picked up a few more Canadian clients. He said he'd be back in time for poker. I didn't argue this time. My only goal was to figure out how to get through to Millie and, as much as driving to her place and throwing her over my shoulder sounded like a good idea, I doubted it would work. As I walked Mitch out, his words crossed my mind. Maybe leaving was a mistake.

Time for a new plan, a real plan. Good thing I had Brody, because I had a task for him.

An hour later, I got a call from a random Toronto number. "Hello?"

"What do you mean, you're not coming to the wedding?"

"Who is this?" I peered at the screen, trying to recall if I knew the number, or the voice, from anywhere.

"It's Sam."

"Sam?"

"As in one of the brides from the wedding that you're not coming to."

"Oh." *Millie's friend. How do I respond to this?* "Uh..."

"My question still stands."

I sat on the sofa and blew out a breath. "I was invited as Millie's date... And since we're not dating—"

"You're an idiot," she interrupted.

"Shit, tell me how you really feel."

"I love Millie. She's practically family. I'd stand by her without question, but I don't agree with her. She can make whatever excuses she needs to, but she's miserable, and it's all because of Nick, not you. We tried to stay silent, but she's a stubborn mule." We both laughed in agreement. "Do you love her?"

Just the mention of her name made my heart squeeze. It was no use in denying it. I had fallen in love with her a long time ago.

"Yes," I said, as if saying it out loud relieved some sort of pressure off me.

"Like actual love? Not lust..."

I stopped her mid-sentence. "Sam, she means everything to me. I'd give up baseball for her." I meant it. I would give it all up for her, for them.

I heard her clap and shriek in triumph. "Get your ass to my wedding. I'll send you the details."

She hung up on me before I could say anything else. Exactly ten minutes later, I had a copy of the wedding invitation. Immediately, I emailed Brody back with an update on our plan. Sam was right. It was stupid of me to let the time pass without fighting for her.

* * *

Four days later, I paced nervously outside the conservation center, staring at a large rustic chalkboard sign with bold hand-writing, The Union of Samantha Clark and Gia Savino Reception, five-thirty in the evening at the Glass House. An arrow pointed down a candle-lit path through the woods.

My hands were sweaty, and my heart hammered in my ears. What-ifs danced around in my head. What if she told me to leave? What if she ignored me? What if I ruined tonight? Or what if she took me back? It was that last one that gave me hope enough to propel me through the plan I had worked out with the girls.

Laughter floated from the path ahead. It was Millie's laugh. I'd recognize it anywhere. My body moved on autopilot toward it until I came to the bend in the path next to a large building. The bridal party had lined up, talking amongst themselves, while photographers snapped candid pictures of them. They were picturesque in matching champagne pantsuits with a lace halter neckline.

It took all of three seconds to spot Aubree. She stood out in a sequined pink ball gown, twirling with another little girl. I felt like my heart was going to burst watching her. My eyes landed on her purple arm cast. I choked back a tear.

Millie's voice echoed from the crowd as she stepped out from behind a group of women. "Careful..."

My eyes darted to her, and I had to grip the rail to steady myself. She was breath-taking. Her hair cascaded down her back in waves. Her pantsuit hugged her in the right places, showing off her spectacular curves, while the halter high-lighted the swell of her breasts and, if that wasn't enough to take me down, I saw her smile. *How could I have stayed away?*

Movement in the corner drew my eye away from Millie. Sam and Gia held hands as they approached the rest of the group. I felt my lips tug at the sides, watching them take their place behind Millie in the line. Gia was in a similar pantsuit as the bridal party, except it was strapless and black. Sam had on a white fitted dress with long lace sleeves. Both of them were radiant as they laughed and joked with everyone.

Gia stopped dead when she noticed me, smirking as she nudged Sam. A hushed whisper fell across the crowd while each of theirs heads turned toward me.

When Millie turned her head and finally spotted me, time

stood still. The second her gorgeous eyes locked on mine, I had to do all I could to stop from sprinting to her.

Aubree shrieked, causing me to break my focus as she bolted to me. "Jake! Jake! You're here."

I scooped her up and gave her a tight hug. "Of course I am, sweetie." She giggled, and it was the best sound a guy could ask for.

She held up her cast, which had a lot of signatures and drawings on it, like a prize. "See my cast?"

It choked me up. Millie was right, she should have been there. *Fuck, I should have been there, too.* "I love the purple color. Did you pick it out?"

She grinned. "Yup. It's purple like my favorite princess's dresses."

Feeling her stare, I looked at Millie. Her cheeks were pink, and she gave a small nod with moisture in her eyes. I set Aubree down and walked over to Millie. The scent of her smacked me in the heart. I was lost in her eyes. Not a chance was I wasting that moment. I grabbed her around the waist and delicately brought my lips to hers, dipping her back to get the full effect. She tasted like vanilla and mint and, to my surprise, she didn't resist me. It was a kiss that made every fiber of my being come alive again.

"Hi."

"Hey back," she breathed.

The bridal party erupted into applause. Millie's blush intensified. I gave a quick bow, then apologized to Sam and Gia for my tardiness and thanked them for the invite.

When I hugged Sam, she whispered, "Don't let her go this time."

"Not a chance." I grinned before heading into the reception.

Mitch stood up and waved me over. He was sitting with Millie's parents and another couple I hadn't met.

"Cutting it close?" Mitch ushered me to sit down.

If he only knew. I had flown in that morning from Florida. I would have come sooner, but I had some family business that needed attention, but now was not the time to get into it. "Plane delays."

"Did you see them?"

"Oh, yeah..." I chuckled. Thinking back to moments ago.

"Jake, we're glad you're back," Peter said. There was an honesty in his voice that made me feel welcome. It was only a few minutes later when the MC announced the bridal party.

Aubree completely stole the show, smiling and twirling her way into the gigantic glass dome we were in. That kid was something else. Millie's parents called Aubree over to our table. She insisted on sitting with me. My heart swelled with love for her.

Millie bit her lip, tearing up as she took out a small handkerchief and dabbed her eyes. Well, one decision was made. Never again was I letting go. I'd fight every day for her if I had to, and I had a feeling I might.

Chapter Twenty-Two

Millie

Jake showed up. One peek at him, and I was ready to leap into his arms. The way his eyes gleamed when he saw us was everything. I had to hold myself back from running to him. My heart squeezed when Aubree leaped into his arms. He was crushed when he saw her cast, and the remorse in his eyes was evident. Ever since I walked out of the hotel room, I lied and told myself Nick was right. Jake wouldn't stay, there would always be something. Jake didn't need all of my drama. It was better for *him*. It was easier for *him*. I gave myself every reason to walk away and not one to stay.

But with him there, I realized how miserable I had been. It was ridiculous to like someone so damn much that it broke you into pieces. I mean, it had only been a month of dating, and yet, it felt like a lifetime. The sight of him made me want to forget all the reasons for ending it. I was a fool.

Hell, I told myself Nick was right. It was easier to say I had to walk away; it was better for *him*. Easier for *him*. He wouldn't need all the stress from my drama. It didn't help that he didn't reach out. I thought maybe this was the out he wanted, that he just needed some time to realize I was right. It was ridiculous to like someone so damn much that it can break you into pieces. I mean, it's only been a month of dating and yet, it felt like a lifetime. Just the sight of him and I wanted to forget my reasons for walking out.

Throughout dinner, I couldn't keep my eyes off him. He even made sure Aubree had eaten her dinner. Jesus, this man. Not to mention him with Mitch and my parents laughing and talking. It was so unfamiliar. They hated Nick. All the drama between us throughout our relationship had caused a rift and my parents couldn't understand why I always went back to him. We were off more than on. My parents got so fed up they made me choose and banned him from our house. There were so many signs of his shitty behavior, and I willingly overlooked all of them. I had no excuse except for having been young and in love. I really thought that I could have changed him. I was wrong. But, out of all of it, I got my precious little girl. One who I sat watching dance her heart out with a guy who was everything Nick wasn't.

As if Jake read my mind, he stood up and bowed to Aubree, taking her hand and leading her out to the dance floor. I watched Aubree climb on his feet. He made a funny face as if she had stomped on them, making her giggle, and I about died. How did I get so lucky?

Gia nudged me in the rib. "I think your boyfriend's back."

My face flushed. "He took long enough."

This time it was Gia who broke into a wide smile. She put her head on my shoulder. "I hope you aren't mad."

"Not even a little. Thank you." And I meant it. For once, I was happy they meddled.

"Anything for you." She kissed my cheek and then went back to talk to Sam.

The MC announced it was time for the first dance. We watched as Gia and Sam walked over to the dance floor, and my heart burst for them. I was with them to watch their love story right from the time Sam laid eyes on Gia. It was the first time I had seen her fumble over someone. It was adorable.

My gaze lifted over to Jake, and the simple wink he gave me made my heart sputter in my chest.

"Alright, time to join in," the MC called out. Jake scooped up Aubree and came over to me.

"C'mon, Blondie. Let's give them something to talk about." He grabbed my hand and twirled me. I laughed in surprise. Jake wrapped one arm around me, and the other carried Aubree. Jake set Aubree down as the three of us bopped around, holding hands and jumping as music blasted through the speakers. My heart felt full. After a few songs, my parents called it a night and were taking Aubree home.

"Do we have to go?"

"Oh, we can still have fun. Nana brought your favorite movie, and we can have a pajama party." My mom tried enticing her into the car.

"Mommy and Jake, you come, too?"

"Not right now. Mommy has to stay to help Auntie Gia and Auntie Sam," I replied.

"Okay," Aubree said, jutting out her chin in a small pout, leaning over to give me a kiss. She turned to Jake and kissed his cheek. He choked up as we walked my parents out to the car.

"Night, sweetie." Jake squeezed her until she giggled.

Jake wrapped his arm around my shoulders. We stood and waved goodbye as we watched them drive off.

"God, she's adorable. She gets that from you."

"Easy, cheese ball." He laughed and grabbed my hand, spinning me around so we were face-to-face. Our lips met without hesitation. His arms closed around me, pulling me tight against his body and did I ever miss it. My body ached to be next to him.

"You're so beautiful," he murmured. "I missed you." He gently lifted the diamond palm leaf charm from my necklace and rubbed his thumb over it. "This is even better on you than I imagined." He smiled.

"I wasn't sure if I should..."

He silenced me with another kiss. "It was for you, no matter what."

"But, why?"

"Why not? I saw it when I was out, and I remembered you talking about your love of palm trees. Now I know it's not a tattoo, but it's just as permanent."

I had no words. I kissed him, knowing I had fallen in love with him.

"Hey, lovebirds. They're asking for you inside." The sound of Mitch's voice startled us. Jake nodded and slid his hand into mine, gripping it like he was never letting go, and I loved the warmth it sent through my body.

When we got inside, Gia and Sam were waiting for us so they could cut the cake. I apologized for being late, but they didn't seem to care. They were too busy gushing over how Jake was with Aubree. Jake had excused himself to sit with Mitch while they waited for Lisa and me to finish some bridal party duties. A few photo ops later, and we had gone to join them.

"Ready to dance?" Jake asked, taking my hand and leading me out to the dance floor.

He pulled my waist against him tightly while a pop song played in the background.

"This isn't slow dancing music," I teased.

"One night we were talking on the phone, and you had music on in the background, so I made a joke about it being our first song, which you instantly scoffed at," he recalled. "You said a song should have meaning. I listen to every damn love song to see if it reminds me of you." Jake playfully squeezed my butt, earning a yelp from me. "One stood out," he continued, as I furrowed my brows in confusion. "Just before we... Uh, New York. I heard a song, and I haven't been able to stop listening to it. Everything about it reminded me of you. Of us."

Jake nodded toward the DJ, and a familiar song played as my breath hitched in my throat.

He pressed his cheek against mine, swaying us perfectly. Unable to speak, I moved along with him. He sang lyric by lyric in my ear, and his watery eyes locked with mine when he sang the words in the last line.

My voice shook. "Jake, this is perfect."

He leaned his forehead onto mine and pulled me tighter to him until I could feel his heartbeat. My heart swelled. When the song ended, he kissed my forehead.

"I think you found our song," I whispered.

Everyone clapped, bringing us out of our trance. I had completely forgotten we weren't alone. We glanced around to see we were the only ones left on the dance floor. It suddenly felt hot, too hot. I walked off the floor and out the patio door.

Jake followed me. "Are you okay?"

Overwhelmed with emotions, tears pooled in my eyes.

"Baby, what's wrong?"

"I saw the picture of you with some girl. I know I had no reason to be jealous..."

He grabbed me into a tight embrace, kissing my forehead. "I don't know her, and I don't want to. She was just at the bar. Josh let her through the VIP section. We were outside, and she was cold. I swear it was nothing. It could never be anything. I'm too wrapped up in you."

Jake brushed his fingertips across my cheeks. " I need to

know something." He stopped and tilted my chin up so we were eye to eye. His lips pursed together. "The night you found my necklace, you sent me a text. You said you love me..." His chest lifted with a deep inhale, and his voice lowered. "Did you mean it?"

I gazed into his eyes, equally scared of saying it out loud and never having the courage to say it. "Yes."

He crushed his lips against mine, pushing further. His hands cupped my face. My body lit up with excitement. Our kiss was deep, and both of us were afraid to let go.

When we finally released each other, his blue eyes were shining. "Amelia Rosalie Harte, I am, without a doubt, beyond in love with you."

* * *

We woke up still entangled in each other. I'll admit I pulled a creeper move and watched him sleep. He was so handsome. His hair was messy and out of place, and his five o'clock shadow darkened. He lazily opened his eyes and grinned.

"I thought I was dreaming, but you're really here," he murmured.

I knew the feeling, almost afraid to open my eyes to find him gone. I didn't realize how much I had fallen for him until I screwed it up.

When he showed up last night, I felt like my heart had returned. I snuggled closer to him, feeling his warmth next to me. He gently kissed the tip of my nose, wrapping his arm around me.

An hour later, I woke to Jake's fingertips grazing along my back. It was delicate and sensual, sending a wave of arousal to my core. Even though we spent the last night making love, I wanted more. How I let him go was beyond me. He leaned forward, kissing my shoulder and neck.

I rolled on top of him. "Since you're so persistent."

Our passion had shifted from hot and heavy and full of wanting and desire to make it last. Our bodies were tight to each other. Neither of us wanted the morning to end. When we finally finished, we lay in bed, my legs over his. I wasn't ready to let him go yet. The questions about what happened next played out in my head.

I twirled a tuft of his chest hair in my fingers and propped my head on his shoulder. "Lisa told me you moved back to Florida..."

He gazed up at the ceiling and let out a deep sigh, nodding. I tried to hide my disappointment. Jake brushed a stray hair out of my face and chewed on his lip.

"Looks like I'm gonna rack up some air mileage points," he said.

"You can't be serious?"

"I was thinking, I'll commute for a bit. It's the off season. I only have a few things on the go. I'll fly down on weekends or something."

"You live in Florida."

"It's only a three-hour flight. It's not like I'm coming in from Europe. Besides, what's the difference in driving from downtown to your place on a Friday night?" I playfully swatted him, and his expression softened. "Give us a chance. I know it's tricky, but I'll do everything I can to make it work."

Thinking about us being apart crushed me. I barely had him back. I wanted him in my life more than on occasional weekends. Only one way seemed logical, but was it too fast? Jake's expression was etched with worry.

"How about you stay with me? Commute to Florida when you need to," I suggested.

His hand froze while twirling my hair. "Are you asking me to move in with you?"

He sounded as shocked as I was when it came out of my

mouth. "Maybe? It's not like you have a place here anymore. It makes little sense for you to fly back and forth."

"What about Aubree?"

"You heard her last night. She wants you here, too."

He kissed me feverishly, as we made love again and, when we were done, I couldn't help thinking about how often that would be a regular occurrence. I blushed in his arms.

My phone chirped, dragging us out of our little bubble. My mom had messaged to say they would be taking Aubree out for the day and to expect us to have dinner with them.

"Time to go," I groaned, not wanting to leave this moment. I was worried about what was to come next.

Driving home, Jake was nervously checking out my car.

"You got it fixed. There were no big issues, right?"

"Huh?" I asked, confused.

"Last time you came to a game, you had your brother's truck. Something was wrong with yours?"

"Oh, yeah... Just a few minor fixes."

He chewed his lip as if he had more to say, but he poked around at the glove box, and the stereo, then shook his head at the lack of USB ports. He was doing a terrible job of hiding his concern.

"Not all of us have five fancy cars. Betty does the job fine."

"Betty?"

"Duh. That's my car's name." I tapped on the steering wheel. "I bought it when Aubree was one. I needed it to get around. It was affordable. She gets me where I need to go. It's not my dream car, but I'll get that eventually. For now, this tough old broad keeps going and going."

"What's your dream car?"

"Oh, no. You're going to make fun of me."

Jake grinned and held his hand over his chest. "I just want to know your taste. I promise."

I hesitated before I turned and said, "I've been dreaming of a Range Rover. They're sexy."

Jake's eyes widened and a big smirk pulled across his mouth. "Nice."

"Really?"

"Yeah. I could see you in that. Also, great for safety." He laced our fingers together. "Betty is great, too."

Jake kissed my knuckles and I relaxed against his touch.

When we got to my parents' place, Jake surveyed the property. "It's way bigger than I remembered."

"That's what she said."

Jake chuckled. As he stood staring at the large navy and stone two-story Craftsman-style house set back toward the beach. "Nice view."

"You should see the backyard, closer to the water. It's amazing to have a bonfire out on the beach."

"I bet."

This was actually my great-grandparents' cottage." I pointed around at the massive property. "They came up here when they got lost on the way to Wasaga Beach. It was barely a town, and they both fell in love with the area. Ended up buying this little run-down shack, and then put down roots."

Jake nodded, catching the lakeside view. "I can see why."

"Mommyyyyy," Aubree squealed. We both turned around. She was standing on the deck with her princess doll.

"Well, morning," my mom called as she stepped out of the house. Amusement spread on her face as she looked at the silent conversation happening between us. "Jake, glad you're here. Coffee's on."

I hightailed it inside. Jake chuckled at my sudden motivation. During dinner, my dad badgered Jake about next season and his stats. Mostly, he grilled him about his off-season plans. I tried to change the topic several times to save Jake, not that it worked. Jake took it all in stride and did his best to answer my parents' inquisition. His hand rested on my leg, encouraging me to relax. By the end of dinner, my parents were quite happy to learn he'd be in town for a while, but I had a feeling it was for an entirely different reason.

Chapter Twenty-Three

Jake

I was on cloud nine. The fact she asked me to stay with her meant more to me than I could have imagined. I emailed Brody to make sure my calendar was cleared, but I only had a few days to stay. There were some endorsement deals and a couple of 'must attend' special events in Florida, thanks to family obligations.

Backing out now wouldn't be good, and I was pretty sure my mother would have killed me. Speaking of family, my sister had been on my ass about meeting Millie, and I was running out of ways to stall them. In my circle, there were plenty of wolves, and I needed to protect Millie from them. How I had kept things under wraps so far was beyond me. My only guess was Brody. He was a genius at hiding me, so to speak.

Millie was putting Aubree to bed on our first night together in the house, and I was a bit of a train wreck. I wanted to share a room with her, but I wasn't sure if it was a good idea with Aubree there. I had never considered how it would work. Do I sleep in the guest room? Couch? We didn't have a chance to discuss it.

I sat flipping through the channels on the television, trying to get my mind off the living arrangements for the weekend. The playoff highlights were on. A twinge of jealousy that I was out for the season washed over me. The Twisters had been close, but not close enough. Mickey, the dog, nudged me and moved to sit at my feet with his head on my knee. A shadow caught my eye, so I turned to catch Millie in the doorway, in striped pajama pants and a white t-shirt. No bra. Instantly, I grew hard. She sat next to me, scooting Mickey over. He grunted at her in response, which was funny.

She nodded at the playoff highlights. "Miss it?"

I shrugged. "Yeah, but I'm also glad for the break. All the travel is exhausting."

"And you wanted to commute from Florida," she scoffed.

"For you? Fucking right." The grin that spread across her face came complete with an adorable light pink tinge on her cheeks. I loved her blush. She climbed on top of me, and I rushed to raise the back of her shirt, my hand resting on her lower back. Her head tilted forward, and her lips brushed against mine. Gentle at first, but it didn't take long to escalate.

"Easy, baby. You said take it slow around Aubree."

She tipped her head back and forth. "I lied."

Our kiss was heavy, and my hands worked her shirt off over her head. Her tits landed perfectly in them.

"Bedroom."

She jumped off of me and grabbed my hand, yanking me off the couch. The woman was eager. I loved it. She passed the stairs and led me to the guest room, and pushed me down to the bed.

"It's further away. We don't have to be so quiet." The

lopsided grin on her face was that of a temptress, and it was working for me.

"Are you sure?" I squeaked out as her hands pushed into my joggers and landed on my dick.

She rolled her eyes at me and kissed me roughly on the lips. "As sure as I love you."

That was all I needed to hear. It felt as if I couldn't get enough of her. She made it easy to get lost in the feeling. She pushed my pants down and cupped my balls.

"Three."

"Three what?"

"Three orgasms before we leave this room."

"Is that a dare or a promise?" She smirked.

"Promise."

"You should get started then."

Fucking sassy. I wanted nothing more than to make up for the lost time. And a sex marathon was only the beginning.

"Up. On all fours," I demanded.

She didn't argue. I positioned under her, planting my face beneath her clit. Instead of gripping her legs, I grabbed each tit and massaged it. My tongue swiped across her. She hissed and clenched tight.

"Stay still." I swiped my tongue again. Diving in. My hands moved to hold her hips in place as she sunk onto me. Her groans grew louder, and her legs shook. She lowered her head into the pillow as she came and, fuck, it was satisfying. I loved making her come with my mouth. It wasn't a skill every man had, but I knew what worked for her. She was never going without. Not with me around.

After her third orgasm and my second, we laid still, wrapped around each other, lost in the moment. Catching our breaths, I held her to me.

"Alright. You kept your promise," she panted.

"You doubted me?" She bit her lip and ducked her head.

"I don't make promises I can't keep."

She rolled her eyes, but said nothing as we went to clean up. She was gone when I returned. I wandered into the living room. She had dressed and was turning everything off.

I stood in the doorframe. "Is this where we say goodnight? Because it feels weird."

She shook her head before taking my hand and leading me upstairs. We crawled into bed, and she nuzzled against my arm.

"When I said stay with me, I meant it," she murmured. It didn't take long for her to fall asleep.

My chest swelled. I kissed her head, smelling the tiniest hit of maple. "Never again am I letting you go... I promise."

For the first time in a month, I felt like I could breathe. Our being apart broke a piece of me I never knew existed. The pain was unbearable. I prayed I could make things work, that she would give us a chance. It would be tricky. Especially in the new year when the season started back up. Scheduling was always problematic, and that was only having baseball.

Jax told me the family was waiting for me to take on more business responsibilities in Florida. It was something that had crossed my mind more since meeting Millie. They knew baseball came first, but in the last two years my game wasn't the same, and with the trade came the reality that baseball won't be forever. The family were circling like vultures. I fell asleep with swirling thoughts in my head.

* * *

Millie's sweet voice woke me as she rubbed her hand over my arm. "Morning. You had a rough sleep."

"A bit." I stopped from saying anything more about my restless night. "I should get going before Aubree comes in. I heard her a few minutes ago in her room."

"I think you should stay. It's not like we're naked or doing anything she shouldn't be seeing. It's healthy for her to see us together, especially if you're living here."

"If you're sure..."

"I'm sure, but if you're not, then please say something." She pinned me with her eyes. "I want you to feel comfortable here with us. Is it weird because I have a kid?"

I shut down whatever train of thought she was about to go down. "Hell no. I love you *and* Aubree. This right here." I swirled my fingers around us. "I want all of it."

Millie beamed just as Aubree came into the room, still rubbing her eyes. She walked over to Millie's side of the bed and climbed in without even batting an eyelash.

"Morning, baby," Millie whispered to her.

"Mama, can we have pancakes? I hungry."

"Absolutely."

Aubree lifted her head and eyeballed me. She said my name as she climbed over Millie, causing her to grunt, weaseling her way in between us. She gave me a big hug. I became a big, sopping puddle of mush.

"What should we do today?"

"Costumes."

I looked at Millie, and she just shrugged. "Halloween is coming up, and she's been begging for a new princess costume."

"Costume shopping it is," I agreed.

Millie sat up. "I was also thinking of taking her to the pumpkin patch and putting up our decorations..."

"You need me for the tall stuff. Right," I teased.

She laughed. "I could call Avery or Alex. They usually help."

"Over my dead body."

"So competitive." Millie smirked. "Alright, let's get going, munchkin. Seems like we have a busy day." Millie whooshed Aubree out of bed to get dressed.

"Mind if I shower?"

"Of course not. Make yourself at home. Although, I can't say I have any manly scented things in there."

I winked. "I guess maple will do today."

* * *

I thought extra innings after a travel day sucked, but shopping with an almost five-year-old wiped me out. The girl was all energy.

Hell, I even felt like I hit dad mode. I was overbearing, worried, and about to lose it. I was afraid she would get hurt on the bouncy pillow things or from running too fast. She still had on a cast, for Christ's sake! And when I thought I'd lost her in the corn maze, my heart moved to my throat until we found her. The little turkey had crouched down to jump out and scare me. *She did all right.* The panic was real. I don't know how Millie stayed so calm. She spent half of the time trying to comfort *me*.

When the day was done and Aubree had fallen asleep in my arms on the walk back to the truck, I realized how easy it was to adjust to family life. It felt seamless, even though I had never experienced that before. I grew up with nannies and maids. Not to say my mom was awful or anything, because she wasn't. She was hands-on, but with help. That's just how things were for my sister and I.

"You okay?" Millie asked, as if she read my mind.

"Yeah. Just thinking about Monday." *And the lack of desire to leave.* I had no interest in that forced trip, but time ran out and there was a conversation that needed to be had.

"Need a ride to the airport?"

I shook my head. "Nah. Brody will come to get me."

"I can drive you," she protested.

I rubbed her arms up and down. "Aubree has school, and it's an early flight."

Her shoulders slumped. I knew she wanted to help, but it would be too much to ask. "That's what Brody is for." I nudged her shoulder with mine, hoping to lighten the mood. It worked a little bit.

The weekend ended faster than either of us wanted. I kissed Millie goodbye and tiptoed out of the house, careful not to wake Aubree. Four days. Four days with them, and I wanted to stay forever. When I got in the car, Brody had coffee waiting for me.

"Slight change of plans," he informed. "Your mother has requested to see you before you head into the office." I groaned. *Here it comes.* The drama. The things I had been avoiding. There was only a matter of time before I had to face the truth. There were some things that I needed to tell Millie about, and I wasn't sure how it would go.

We headed straight to my mother's. The limo pulled up to the expansive white waterfront estate where a brand-new Lamborghini was parked in the driveway. I rolled my eyes. Luis, lucky husband number four, must have been a good boy to get such a gift. Unless Jenna's new boyfriend was over. I punched in the code to the front door.

"Mom? Jenna?" I called out. My voice echoed through the large foyer.

Nothing. I went through the house, noting she had changed the furniture again. Everything was now cream or beige with silver trim. Nothing was out of place. The house appeared staged, unlike Millie's house, which was full of rich colors, family pictures, and scattered toys. God, I already missed them. Wandering through the house, I saw my mother sitting poolside, on the phone.

"Gotta go. Jake is here," she said, hanging up abruptly. "Hi, sweetie." I parked myself in the lounge next to hers.

My mother was not like most moms; she was a bit of a rebel. Only fifty, yet she looked like she was still in her thirties, some of it thanks to Botox, the rest thanks to perfect genetics. "Jenna will be here in a minute."

"Where's number four?" I asked, referring to her latest trophy husband.

"Off getting manscaped. I hate when fuzz gets caught in my teeth." She deadpanned.

"Jesus, Mom. Gross."

"You asked," she laughed in her high-pitched tone.

Jenna called down from the second-floor terrace, saving me from the conversation. "Hey, look who finally came home." She lowered her designer sunglasses over the bridge of her nose. "What brings you here straight from the flight?" *As if she doesn't know...*

"Brody informed me the lawyers were circling," I said dryly. Hugo, the family butler, brought out a tray of drinks.

"Welcome home, sir." He nodded, then passed me a whiskey neat. My usual order when it came to 'conversations'. Jenna and my mother each reached for their white wines.

"What did you expect, big bro? Rumor has it you're living with Amelia."

That didn't take long. This family news travels as it does in Millie's town.

"It's only been a few days."

"It must be serious." My mother arched her perfectly shaped brows.

I twirled the glass in my hand. "Yeah. It is. She's unlike anyone. I'm in love with her."

My mom straightened in her chair. "When do we meet this phantom girl?"

"I don't know. It's complicated."

"Why?" Jenna chimed in.

"She's not like us, Mom. She works and has a schedule."

The memory of New York came to my mind. "The last time we traveled, it didn't go so well..."

"Fine. I'll come there."

I coughed on my drink. The image of my mom in Millie's town was quite visual.

"Why are you so hesitant? It's never been a problem before."

"It's different with her."

Jenna's eyes widened as she turned to me, silently asking if my mom knew Millie was a single mom. I nodded at Jenna.

"Do you think she's after money?" she asked.

I snorted. "Not likely. She doesn't know about all of this."

They gaped at me like I was insane. I was terrified of Millie seeing all of this. She was already skittish. My family was not normal.

"Don't you think it's an important thing the love of your life should know?"

Guilt smacked me. I was never planning on keeping it a secret, I just didn't know how to approach it. "She will, but she's not going to care."

"Didn't you say that about Haley?"

I glared at my sister. She had to bring her up, although I really should have expected it. "Haley was happy to have things end. She had already found someone else," I retorted.

"Touché." Jenna raised her glass as if she didn't just instigate something.

"Now, you listen. You can't come in here, spouting how in love you are with this girl, dangle a little girl over me, and expect me to wait patiently." Before I could interject, she held up her hand to silence me. "I expect to see all of you through the holidays. You have never missed one of my charity events, and you're not about to start because you moved to Canada." My mother's tone wasn't friendly. I nodded and finished my drink in one gulp. *Great. One more thing to add to the plate.*

Chapter Twenty-Four

Millie

It had been five days since Jake left and I missed him. We talked constantly, or at least when either of us wasn't in a meeting or busy doing stuff. He was going to be back tomorrow night, and I already had it circled in the calendar in bold to pick him up at the airport.

I had rushed Mickey's walk since I was running late to meet Nick and Aubree at her swim class. When I opened the door, a young guy standing there startled me. "Miss Harte? I'm Brody. I have a delivery for you." I racked my brain, wondering from where I knew his name. "Jake's PA," he added.

"Right, sorry. I didn't recognize it at first."

"I'm not surprised. You have direct access." Before I could ask him what that meant, he handed me a large envelope.

"What the swizzle sticks? Are you kidding me?" I said, fishing out keys.

Brody broke into a chuckle. "Umm... There's a note in the envelope with the keys."

Betty deserves to be retired with grace, not dead on the road somewhere... I Love you P.S. We can fight about her later.

Holy Crap. This can't be happening. I shook my head, staring at the white Range Rover parked in the driveway. "Is this for real?"

"Yes."

I was angry and excited at the same time. "I can't accept this."

"No returns. Sorry," Brody whispered, raising his hands in surrender. "Don't shoot the messenger. And, just for the record, she drives incredibly smoothly."

The white color screamed luxury as I walked over and slid my hand along the hood. Brody walked down the driveway to a waiting car. My brain went into a state of shock as checked out *my dream car.*

When I opened the rear passenger door, there was already a car seat installed. Oh, Jake. I wanted to be mad, but this pretty girl was begging to be driven.

Holy crap, he wasn't kidding. The car was fabulous. I should have known better than to mention it when we were talking about Jake buying a car for when he's here. We even made plans to go car shopping when he got back, the sneaky little bugger. Several heads turned in surprise when I got out of the car, including my brother.

"Nice ride. I checked twice to make sure it was you. Mom and dad give you a raise?" Avery chuckled, walking over from the other side of the street.

"Yeah, right." Not that they wouldn't if I asked. "What are you doing here?"

"I was dropping off a few things for Cliff across the street. It was the only time I could meet up with him." Cliff was one of our dad's friends, who Avery helped once in a while after he had a stroke. Avery chewed his lip. "It looks good on you, Mils. All of it, including that smile permanently plastered on your face since Jake came around." I blushed, feeling truly happy for the first time.

Avery offered to come to watch Aubree's swim class. It wasn't a bad idea since Nick would be here. He'd Aubree last night for a sleepover and we agreed to meet there. I was shocked he had asked to take her. Maybe we were heading in the right direction.

When we entered the community center, we rounded the corner to the pool area where Nick was sitting, watching through the glass. He saw Avery with me, and he instantly tensed. I hesitated, not sure I should go over, but Nick grabbed his phone and made it seem like he didn't want to be bothered. Avery and I remained at the window, watching Aubree stand with three other kids.

After class, Nick came over with Aubree between us.

"Did she have dinner?" I asked.

"No. She had a snack, though."

"Okay." It felt awkward. Like he wanted to say more, but didn't.

He shoved his hands in his pockets. "I'll pick her up next weekend."

"Sure." I said as he squatted down and hugged her goodbye.

"Mama, is Jake home yet?" *Shit*. I swallowed hard. Nick's stare flicked up to mine, anger evident.

"Not yet. Soon."

Nick opened his mouth to say something.

"Don't even think about it," Avery growled, shutting him down. Nick stormed off. I grabbed Aubree's hand and led her out to the car. Nick was sitting in his pickup truck, mouth agape, as I loaded her into the new SUV. This wasn't going to be good.

"How about we go for pizza?" Avery asked Aubree, and it sounded like a great idea.

* * *

At bedtime, it was hard to get Aubree to focus on the story I was trying to read. She kept going on about our pretty new car and kept asking when Jake was coming home. After three pinky promises, she finally believed me that Jake would be home tomorrow after school. I tucked her into bed and went back downstairs.

When I came around the corner, Nick was standing in the front hall with a grave look on his face.

He startled me. "Crap, Nick. Don't you know how to knock?"

"The door was open."

"It wasn't open, it just wasn't locked."

"Is your boyfriend living here?" he asked, a hint of sadness in his voice.

I clenched my fists at my side, refusing to answer.

"So, what, he buys you a car, and you shack up with him? What the fuck? You just met this guy."

"I'm not going nine rounds with you over this. You already got in my head once, you won't do it again. We are none of your business."

"You are my business. You and our daughter, always. Remember?"

"*Always* went out the window when you knocked up my best friend!"

"It was a mistake."

My face scrunched. "What?"

"All of it," he added, stepping toward me. I rolled my eyes. I'd heard that all before, when I first found out. He begged me to stay, but I left.

"I'm tired of all of this." I waved him off, trying to push past him to the door, but he grabbed hold of me and planted his lips on mine.

It took a second to register. I tried to push him off, but he had a firm grip. My reflex was to stomp on his foot, which worked as he let go.

Gross. *Did he always kiss like that?* I wiped my mouth, backing away.

"What the hell are you doing?"

He stood across from me, running his hand through his shoulder-length hair. "I should have fought for you. I should never have married Misha... You were it for me. I knew it then. I was just being stubborn. Now, seeing you with him and our daughter is killing me."

I needed to hold on to the banister. *What the hell was he saying?* He lunged at me. I put my hand up and pushed him back. "No, Nick. NO! You need to leave."

"I'm not leaving here. Did you hear me? I'm sorry, I made a mistake. I want to be with you and our daughter. We're family."

Family? He was delusional. I lowered my voice not to wake Aubree. "Nick, you're married and you're about to have another baby. Go home to your wife."

His voice cracked. "It was supposed to be us. We should have gotten married. I lied to you when I said I didn't want marriage and kids. I did. It scared me. Mils, I can fix this, fix us. I'll divorce her so we can be together."

Has he lost his mind? The words coming out of his mouth were unreal. How could he think I'd go back to him?

"Are you high? You're crazy to think we can forget everything that happened. There's no going back." I paced, waving my finger at him. Angry over his confession and entering my home, I raged. "*YOU* made a choice, not a mistake. *You* chose to fuck her behind my back for years, then married her weeks after it all came out. You already chose a family."

He shook his head. He was close enough to grab my wrist, and I wasn't quick enough to pull away.

"Let me go." I tried to wiggle free, but he was stronger than me. Panic hit me. "Stop. Please."

Nick was yanked back, making me lurch forward and trip on the carpet. I fell to the ground, smashing my nose against the hardwood floor. Warm blood dropped from my nostrils.

"Ouch," I groaned, lifting my head to see Jake shove Nick out the front door by the scruff of his shirt.

"She told you to leave," he bellowed. Nick stumbled back, anger flaring in his eyes. Jake planted himself in the door frame.

"You don't belong here. This is my family!" Nick yelled before he charged at Jake. Jake dug his heels down and shoved Nick hard enough that he tumbled down the steps.

I watched in horror at the scene in front of me.

"Stop," I moaned, holding my nose.

Jake turned to me and held his breath. His fists balled, ready to swing, but he took a steadying breath.

"Look, man, you need to walk the fuck away and cool off before you wake up Aubree." The tension in Jake's body told me he was using every measure of self-restraint he had left in him. "If you ever lay a fucking finger on Millie again, I won't hesitate to beat the ever-loving fuck out of you, and then call the cops. Get out of here now before I do it, anyway."

Nick glared at him with contempt, then lifted his gaze to me. "This will never be over. He won't be here forever." He got in his car and sped off.

I sat up, woozy from the fall, and wiped my nose.

Jake kneeled down next to me, helping me up. "Christ, baby, are you okay?" He grabbed onto my arms, studying the red mark that was forming on my wrists from Nick's grip.

"What? How? Are you here?"

"I wanted to surprise you."

I gave a half smile. "Surprise…"

He rolled his eyes. "What the hell just happened? Why was he here?"

"Does it matter?"

His eyes narrowed. "Yeah, it fucking does. I may have only caught the tail end of it, but I didn't like what I heard. And don't sugarcoat it." Jake helped me stand and brought me over to the couch before he grabbed a bag of peas from the freezer. He gently put it on my nose. I told him about everything from Aubree's swim class, and then how Nick was here when I came down from putting Aubree to bed.

Jake was furious, but said nothing.

"I told him to leave, but it made him worse. He was never good at rejection."

"How many times?"

"What?"

Jake's voice shook. "How many times has he shown up unannounced?"

I didn't want to answer. It was only going to piss him off more. I closed my eyes.

"Silence says it all," Jake snapped.

I blew out a breath. "A few, and nothing like tonight. We just argued last time." Jake tensed, and he ran his hands so hard through his hair that I thought he took a chunk out.

I dropped the peas on the table and scooted forward. He wrapped his arm around me, and neither of us said anything for a minute. When he relaxed, I squeaked out, "Thank you for helping me."

"I'm sorry I wasn't here. He wouldn't have tried it if I was. We're putting in a security system," he gruffly murmured against my hair.

Chapter Twenty-Five

Jake

When I saw the pickup truck in the driveway, I thought it was one of her brothers until I heard her yelling for Nick to let her go.

I didn't know he had a hold of her until she hit the ground. I felt like shit, and I needed to punch something. Still, I was reeling with anger. How dare he come into her home and attack her? Thank fuck, I came home early.

It was hard to keep my cool and not drill the fucker. Let him come at me again, and that was it, I wouldn't hold back. At that point, it was self-defense.

What cut even more was hearing it wasn't his first time. How the fuck can I protect her if I'm thirteen hundred miles away?

Millie had gone to check on Aubree, even though I offered. I stewed on the sofa, researching security companies.

Everything was already closed. I emailed Brody, asking him to take it on, explaining I would pay double if they could do it within twenty-four hours.

The vision of Nick holding Millie while she screamed for him to let her go made my chest feel like it was being crushed. This asshole was not only emotionally blackmailing her by using Aubree every chance he got, but now he was physically assaulting her. What the hell did she ever see in this dick?

With his ears down and tail tucked in, Mickey sauntered over. He sat next to me and nudged me with his head. Absently, I scratched his ear. "Why didn't you bark and warn her?" I asked, as if he would answer.

"Mickey was his dog, too. He never barks when he shows up," Millie said in a soft voice. She walked past me, and I grabbed her and pulled her on top of me. My hand went behind her neck, bringing our foreheads together.

Her eyes were red-rimmed and ten shades brighter from crying. A tear fell down my cheek. "What would have happened if I didn't come to surprise you?"

"Shhh," she whispered. "You were here."

"Amelia, I need to ask you something. Please be honest." My palms sweat, unsure if I was ready for the answer. "Has he ever..." I collected myself, running my palms along my thighs. "Has he ever hurt you before?"

Shame crossed her face instantly, and she moved away. *Argh. I knew it.* I gripped her tighter to steady my temper.

"Once, a long time ago. Some girl called our house phone, not his cell. She was a real bitch to me. I didn't take kindly to it. I told her she was calling my house, for my boyfriend, so she better be nicer when she speaks to me. When I asked him about it, he said it was someone interested in booking the band. It sounded like she was interested in *him*. He told me I should have been nicer, so they didn't lose the gig. It started a nasty fight. I screamed at him and grabbed his guitar to throw it outside. He pushed me away from it. I stumbled sideways and hit my head on the coffee table."

She pulled a patch of hair near her temple, making a small scar visible. "Three stitches."

"Jesus, Amelia... Why didn't..." I stopped from going any further down that thought.

"Somehow, it felt like it was my fault. If I had been calmer about things, then it wouldn't have happened."

Is she kidding me right now? He pushed her and it's her fault? What the actual fuck had this guy done to her? My anger boiled over. I pushed out from under her and went straight outside to the deck to punch the rail a few times. "Fuuucckkk."

My breath billowed across the frosty night air. My chest heaved. Amelia embraced me, as she buried her face in my back.

"Baby, please don't.... It's not worth it."

I turned, locking my arms around her, breathing in her familiar sweet scent that calmed me. The thought of what Nick did had me torn up. I was incredibly proud that she got away from him as much as she could. What she did, and what she puts up with for the sake of Aubree, showed her true strength. As angry as I was at all of it, I knew I would do everything I could to protect them.

"I don't want him coming here anymore. I can't imagine anything happening to you and Aubree." I lifted her face, scanning her eyes as she slowly nodded in agreement. I was stunned that she didn't even attempt to argue.

"I can't have him coming here and hurting us anymore."

"That will never happen. I'd hire security for you and Aubree before he ever thinks of coming after you again. Hell, we should report his ass to the cops tonight."

She stared at me blankly. "You're kidding, right?"

"Seriously? Amelia, look at your wrists. If he comes even once, you will have security posted in the driveway."

She stilled, terrified. I rubbed my hand down my face as I struggled to breathe at the thought of any harm coming to them.

"It won't happen. We're okay."

I kissed the top of her head. Not the least bit confident she was right.

The next morning at ten, a security company installed a state-of-the-art system

"You okay?" she asked as I handed her a cup of coffee before sipping mine.

"Better now that I know there's some sense of security for you." I kissed her on the cheek. Aubree was playing with her toys off to the side, oblivious that anything had happened. I was grateful she was none the wiser.

When my eyes drifted back to Millie, her eyebrow raised. *Oh, crap...What did I do?*

"Last night, with all the fuss, I forgot I was mad at you."

I let out a sigh of relief. "Oh, yeah? What did I do?"

She narrowed her eyes at me. "You didn't message me at all yesterday. I was worried, you big jerk."

I placed my coffee on the counter and pulled her into my arms. "Sorry, babe. It killed me, too, but I was trying to finish up and come home earlier to surprise you." I chuckled.

"I thought you were going to ball me out for buying you a car."

"I was going to, but who am I kidding? I love it." Her eyes went big and bright. "She's so fancy and pretty. Also, I didn't realize it had butt warmers in it. On my way home, I thought I peed my pants before I realized I had turned it on."

I nearly choked on my coffee as I coughed on the scorching liquid. She was something else.

"I was supposed to pick you up at the airport," Millie added. "How did you get here? I hope you didn't bother poor Brody."

My turn to fidget. "It's kind of his job, but no. I drove." I walked over to the window and nodded to my new classic green Defender parked next to Millie's new white Velar. A perfect matching pair.

She chirped. "Boys and your toys."

"What? It's practical. You weren't impressed with the sports car... And we needed something built for handling the harsh Canadian winters." I grinned ear to ear. I had wanted one for a while. I was more of a truck than a sports car guy, so when we had talked about me buying a car, that was the first one I thought of. It helped that Millie's dream car was also a Rover.

Millie rolled her eyes. "We're not in the Arctic."

"Close enough," I teased. She swatted at me.

"We were supposed to go shopping together."

"Yup. Then you would have talked me out of it and not let me buy the Velar and I had to buy it. They were parked next to each other. One of them whispered they were a pair, and I had to take them together. How was I supposed to refuse?"

She rolled her eyes so high they could have hit the roof. "You're nuts."

"Besides, I wanted it. You gave me a good reason. Safety for my girls." I snaked my arm around her. "Are you mad I bought it?"

"No. Why would I be mad that you bought us matching cars? It's cute." Millie stepped on her tiptoes to kiss me.

* * *

After I dropped off Aubree and Millie, I leashed up Mickey and went out for a run. Millie's town was cute, and no one bothered me. It was peaceful this morning as I ran down by the lake at a slightly slower pace.

Mickey was lagging. *Poor guy.* I changed my plan and headed into town instead. It was only a fifteen-minute walk. I wanted to grab some of that coffee Millie loved. My phone beeped with a message from Jenna, so I stopped to check it out.

Jenna: Hey, stranger.

Me: What's up?

Jenna: You bolted awfully fast. What did Uncle Julian have to say?

Me: The usual...

Jenna: What are you going to do?

Me: Nothing. It's not his choice.

Jenna: ...

Jenna: Is it serious?

Without a doubt, I knew it would be, which was why it was going to complicate the fuck out of everything else. The conversation about family obligations and expectations replayed in my head. My dick of an uncle even brought up my past to make a point.

Me: Probably

Jenna: Don't worry. Mom and I will help.

Jenna: I ran into Haley. She said to say hi. She looked good.

Me: Haley always looked good. We just went different ways...

Jenna: I guess it's good that things ended, right? You have Amelia, now.

Me: Yeah, I do. I hope so.

Lost in my thoughts, I ran into Millie's mother coming out of the coffee shop. She bent down to scratch Mickey's ears.

"Jake, walk with me," she directed, roping her arms through mine. I nervously tucked my phone into my pocket.

"Millie hasn't been this happy in years. It's like you brought the light back into her life, but I worry about her when you're gone. I would like to think you're not just playing house while you're here." She waited for my response.

"Absolutely not. I love your daughter and granddaughter."

"That's pretty obvious in the way you are with them. But I want to make sure you understand exactly what you're getting into. What did she tell you about Nick?"

This felt like a trap, but one I couldn't avoid.

"Nothing really." It was the truth, and I despised what I knew about him. "She simply said they broke up before she found out she was pregnant."

She scoffed. "Well, that part is true. There's a lot more, but we had a falling out during that time. I'll skip the nitty gritty of why, but you can bet your ass it came down to him. He was a terrible person to her. We wouldn't watch her suffer anymore. It broke our hearts, but she needed to learn on her own." Her mother sighed. "I swear she chose him just to spite us sometimes, to prove to herself that she wasn't wrong about him. The girl is stubborn."

I chuckled to myself, agreeing wholeheartedly that Millie was stubborn as hell.

"It's going to be rough. Nick doesn't like to lose. And since you came into the picture, he's gotten a taste of his own medicine. He will do anything to manipulate her, and his favorite thing is to use Aubree. I love my granddaughter and she's the only good thing that came out of the two of them, but I know how hard it is for her and how much she sacrificed coming back. Don't be one of those things."

The way she spoke made me wonder if she had heard about the other night. In this town, I wouldn't be surprised, but on the off chance she didn't, I wasn't about to open my mouth.

"I like you, Jake. You're a good man. I don't know how long you're staying, but I hope it's for the long haul."

The anguish in her mother's eyes was clear. I still didn't understand what Nick had on Millie. What happened to them? Why did she choose him over her parents?

I nodded, feeling the same sentiments as Millie's mom. Leaving in a couple of days for meetings and charity events was heavy on my mind. I pushed the meetings off as long as possible. I had to go, ready or not.

"I promise, I never want to lose either of them. I'll do everything for them to know how loved they are."

She smiled gently and tapped my arm with a slight glimmer of a tear in her eye. We walked back toward her car. I waved as she drove off, leaving me with dozens of questions about their relationship. I couldn't piece it together. Nick was an absolute dick. None of Millie's friends or family liked him. How long was she with him? Why did she stay despite everyone's warnings? And why didn't she tell me more?

When I picked up Aubree from school, she was excited to go trick or treating. I told her we had to wait until after dinner. Oh, the eye roll she gave me. A replica of Millie. *Priceless.*

The girls left to put on their costumes while I did the same. I stood in front of the mirror in a full character costume complete with tights. *If Carlos could see me now.* I chuckled. Personally, I wanted the snowman costume, but Aubree persuaded me with her giant blue eyes during costume shopping, and whispered in my ear, "Do you love Mommy?"

So, there I was, dressed in blue tights and fuzzy boots, with a blonde wig. I felt like the male version of a Bavarian beer wench. Thank God the shirt was long enough to cover my junk. It was so damn cold that I swore my dick was going to freeze off.

Millie suggested Aubree wear a snowsuit under her

costume. I laughed until I realized she was serious. Millie said it wasn't uncommon, and that she bought the costume a size bigger, just in case. I shook my head. *Oh, Canada*.

Chapter Twenty-Six

Millie

Avery invited us to the Halloween costume party at the pub. I was skeptical, but he said he felt bad for Jake being stuck in the house. He was right. Jake probably wasn't used to being home every night. I'd convinced myself a date night would be good for us. My parents were more than happy to stay with Aubree.

Jake glanced around. "Damn, it's packed. Is anyone not here tonight?"

"Probably not." I saw Avery in the back with a group of people. I shook my head while looking at his costume. Jake offered to get us drinks as I went over to them.

Once Avery saw us, he shook his head and waved his hand up and down at me. "Really?" he questioned, laughing.

"Your niece picked it out," I defended.

"I sure fucking hope so, or there's something wrong with you." He greeted Jake, who approached with some drinks in his hands. "I've got to give it to you. The blue tights are working for you, man."

"This from the guy in the loincloth," Jake rebuked, playfully flipping off Avery. My smile stretched across my face, loving that they got along. A stark difference from Nick.

"Where's Alex?" I asked. Avery nodded to the bar where Alex was hanging off of some woman barely wearing anything. I rolled my eyes. *I'll catch up with him later.*

Avery had brought Piper with him. She was the new florist in town. So far, she was hilarious, and I enjoyed hanging out with her. Piper was nothing like Avery's usual type, with her pinup style and curves. The way he was sneaking glances at her made me think they might be more than friends.

My gaze flicked to Jake, who went to sit with Avery and his buddies. I noticed a few women batting their eyelashes and laughing like hyenas. I tried not to be jealous, but the memories of Nick talking to "fans" after his gigs played on my insecurity.

Jake caught my glance, as he'd been doing all night. He excused himself and, without hesitation, cupped my face and kissed me so deeply that my toes curled.

When we finally parted, I sighed against him. "You have a fan club."

"So do you." My eyebrow raised, and I took a step back. He brought his face close to mine and licked his lips. "Me."

The grin that washed over my face was unmistakable.

"It's hot how jealous you just were," he said, taking my hand and tugging me onto the dance floor. My ass tucked against his groin as he peppered kisses along my neck to my shoulders, sending tingles down my spine. For once, I didn't shy away from the PDA.

Jake's fingertips firmly held me in place as we moved with each other to the point I had forgotten we were in the middle of a crowded bar. It was hot and heavy until, out of the corner of my eye, I saw Misha and Nick walk in. My breath caught as I watched them walk over to a group of people on the other side of the bar. *Damn. All I wanted was one night of peace.*

Jake stiffened behind me, whispering in my ear, "Let's go home."

He spun me around and I saw the fury he held for Nick and the concern he had for me. *This isn't fair to him.* It was our night out.

Leaning my head against his shoulder, I replied, "No. We were here first, and I'm having a great time. You and my brothers are here. He won't start anything."

Jake hesitated. "Amelia... If he does, I'll finish it."

I nodded to him, welcoming his kiss before heading over to Avery's table.

"Want to grab a round?" Piper asked me.

"Sure."

"I'll come," Jake offered.

"No. It's okay. I promise. Relax and have fun." I winked as I left with Piper.

The bar was packed. It took nearly five minutes before I could squeeze between people.

"I'll try from the other side," Piper shouted over the loud music. A few minutes later, she came back with a handful of beers. "Hey, do you know her?" She nodded toward Misha and her group of friends. I lolled my head, wondering why she was asking. "She's a bitch," Piper scoffed, taking me by surprise.

"Did she say something to you?" I questioned, worried, as I took two of the drinks she carried.

She shook her head. "I overheard her saying something about you refusing to let Nick see his daughter now that you have a rich boyfriend. Suddenly, you think you're better than everyone when you're just a glorified groupie." She wasn't holding back. "Oh, and she can't wait to see how fast he drops you when the season starts. What does she mean?"

"Jake plays for the Twisters," I told her, trying to hold back my anger.

"Like for real?" She grinned as I nodded. "No wonder she's jealous."

As much as Piper's comment took my side, rage engulfed me. The hurt and anger over everything that happened had never settled between us. Why the hell was *I* the bad guy?

I'd had it. I stormed over to Misha, causing her to startle.

"Listen here, you cold-hearted bitch. You used to be my best friend. Why are you so hell-bent on trying to ruin my reputation? I wasn't the one who did anything wrong."

She stared at me, narrowing her eyes. "Maybe if you pulled your head out of your ass, you would have seen the truth."

"So callous, Misha. You were always the girl who wanted what everyone else had. It wasn't enough that you were the cheerleader, the pretty one, or the *easy* one." She reeled back as if I had slapped her. "No. You wanted the one thing I had."

She laughed. "I didn't go after him. He came for me. If you knew how to keep him happy, he wouldn't have."

It was my turn to feel slapped. How could she stoop so low? She was like a sister to me. The one person I truly confided in.

"If you weren't pregnant, I'd knock you on your ass right now." Her friends scurried away from us. "You could've just asked, and I would have let you have him, but no. Instead, you lied and betrayed me, then made *me* look bad. And now you spread lies about me keeping Aubree from Nick!"

She crossed her arms over her chest. "It's not a lie. That's why you're here, drunk in a bar, and making out in the middle of the dance floor like a teenager, instead of home with her. You didn't even ask us to take her."

Is she kidding me? Ask them? I was shaking with rage.

"You're pregnant and here!" I rebuked. "As for the making out part, yeah I am. I don't have to hide it. He's my man. You may need to find yours. He's probably off in the corner, stalking some young fan."

She slammed her hands down to her sides and balled up her fists. "You're a jealous bitch because he chose me. He doesn't need anyone else. I keep him plenty satisfied."

The gloves had come off, and I was done taking their shit. All the puzzle pieces about our sordid love triangle were about to be spilled. I actually laughed out loud at her.

"He chose me, but you couldn't take it, so you trapped him."

Misha's mouth fell open. "That's a damn lie."

By this point, everyone in the bar stood still, and the music stopped. We had become the main attraction.

"I don't lie, Misha. I'm not you." I scowled, narrowing my eyes at her. "How did you *suddenly* get pregnant after years of sleeping with him? I'm guessing it was because you stopped taking your pill. Something about it caused too many side effects. Well, at least that's what you told me. I'm guessing Nick never got that story." She paled. *That's what I thought.* Misha must have forgotten that she confided in me once upon a time.

Nick appeared in front of Misha. "Enough, Mils."

"Enough? No. It's not. Why don't you tell your pregnant wife here what you told me a few days ago?" His eyes widened. "Go on, Nick," I said, goading him. "Did you tell her you kissed me and spouted some shit about her and how she was a mistake? You wanted to divorce her and come back to me."

Misha's mouth dropped open and her eyes doubled in size. Nick immediately glanced between us.

"I said enough," he warned through gritted teeth.

Too bad I didn't give a shit. I had held back for years and I was done with it. One question had plagued me since I found out about my pregnancy, but I wasn't sure I wanted to know the truth. For if I was right, it would devastate me. But now I needed to know just how fucked I truly was by them. Ignoring Nick, I continued with Misha.

"Ever wonder how our kids are so close in age? I know math isn't your strong suit, but something must click in that pretty little head of yours."

My pregnancy couldn't have been accidental. I had calculated over and over, and only one answer made sense.

"The girls are three weeks and two days apart." I paused, hoping she was following along. "I had Aubree after you..." Her face scrunched like the wheels were turning. *Seriously?* I tossed my hands in the air. "He knew you were pregnant, and yet he continued to sleep with me."

I was overwhelmed with vindication as Nick's face turned a putrid shade of green. The asshole knew exactly what I was saying. For years, I remembered the day we conceived Aubree. We were living together, and we had had a nasty fight after he stayed out all night the night before, telling me he was helping a friend move. It was all a lie. He never called, messaged, or anything. He came home the next morning as if nothing happened. I was furious. I packed up all his stuff and tossed it out. He begged me to give him another chance and made every promise he could so I would forgive him.

I even bought his lie that I was the love of his life. He had screwed up, but couldn't lose me. It was nothing he'd ever said to me, and I bought all of it. How fucking stupid was I? He had screwed up, but not in the way I thought. Thinking back, it must have been the night she told him she was pregnant.

"You knew about Misha's pregnancy before Saint Patrick's Day?"

Misha clasped her hand over her mouth and she leaned against the bar when Nick refused to answer.

My glare met his wide eyes. "You made sure we had sex,

that day, that week. Why would you sleep with me, knowing Misha was pregnant? Was this some game to you? Did you think we would live happily ever after like a big fucking throuple?" He squared his shoulders while his jaw tensed. I couldn't control my anger. I lunged forward and punched him square in the nose. My fist throbbed as Nick stumbled backward. Gasps filled the room, then someone laughed, breaking the tension.

Jake pressed his hands into my waist as he hoisted me into the air, pulling me away from Nick and Misha.

"You're a fucking coward!" I screamed at Nick, squirming as I tried to free myself from Jake's powerful grasp. "You trapped me into a life with you and Misha."

Jake tried soothing me, but I couldn't hear him, so he held me tighter.

"You fucking bitch!" Nick shouted, holding his bleeding nose.

"Never call her a bitch," Avery roared, slamming Nick to the ground while Misha shrieked at his side.

"Dammit," Jake groaned, letting me go. He and Alex pushed through the crowd and to pull Avery off of Nick. Avery was wildly swinging and kicking, trying to get back at Nick.

"Never come near my fucking sister again," Avery barked.

"I'd stay down if I were you," Alex warned. "We'll be dropping off and picking up Aubree from now on. And one more thing, stop spreading lies. Millie isn't withholding Aubree from you, you prick. You canceled seeing her after you assaulted her."

I heard a collective gasp from the room, then Jake's warm voice filled my ears. He lifted my throbbing hand to his lips, softly kissing it before asking if I was okay.

I whimpered, burying myself in his chest. I had never confronted them because I didn't want to hear the truth. It was easier to believe his lies and to think Aubree was a beautiful accident. It brought more anger out of me. I pushed away from Jake and yelled at Nick, who was leaning against the counter, holding his bleeding nose.

I pointed my finger at him. "How could you do this to me? Do you have any idea what I've endured because of your selfishness? The two of you ran around town, acting like I was the mistress who ruined your lives." I turned to the crowd, "Did everyone forgot he was my boyfriend when he was sleeping with her?" A few people hung their heads. I took a deep breath and turned to Misha. My voice shook, as I could barely hold my composure. "What was it you told people, Misha? That I was too busy with work and school, and you and Nick just found comfort in each other, or some shit like that. Like it was my fault you two cheated."

Tears rolled down my face, thinking of how much I loved Aubree, and how horrible Nick and Misha were. "Do you have any idea how hard it was to explain to Aubree why daddy lives with Misha and Gracie, not with us? It's heartbreaking. She asked me if her daddy loved Gracie more, and if he will still love me when the new baby comes." I wiped my tears away, flinging them to the floor.

"You coward," I sobbed. "I hate you. And Misha," I glared at her through my blurry vision, "you're worse than him. He was an idiot, but you were manipulative and deceitful, and your plan backfired. He was trying to end things with you, so you trapped him, and then he trapped me in a sick attempt to keep me. Both of you are despicable and pathetic. If it wasn't for Aubree, I'd never see either of you again."

I wiped my snotty nose on my sleeve. Barely able to speak, my voice was raw. "I deserve better. Aubree deserves better. One day, she'll have someone there for her every day and every night. He'll play dress up and have tea parties, or teach her sports or anything she wants because he'll only take away her pain, not cause it. He'll be the daddy she deserves."

Nick glared at me, but kept quiet. Misha cried as she sat on a chair. I walked out of the bar and into the freezing night air, feeling like it was the first time in years that I could really breathe.

Chapter Twenty-Seven

Jake

I let out a long sigh. *Jesus, what a night.* No wonder Millie had trust issues. My little family drama, among other stuff, was nothing compared to the shit I heard in the bar. It was enough to make my stomach drop. When she asked Nick if he knocked her up on purpose, I stood there like everyone else, waiting for him to deny it, hoping it wasn't true. But he didn't. He stood there as if he had seen a ghost, petrified. I was in a state of disbelief. *Who does that?*

When we got home, Millie's dad was waiting for us.

"How was your night, kiddo?"

"Shit, Daddy... It was shit," she replied, stumbling away from me and into her kitchen.

"I see," he whispered, following Millie. "Let me guess... Nick?"

"You got it."

"What happened?"

"Daddy, I can't. Maybe another time." Her dad's face morphed into worry as we watched her reach for the vodka she had in the top cupboard. She took a swig right from the bottle and walked out of the kitchen. *Damn.*

I stayed behind to talk to her dad, worried about his pleading expression. I put my hand in my pockets and leaned against the counter.

"I think it's best coming from Millie," I stated. "No disrespect, Sir, but if it makes you feel better, she confronted him and Misha. A lot of shit went down." His eyes widened. "She punched him in the nose. Pretty sure she broke it, but if she didn't, Avery got to him before I could."

I thought he was going to be angry, but he surprised the shit out of me when his face lit up and he clapped his hands together.

"Oh, I bet it felt so good to hit that son of a bitch. I'm gonna call Avery in the morning and live vicariously through him. The lucky bastard," he chuckled. I shouldn't have laughed, but his reaction was priceless.

Taking a breath, his laughter stopped, and his tone grew serious. "This is the third time in her life I've seen her broken. When Nick married Misha, then whatever happened between you two. And now. That's far too many times for me to see my daughter that way."

"I promise she won't feel this way ever again if I can help it."

He gave me a clap on the back, nodding once before leaving. Once I locked the front door, I went upstairs and checked on Aubree, who was sound asleep, then headed into our room.

The sight of Millie curled up on her side, crying, was more than I could take. I climbed in bed behind her, enveloping her in my arms.

"What can I do?" I whispered in her ear.

"Nothing."

She was right. Nothing I could say or do was going to fix her heartbreak. I felt it deeply, holding her as she cried herself to sleep, hoping my presence helped ease some of her pain.

* * *

The next morning, Millie was on the other side of the bed, instead of snuggled against me. She seemed small and frail. My heart ached for her. I heard Aubree playing in her room, so I let Millie sleep while I went to check on Aubree.

"Morning," she said when I opened her door.

"Morning, Princess," I replied, hiding my sadness from her. I hated how Nick couldn't appreciate what an amazing kid she was. He was more interested in playing games.

"Can we watch cartoons?"

"Sure, but it's gotta be quiet. Mommy's sleeping."

We went downstairs, and I let her pick out some cartoons. I put Mickey in the yard, then sat on the couch next to Aubree.

She turned to me with big, wide eyes. "Jake, are you my other daddy?"

"Other daddy?"

"Like Momma Misha?"

I sat up straighter on the couch. "Umm... No?" *Am I?*

"Why?"

I scrubbed my hand down my face. "It's complicated."

"Why?"

She was killing me. How could I explain it to her? "Well, your daddy and Misha are married, and Mommy and I aren't."

"Oh..." She tilted her head to the side, putting her hand under her chin. "Why?"

Good question. I pinched my brows together. "I love Mommy very much, but sometimes adults have to wait a while before they can get married." *That sounded better in my head.*

"Like Misha and Daddy, they loved each other forever."

I suppressed an eye roll, recalling Millie's heartbreaking story. "Something like that," I mumbled.

She tapped her chin, making a face. "Okay."

She gave me a big hug and a kiss on the cheek. I mulled over what Aubree said. It was a good question. *Why weren't we married?* Shit, she was smart. Her eyes lit up when I asked if she wanted to go pick up some treats for her mom.

We drove into town to pick up some of Millie's favorite things, and cookies and milk for Aubree.

The bakery was busy early Sunday morning. A hush fell over the place when we entered. *Wow.* Millie was right, the gossip mill was quick.

"Morning," I said, nodding at everyone watching Aubree and I.

It was clear they all knew what had happened last night, and I hoped Millie would talk to her parents quickly before they heard it elsewhere. People were staring at me with mixed emotions of pride and sympathy while Aubree picked out her favorite cookies.

"Five," she said, holding up her hand.

"How about two cookies? Mommy will be mad if I sugar you up too much," I chuckled. I placed our order, getting an assortment of butter tarts and coffee for Millie.

I finished paying when Aubree shrieked, "Nana, Papa!" I whipped around to see Rose and Peter walking in. As they walked to us, the crowd got eerily quiet, and I noticed several of them avoiding eye contact.

"Hey, sweetie," Millie's mom said cheerfully. "You guys are out early. Where's Millie?"

"Sleeping."

Her mom sighed heavily. Her eyebrows furrowed, but sensing it wasn't the right place, she turned her attention to Aubree instead.

"Want to join us for a while?" she asked. "Mommy needs rest. I think we can talk Papa into a special lunch today."

Aubree's eyes nearly doubled in size with excitement.

"Okay with you?" Millie's dad asked me.

"As if I could say no," I replied, smiling at Aubree while gently tousling her hair.

Millie was still in bed when I got home. She asked where Aubree was. I told her about running into her parents and they asked to take her. She nodded and sat up to take the coffee. I noticed her eyes were red and swollen, as if she had cried again. It was crushing me to see her this way.

"I guess I owe you that story," she murmured.

"You owe me nothing." I sat on the bed, squeezing her thigh.

"Yeah, I do. You've been patient enough. I should have said something before, but I was ashamed."

My stomach dropped. "You have nothing to be ashamed about."

As much as I had questions, I wondered if not knowing was better. After everything I heard last night, I didn't know if I could take it. She tapped the spot next to her, so I moved closer. She brought her knees up to her chest and hugged them.

"I guess you know some of it from last night, but let me fill in some gaps." Her voice was shaky, and I reached out for her hand, interlocking our fingers. Millie shook her head as if encouraging herself to go on. "Nick and I were on and off for eight years before Aubree." *Eight years? Holy fuck.* I sputtered on my coffee I had taken a sip from.

Millie bit her lip while watching me. "I met him through Avery at some party. He was older, a musician, and had that *I don't give a shit* attitude. Everything I could dream of. We kept it under wraps for a bit because of the age difference. I was almost seventeen, and he was nineteen. Christ, when my parents found out... Well, let's just say it didn't go well." I bobbed my head, listening to her. "Our relationship was juvenile and took a toll on everyone, including Misha and I. We had been best friends since kindergarten. We were exact opposites. The tomboy and the cheerleader. She was an only child. We bonded like sisters. We had our ups and downs like all long friendships. She could be a bit much sometimes. She was a diva, and everything had to go her way." Millie paused and turned her head away, staring out the window.

I brushed my thumb across her knuckles, urging her to go on.

"We never had the same interest in guys. Misha dated the jocks and the most popular guys, and I didn't date at all. Until I met Nick." Millie shrugged, reading my mind. "They never got along. Hell, they even refused to be in the same room together, and it caused a lot of fights between us. I always had to choose. It wasn't until Nick and I moved to Toronto on our own, away from everyone, when we grew out of our issues. I was happy they were getting along. I gave her a key to our place. She stayed over often. Now I see that I was a fool."

I clenched my jaw, uncomfortable listening to the harm they'd caused Millie.

"What's worse is that it was Misha who told me. I came home from work, and I overheard them arguing about why he hadn't told me yet. It all came out. Turns out they had been sleeping together for longer than he and I were. They hooked up whenever we broke up, or that's what they said to justify it, like it wasn't cheating until she got pregnant."

I pulled at the top of my hair in frustration. I opened my mouth to say something, but nothing came out. What the hell do you say to that?

She picked at the bed sheets. "They got married three weeks later. Everything had happened so fast, and I didn't even know I was pregnant. Between school, work, and our breakup, the skipped period went unnoticed. Pregnancy never crossed my mind because Nick was adamant about not having kids, let alone getting married. We lived together, and that seemed enough. I gave up everything for him. Even though my family didn't approve of him. When he married Misha, it broke me. She took everything I wanted and waited for."

"Amelia, they are idiots. It's not you, it's a power move from some girl who was never really your friend. You're better off without her."

She wiped her eyes, then shook her head in defeat. "He wasn't even there for Aubree's birth. When I went into labor, Avery and Lisa were with me. Nick came the next day and said that he couldn't get away from Misha. I knew then that I was always going to be his second choice. My beautiful daughter was going to grow up in the shadows of her half-sister."

I pinched the bridge of my nose, willing back my own tears of frustration for her. That part was killing me. It was worse than the cheating. "I'm not supposed to ask, but did you consider not having a baby?"

"For about five seconds, until I saw the tiny heart on the screen. I loved it immediately."

"Was he there for you at all?" Shaking my head, I already knew the answer.

She shrugged. "Sporadically. He brought a case of diapers every month and sometimes a toy for her, but I felt like I was a dirty secret or, worse, a charity case. I'd asked him to stop bringing supplies. I could manage it, but I spent a lot of lonely nights with a screaming baby, and I was too proud to ask for help. The girls were my only saviors. They were with me the entire way."

"What about your parents?"

"Oh, they were supportive, but I refused to take anything from them. I made my choice when I chose Nick. It was difficult to come back."

"Christ, baby." I had no words. I hugged her while she sobbed into my chest. I could only imagine the head games Nick and Misha played with Millie. No wonder she wanted nothing from anyone. The heartbreak that she endured. Cheating was one thing, but with her best friend? Both of them used her in their own personal sick game. Nick deserved way worse than what Avery gave him last night.

* * *

I couldn't sleep. Thoughts of what Millie went through tore me apart. How or why she stayed almost a decade was beyond me. It was enough to make me want to punch the ever-living shit out of him.

What a manipulative prick. Impregnating her on purpose, so she was bound to him for life? Who fucking does that? Hell, I'm a pro athlete. My family warned me against 'the trap', usually for money or fame, not because you are an asshole who impregnated her best friend. The more I thought about it, the angrier I became. My hands trembled with rage. I held onto Millie tighter until she finally fell asleep beside me. I crawled out of bed to get water in the kitchen.

In the quiet house, I thought about Millie and Aubree, and how they deserved everything Millie said last night, to be loved every day and every night. Someone who was there for the good days and the bad.

But then I felt helpless. I couldn't whisk them away, even if I wanted to, and I couldn't be there physically every day to protect them. Since we got back together, we had only been apart for a handful of days, and it was getting harder and harder to leave. After Nick's attack, I became overprotective, not wanting him near them at all, and the security cameras wouldn't replace me being there.

I hung my head in my hands, so lost in thought that I

didn't hear Millie come down the stairs. She asked if I was okay, and I responded by holding her tightly, burying my head in her chest.

She ran her hand down the back of my neck. "Hey, what's wrong?"

I couldn't bring my face up to hers. For the first time, I broke down. Everything I'd been holding back erupted out of me. I wasn't able to erase the hurt or sweep them away, make sure it could never happen again. I hung my head, barely able to croak out an answer she was patiently waiting for.

"I can't save you from him. He's the father of your daughter. He'll forever be in your life. Listening to the torture he put you and Aubree through is killing me, and I can't do a thing about it."

She curled her fingers in my hair and tilted my head up, forcing our eyes to meet. "Jake, I don't need you to save me. You do way more by loving me, even when I'm pushing you away. You have done nothing but *show* me what love truly is." She grazed her nose against mine and it was like a lightning bolt hit me square in the chest. The second my lips hit hers, it all came to me.

"I love you so much," I groaned.

A small smile tugged at her lips. "I wish there was a level above loving you. That's where I am."

God, she's something else. Even after everything, she took a chance on me. I leaned my forehead against hers and gripped her tighter, my nerves on fire, breathing her in. She still smelled fresh from the bath with her familiar maple scent. Aubree's conversation floated through my thoughts and, before I could stop myself, I whispered, "Aubree's going to have the dad she deserves. Someone who loves her and plays with her, who takes away all her pain.... In fact, she already has one. A guy so in love with her mother, he would die before letting her suffer any more pain. He loves her to no end, and he wants to spend every minute of his day showing them how much they mean to him." I took both of her hands in mine, bringing them up to my chest. "Aubree asked me this morning if I was her other daddy."

She blinked at me. "Wh-what?"

"Baby, I desperately wanted to say yes to her." She sucked in a breath. "I'm that man for you, and for her. Forever.... Amelia Rosalie Harte, I will love, adore and cherish you for a thousand seconds, days, minutes, hours, months, and years, if you'll let me."

I paused, all choked up. My eyes locked onto hers and, with her blue eyes piercing me, I whispered, "Marry me?"

She clasped her hand over her mouth. "It's so soon."

I shook my head. "I don't need to spend a decade figuring out how extraordinary you are. I knew the first night we were together, and every moment since has only proved how right I was. I've been waiting for you to catch up."

Her expression melted into the most precious smile. "That smile of yours is what I live for."

She leaned forward, whispering against my lips, "Yes."

"Yes?" I asked in amazement. She nodded at me with a smile shining brighter than the sun. My chest felt like it was going to explode. I picked her up and kissed her feverishly. She was about to be shown just what I meant by loving her.

Chapter Twenty-Eight

Millie

Jake carried me bridal style into the spare room, our lips never leaving each other. All the feelings of self-doubt washed away. He was right; he was everything I deserved. *And everything I wanted.*

My desire for him was off the chart. He put me down next to the bed and kneeled down in front of me, and I was already wet. He slid his hands up my thighs, his thumb running on the inside with the faintest bit of pressure. It was sensual and doing all the right things already, and he hadn't even started yet. His fingers inched up to the fabric of my underwear, and dragged them slowly down my legs, Jake's eyes on me the entire time. My breath quickened when he nudged my legs apart, lining himself up beneath me. He firmly gripped my ass, pushing me forward until his lips made contact. I twisted my hands in his hair as he worked his tongue around in circles.

"Yes," I moaned, my hips twirling with him.

"I love how you taste," he said, his voice muffled. The vibration in his voice was something else. God, it felt good. I bucked into him.

"Baby, I want you," I begged. He swiped across me faster, pushing down. It was hard to fight my orgasm, but I pulled myself away. "Bed." I pointed.

He raised his brow at my forceful tone, but the small smirk tugging at his lips gave him away while he followed my command.

His eyes trained on me, I unbuttoned his jeans, opening them and then kissing the deep V that was exposed. The sight of him was enough to make my nipples harden.

He lifted his ass enough so that I could take everything off. I stood in appreciation of his thick cock that begged to be ridden. I took the shaft in my hand and then lowered my mouth.

"Easy, babe," he hissed when I took him all in. "I want to make it inside of you."

I did, too, but not until he was on the brink of coming. I licked him from top to bottom until his toes curled. It only lasted a minute before he yanked me on top of him.

He palmed his face. "Shit. Wait."

"What?"

He sat up. "The condoms are upstairs."

"Oh." Suddenly I felt sheepish. I bit my lip. "Do we need them?"

His mouth opened and closed. "I'm on the pill, I promise. And I've only been with you..."

He wrapped his hands behind my neck, nuzzling against me. "Fuck the condom. I'm clean and there will only ever be you."

How could one sentence do to me what it did? I slid myself onto him, inch by inch, taking a moment to feel him. I wound my hips in circles, working him. His head fell back and his large hands grasped my thighs.

"You're all mine, Amelia," he breathed, digging his fingertips into me.

"You're mine, too." He flipped me over and landed on top of me, our lips connecting feverishly.

"You're the best thing that ever happened to me," He said between kisses.

Every inch of me was humming with ecstasy as we climaxed together. It was powerful and sensual. It was perfect.

* * *

Did he really ask me to marry him? *Please don't wake me if I'm dreaming.* Jake was sprawled out next to me when I opened my eyes. When I found him in the kitchen last night, it was like my past shattered his soul. Seeing him break down in my arms was beautiful and sorrowful. Never had someone loved me so intensely that it radiated off him.

If he only knew he had saved me long before I realized I needed it. With all the simple things he did every day, from making me the perfect cup of coffee, down to the snuggle goodnight, I felt loved.

"Hi, beautiful," he murmured through a smirk.

"Morning," I whispered, still choked up about last night. He turned over and kissed me.

"How did you sleep?" He tickled my neck with his scruff.

"Amazing. You?"

"Better than ever." He grinned, and I playfully jabbed him in the ribs. "Ow."

"Don't be a baby."

"Oh, yeah?" He snagged my waist and tickled me. I squirmed to get free.

"Stop, stop, I give up," I huffed, trying to catch my breath.

He bent down and swiftly kissed me on the lips. "I love hearing you laugh." Just as his hands wandered up my shirt, his thumb rubbing under my breast, Aubree came into the room, rubbing her eyes.

"What's so funny, Mommy?"

I whooshed his hand away. "Jake was tickling me."

Her eyes went wide, staring at him. Suddenly, he leaped out of bed to chase after her.

"The tickle monster is going to get you," he roared playfully as she ran down the hall.

Not that I expected either of them to hear me, but I told them I was taking a quick shower. Jake was making us coffee when I joined them in the kitchen later.

Jake was staring out the window into the backyard. "It snowed last night!"

I moaned, "It's too early for snow."

"My first Canadian winter." Jake sounded proud as he stalked over, placing a chaste kiss on my lips and handing me a cup of coffee.

I scoffed. "Sure, it's beautiful now. White and fluffy glittering on the treetops, but just wait until you're shoveling the driveway for the fifth time in one day and freezing your nuts off."

"Wow, really selling the winters here, babe." He shook his head, then he clapped his hands together with a gleam in his eye. "Okay, get ready. I have plans for us today."

I raised an eyebrow at him, and he shrugged.

"Actually, we're winging it, but let's pretend I made the best plans ever." His eyes cast down, and his face etched in worry. "It's my last day before I leave for a few days." The worry in his voice wasn't missed.

I grabbed his hand and squeezed it. "We'll be okay." He nodded at me and gave me a small smile. "The girls are coming this weekend," I reassured him. The tension in his shoulders eased.

We spent the day making the most of the time we had before he left, Jake making sure Aubree and I felt his love every moment.

* * *

"It feels like forever since we got to do this," Gia squealed as she hugged me.

"How was the honeymoon?" I asked.

"Spectacular. Italy was amazing. The food was to die for."

"So were Paris and Greece. I swear I never wanted to come back." Sam smiled, coming in behind Gia.

"What about you guys? What did we miss? Millie, please tell me you're with Jake?" Sam asked eagerly.

Gia clapped. "Gah! Your face when he showed up at the wedding was priceless. The song he picked was beyond perfect. I wanted to die. He's so damn sweet."

"Fill up the drinks, girls. This is going to take a while," I teased, grinning as I thought about my man.

I started from the beginning, telling them about Jake moving in, Nick's attack, and his speech about how he should have chosen me. Then, I filled them in about the costume party, and how all of Nick and Misha's lies came out, and left it off with me punching Nick. Although that may have been the highlight, a sadness filled me while recounting the story, and how all my deepest fears were exposed. The hurt and betrayal were devastating, like I was living it all over again.

"You punched him? God! Why wasn't I here for this?" Sam laughed. "I'd give good money to watch that. Please tell me if someone in this town has a video or something."

Gia applauded me. "Well done. I love that after all these

years, you finally stood up to Misha. That bitch was never a choice. She was just easy."

Not wrong. "Well, they can keep each other. I'm done with them."

"About damn time!" Lisa raised her glass.

"How did Jake take all of it?"

My shoulders slumped as I recalled Jake's reaction. "Jake was distraught. He had heard so much shit, and there wasn't a thing he could do to make it stop."

"Who wouldn't be Mils? Everything they put you through was awful," Lisa offered, quietly.

"Jake kept going on about wanting to save me and how he couldn't. Nick's her dad. No matter what, I was bound to him. Jake said he was the guy I was talking about, the dad who would take away Aubree's pain and be there every day. If I let him, he would love me for a thousand seconds, days, minutes, hours, months, and years," I recalled what Jake told me, tearing up. "It was beautiful, honest, and filled with so much raw emotion that saying no wasn't an option."

"Saying no to what?" Sam choked, staring at me.

I felt nervous. *Do I tell them?* We hadn't even talked about it after. My silence was filling the room until Gia slammed her hand down on the counter before pointing her finger at me.

"Wait, what? Are you telling us you're engaged?"

I bit my lip, unable to contain myself. "Yeah."

"Holy fuck." Lisa jumped on me, wrapping her arm around me. "I'm so damn happy for you."

Gia grabbed onto my naked hand. "Where's the ring?"

"Here's the thing... I don't have one. It was so sponta-neous, I don't even think he was prepared to do it."

"That's so god damn romantic, Millie." Gia squealed and hugged me.

"I doubt he hadn't thought about it. That's not some-thing you just jump into," Sam said.

"I don't need a ring. I was happy to say yes without it." I felt warm and gushy saying it. It was true. I didn't need anything from Jake he hadn't already given me.

* * *

Jake called me earlier to say that he was picking Aubree up from school. He had refused to stay away from us longer than twenty-four hours. When I got home from work, the house was dark. *Odd.* There was a note taped to the front closet door.

Leave your stuff there, and head to the right.

What are they were up to? I kicked off my boots and hung up my coat. The tiny sounds of Aubree shushing Jake with a giggle gave them away. As I turned my head to see where they were, the fireplace lit up.

"Come, Mommy." Aubree waved me over. I tilted my head, curious why she was decked out in her princess outfit. Jake was standing in a black suit with one button undone on his shirt. He looked like a god next to the roaring fire, but it was Aubree who snapped my dirty thoughts from forming when she whispered something in his ear. He nodded at her and she jolted away from him, running past me and upstairs.

"What is going on?" I asked Jake out of the side of my mouth. He shrugged his shoulders with a wicked grin that send a flurry of butterflies to my stomach.

Aubree rushed back, something hidden behind her back. She peered at Jake in exchange for some sort of silent conversation before she held out a blindfold.

"Mommy, put this on," she demanded. I glanced between the two of them. Playing along, I put on the blindfold.

I was tempted to cheat and see what they were up to, since I could hear them moving around the room, but I resisted the urge. After what felt like an eternity, Aubree tapped my hand.

"Mommy, you can see now," she whispered excitedly. A bundle of nerves hit me and I had no idea why. Slowly, I lifted the blindfold to see the living room covered in rose petals and dozens of candles lighting the space.

Aubree stood in front of me, beaming, as she handed me a folded note.

My hands trembled as I opened it.

In case you thought I'd forgotten the ring, you'd be mistaken. You stole my heart the minute we met. This has been a long time coming for me.

I stared at Jake, his eyes gleaming with delight, and his usual cocky smile wasn't there. In its place was a timid guy with a sparkle in his eye. Holy shit, that was even sexier. Aubree tugged my hand and placed the second piece of paper in my palm.

Clue 1: Our journey began with our toes in the _ _ _ _ ?

Confused, I scanned the room.

"It's a game, Mommy," Aubree said.

Oh. My gaze landed on the bookshelf. There was a small glass jar in the cupboard filled with sand I had taken from my first-ever trip to Florida. There was another piece of paper tucked behind it.

Clue 2: The next time we met, I could never forget. The way you danced in the dark it captured my _ _ _ _ _ ?

I noticed the heart-shaped box of chocolates on the window bench. Slowly, I walked over and examined it to see another note taped in it. I felt nervous and excited as I read it.

Clue 3: Winning you over, took patience and _ _ _ _ ?

I ran to the clock on top of the fireplace. There was a note underneath it. My heart was pounding so loudly in my chest that I was sure they could hear it. With each clue, Jake's smile widened.

Amelia, you were nothing I ever expected. In one night, my whole life changed, and nothing could make me regret it. You are beyond beautiful, loving, and fierce. You have made me a better man and, if you let me, I will spend my whole life loving you the way you deserve.

Tears spilled from my eyes. When I opened them, Jake was in front of me on bended knee. He held out a small black box. When he opened the lid, a flawless emerald-cut diamond, flanked by diamonds on either side, was gleaming in the candlelight. My legs shook as I clasped my hand over my mouth.

"Our thousand years, hours, and minutes start now, if you'll marry me," Jake murmured, patiently waiting for an answer. Aubree was next to him, holding his hand. My voice was caught somewhere in my throat.

She shook my hand. "Mommy, say yes or no." Breathless, I nodded.

He slipped the ring on my finger. Unable to move, everything stood still. Aubree giggled as Jake spun me around in a hug. She held out her arm, telling me she got a present, too. A tiny silver charm bracelet dangled from her wrist, the word "daughter" engraved on the charm.

I sobbed, smiling proudly at her. "It's beautiful." I kissed her on the cheek and swooped her into a hug.

"Why are you crying?"

"Mommy is happy, sweetie. Really, really, happy."

I leaned over, softly kissing Jake on the lips. "Thank you."

He had tears in his eyes. "I love my girls," he declared, then asked if I liked the ring.

"It's stunning," I said, staring at it. "But when? How?"

He bopped his head back and forth, nervous to say something. "Actually, I've been carrying the ring for a while," he confessed, taking a big breath. "Like after we broke up."

"What? How did you know we'd get back together?"

He guffawed. "There was no way I was letting you go

forever. I was coming back to you, no matter what. I meant what I said to you. You are everything to me."

"Jake..."

"I've whispered it to you in your sleep every night, trying to build up the courage to say it when you're awake. The other night wasn't a spur-of-the-moment decision, it was perfect timing. And if you had said no, I would have just asked you every day until you gave in."

I let out a small laugh, knowing how persistent he was. He leaned over, kissing me softly.

"How did you know my ring size?"

"Lisa." He smirked, brushing some of my hair over my shoulder. "I'm glad she told me." His eyes darkened as he leaned to trail his lips down my neck. "I have never known genuine happiness until you walked into my life."

"I love you."

"I love you," he whispered into my ear, sending a shiver down my spine. He was everything I never knew I wanted. What a fool I was to almost have let him go.

Chapter Twenty-Nine

Jake

I woke up with a feeling of utter euphoria, like I'd accomplished all my wildest fantasies in one giant explosion. Millie nestled in the corner of my shoulder, her hand resting on my chest with her ring gleaming in the sunlight. It was a thousand times better than I pictured. A goofy grin spread across my face.

I remembered picking it up even though we had broken up. Mitch coaxed me out for a chat, which included shopping for a gift for Lisa. I suggested shoes or a handbag. Women loved that shit, but apparently Lisa was against shoes. Mitch told me it was a superstition of hers, that it was bad luck to give someone shoes, because it meant you're allowing them to walk out the door. I couldn't believe he considered that horse-shit, but he was adamant about not taking any chances with Lisa.

It made me think back to my past relationships, and there

were a few Christmases that involved shoes. By spring training, they were gone. I couldn't argue with logic like that.

He dragged me into every damn jewelry store, debating between earrings versus a bracelet. I'd been nursing a broken heart, and he brought me jewelry shopping? What kind of sick fucking friend was he?

I needed a drink, and Mitch was on the phone with Lisa *again*. She yelled out Millie's ring size, which the sales lady heard through Mitch's phone. She perked up from the counter and came over within three seconds.

I rolled my eyes hard and hightailed out of the store. Not for any reason other than if she had opened her mouth, I would have ordered one of everything. Seriously, I would have sent one to Millie every damn day if I thought it would work.

I had found myself outside of the jewelry store when Mitch found me again. He eyed the diamond-encrusted watches when my eye caught something glittering in the corner showcase. It called to me, like one of those unrealistic scenes where the object had a halo around it, pulling me closer. It mesmerized me. The image of it on Millie's finger hit me like a ton of bricks. I left the store empty-handed, but after a day of arguing with myself, I went back and bought it. I had to, and I was glad I did.

Millie shifted against me. She lazily smiled without opening her eyes. "Morning."

"Morning, fiancée," I said, kissing her softly on the lips.

"I still can't believe it's real," she whispered.

"Me either." I cleared my throat. With the reality of us being officially engaged, there were going to be some adjustments to our life, and I'd held off as long as I could. I checked the clock on the side of the bed. Time is literally running out.

"Brody and I have a call in half an hour, and we need to discuss our schedules. It's charity season, and I've already committed to a few events that have come up in the new year. By the way, I'll need a schedule for you."

She propped herself up on her elbows. "A schedule?"

"Yeah. There's going to be some stuff you're expected to come to." Her mouth opened and closed. "Awards and stuff," I clarified.

"Oh, right."

"You want to talk about it?"

"I just, I guess I didn't realize this side of it. Like, I want to keep you in my little bubble."

I grinned. "I like your bubble."

She rolled her eyes. "Not like that."

"So, now that it's truly official, we should talk about a date."

"Really?"

"Kind of the point of an engagement babe, to plan a wedding."

She swatted my stomach playfully. "I didn't realize we would need to jump in so quickly. What are you thinking?"

"Well, baseball season takes away most of the year. It really only leaves the fall or winter. I don't want a long engagement."

"Jake, it's already almost Christmas."

"I'm not opposed to a Christmas wedding. How fast can you bridezilla up?" I chuckled.

She smacked me with her pillow. "Get real, you turd."

I let out a deep, rumbly laugh. "Okay, no Christmas wedding... What about our anniversary?"

She tilted her head. "Which one? We met, then re-met, broke up, got back together, then engaged. We only have anniversaries."

My smile faded. "Fuck. You're right. Okay, how about the very first one? It was the most important one. Without it, there is no other one."

She hesitated and chewed her lip, a sly smile creeping across. "It would be one way to top last year's birthday."

My hand that had been rubbing her back stilled. "Wait, it was your birthday trip?" She simply shrugged, and I sat up. "Like that actual night?" She nodded. "Why didn't you say anything?"

"Like what? Hey, I don't know you, but it's my birthday, so do you want to have sex?"

I rubbed my face. "Well, something. I don't know."

"I didn't need to tell you. You gave me a present instead. A great one, if I recall."

"Funny."

"Oh, don't be like that. It was a don't ask, don't tell moment that I insisted on. I didn't want you to feel weird or obligated to know it. Besides, I never asked you about your weekend. It was a bachelor party, right?"

I swallowed hard, feeling queasy. Aubree yelled for Millie from down the hall, just as Millie asked if I was okay.

"I'll bring up a coffee when it's ready," she offered, getting ready to tend to Aubree.

"Thanks." She placed a chaste kiss that engulfed me in guilt.

When she left the room, I had sunk into the side of the bed, rubbing my temples. She was going to lose her mind when she knew the secret I'd been keeping. I'd been avoiding the conversation with her for so long I'd forgotten about it. But my past was about to come to bite me in the ass. One thing I loved about Millie was her refusal to research me. She said my past was in the past. I was an athlete, and she was sure there was plenty of shit the media could spin. She wasn't interested in seeing me with any exes or splashed on tabloids.

I had been on the bad side of the media plenty of times, both professionally and personally, but this was different. It was going to change everything. *How is Millie going to feel about my family, the money, and everything it comes with?* My stomach turned with each piece of the puzzle that brought us together, and I feared how it could tear us apart.

At precisely nine o'clock, my phone rang. I grumbled incoherently to myself as I swiped it open. "How bad is it?" I asked Brody in greeting.

There was a long pause. "The engagement isn't public knowledge yet, but news of your trip to the jewelry store has circulated to the lawyers. I held them off, telling them it was Mitch who was buying. You were just moral support."

I rolled my eyes and blew out a heavy breath. I knew exactly what the conversation was about, the fucking prenup. It was standard practice. I never cared before. It was smart, but now the thought pissed me off. I didn't want one. We didn't need one.

"Your uncle and your mother have both been calling. Hourly."

I rubbed my hand down my face. "I bet." *I better tell my mother she is going to have a daughter-in-law and a granddaughter.* "Anything else?"

"Yeah, do you still want to meet up with the real estate agent?"

The question surprised me. I had forgotten about wanting to find a new condo in the city before the spring rush, but since Millie and I had gotten engaged, where we lived was something I needed to discuss with her.

"Hold off for now. Can you get my mom on the line?"

"Yup. Hold on," he said while the line clicked. There was a pause before it rang.

"Jake?"

"Mom."

"Please tell me you convinced Millie to come for Thanksgiving," she stated.

"I doubt it, Mom. Aubree has school," I explained. "Canadian Thanksgiving was in October."

"Try, please. I'd love to meet my future daughter-in-law before the wedding..." Her sarcasm wasn't missed. My mouth opened and closed. She chuckled at my silence, continuing. "Oh, please. That jewelry store was no joke. Are you going to tell me it was for earrings?"

"No, it was not for earrings and yes, I proposed. Twice in fact."

"Did she reject you the first time? Shit, I love her already." Jenna chimed in.

"Jenna?"

"Yes. It's on speaker."

Of course. "Long story," I huffed.

"JJ, it's official, right? She's got the rock?"

I felt the swell of pride in chest. "Yeah."

"You're going to have to face the firing squad."

"Comforting, sis."

"What's the big deal? It's not like you haven't been through this before." I felt like someone had punched me in the gut with the mention of Haley, even though she wasn't wrong. With my ex, it was no big deal. Everything was like a business transaction. Not that we made it down the aisle. *Another thing Millie needs to know... Except this one won't be pretty.*

"It's different."

"Right..." I swear I could hear Jenna roll her eyes through the phone.

"Jake, listen. You love Amelia. You're very protective of her. If you say she's not in it for the money, then what's the fuss? She won't care about signing a prenup." My mom spoke rationally, pissing me off further because Millie would sign it without flinching, but I didn't want her to. Sure, I'd make sure I set her for life, but I already knew she wouldn't take a dime of the money. She was too damn stubborn. She won't even take money from Nick. If she did, she put it all away for Aubree. I admired her for it.

"If I ask her to sign one, it won't be the standard one. It will be what I see fit. If that's a problem, I'll take her to Vegas tomorrow and no one can say shit."

"Okay. Let me know about thanksgiving."

"Mom. It's next week."

"Bye." She hung up.

Great. How the fuck do I convince Millie to go meet my family in less than a week?

Chapter Thirty

Millie

I stood in the kitchen, putting bacon in the pan, when Jake came downstairs.

"Where's Aubree?" he asked, peeking around.

"Playing in the snow with Mickey." I nodded toward the backyard. I looked out the window, seeing her toss little snowballs in the air while Mickey chased them, barking at her.

Jake planted himself next to me, leaning against the counter with his back so he could watch them.

"How did your call go?" I asked.

"Uh, good. I guess."

I cocked my eyebrow at him. "You guess?"

"My mom wants us to go for Thanksgiving."

"Next week?"

"Yup. News traveled fast about the engagement." I opened my mouth to say something, then closed it. I blinked at Jake, the realization of our engagement sinking in. "We're so absurd. We got engaged and I've never talked to your mom. What if she doesn't like me?"

"Woah," He rubbed his hands up and down my arms. "They kind of already love you."

"Jake!"

He laughed. "Babe. We don't have to go. Maybe over Christmas?"

"No, no. I think I can make it work. I'll see if Nick will switch weekends and take Aubree."

His eyebrows scrunched, causing a deep crease. "What? No. She comes, too."

Crap. I hesitated, knowing this was going to be awkward. "I'd have to ask Nick."

"What? Why?"

"He has to sign off."

His expression fell flat. "You have to be shitting me."

"It's the rules." I hated them, too. We hadn't spoken since the bar. It was going to be a battle.

"Well, then we can figure it out together."

Oh, Christ. He's not going to like what I'm about to say.

"Hold that thought," I said, staring into my steaming cup, avoiding his penetrating gaze. I tensed, bracing for the argument we were about to have. "I'm going to drop off Aubree with Nick. It's better if I'm alone."

Jake's entire body stiffened. "No. Millie, no fucking way," he snapped, pacing.

Calmly, I replied, "Jake, it's already tense enough. Let me go on my own."

"His track record fucking sucks. No way are you going anywhere near him without me." He clenched his teeth and ran his hands through his hair.

I wrapped my arms around his waist, forcing him to look at me. His deep blue eyes pleaded with me not to go.

"Work with me, honey. You want us to go to your moms, right? I have to do this."

He embraced me tighter, taking several long breaths. I knew he didn't like it, but I was right. If Jake came, Nick would deny us taking Aubree.

"I hate how this shithead gets to dictate your life," he grumbled. "What if I come, but stay in the car?"

"What, are you a dog?" I rolled my eyes and softly chuckled, trying to lighten the mood. "I promise I'll call the second I get to the house and when I leave."

"Take Avery? I'll call him now and have him meet you."

"No. No one comes. They asked to take Aubree for dinner, so I'm trying to be a better person."

"Can't you be the shitty person?"

I didn't even respond. My face said it all. He groaned and pulled me tight to his chest, our foreheads touching as the air between us thickened.

"Go," he huffed, but he didn't let go of me.

I quickly kissed him and squirmed out of his embrace. I brought Aubree in and had the quickest breakfast possible before I bolted out of the door.

"Love you!" I shouted over my shoulder and left without glancing back. Mostly because I thought he would be behind us.

Aubree was excited to have play time with Gracie as she chatted incessantly. I did my best to smile and nod, or respond appropriately, but facing Nick again distracted me. My hands trembled as I pulled up to their house and put the car in park, taking a minute to gather my nerves.

"C'mon, Mama. Let's go," Aubree said impatiently. I cringed. *Sure, kid. Mama's just trying to grow a pair.*

When the door swung open and I was met with Nick's icy glare, I wished I'd let Jake come. Nick ruffled Aubree's hair, opening the door wider for her. I passed him her backpack. Aubree ran into the back of the house, calling out for Gracie.

"I thought you would have stayed in the car," he grumbled. His face turned ghostly white. I followed his gaze to my ring. "So that's it then. You're going to marry this guy after a few months? Is this why you spouted some bullshit about getting married one day? You were already engaged?"

I wanted to snap back at him, but I was trying to remain calm. "No, I wasn't engaged then, and yes, I'm marrying him. He doesn't need to spend years playing head games, deciding if he's in or out of our relationship."

"Great. Congrats. Anything else, or are we done?"

So much for civility. I took a breath to stop myself from slapping him across the face for everything he has done to me. I stuffed my hands in my coat pockets to cover up my balled fists. "I want to take Aubree to Florida next week for American Thanksgiving."

His eyebrow shot up. He let out a small snort. "Yeah fucking right." He considered my impassive expression. "You're serious?"

"Yeah, I am. We'll be gone for the weekend. You can come get her the weekend after."

He raked his fingers through his hair before throwing his hand up in the air. "I knew you were going to do this!"

How dramatic. "Take Aubree on a vacation? Yeah, parents do it all the time." I forced myself to breathe as I pulled out a folded piece of paper from my pocket. "It's Disney World. I need you to sign the paper."

My hopes of appealing to his soft side died when he scoffed. "What if I say no?"

"Then you really are an asshole. The only person you're hurting is your daughter. How about you explain to her why she can't go meet all her favorite princesses? And don't forget to tell her you already went last year with Gracie."

Anger flashed in his eyes, but I didn't care. I was equally angry. We stood toe-to-toe in the doorway, glaring at each other, when I caught Misha rounding the corner. Her baby bump was now prominent.

She sighed. "Aubree can go."

With daggers in his eyes, Nick whirled around. "No fucking way."

"She. Can. Go," Misha snapped. "It's fair, Nick." She then turned to me. For the first time, she didn't stare at me with disdain. She glanced at my ring, and her face relaxed. "It's for a few days. Sign the damn paper." She gestured at him.

Misha was not in the best mood. She held her lower back as she breathed heavily. She waddled over and thrusted a pen at Nick. He snatched the paper from me, slewing out a string of profanities under his breath before he tossed it back at me.

"Thank you," I mumbled. I turned on my heel, shouting to Aubree that I loved her, even though she was already off playing with Gracie.

* * *

Boarding Jake's jet, my nerves hit me. New York flashed in my head. The last time we were there, shit didn't go well. Jake sensed my anxiety and gripped my hands as we took our seats.

The flight attendant passed Aubree a tablet with earphones, and a few coloring books with crayons.

"Really?"

"It's a long flight, and all the kids her age have their own tablets," Jake assured me.

I rolled my eyes. Aubree was in her glory when she found her favorite movie.

"Tell me more about your family," I urged.

Jake shifted in his seat and grinned. "My mom's young. She was nineteen when she had me. She met my dad when they were in their rebellious teen years. They never married, despite the family pressure to. When I was three, he left. He wasn't into settling down. He was happier with the rich kid party life."

That was not at all what I was expecting. I'm not sure I noticed Jake never mentioned his dad. Now I understood why.

"Husband number two is Jenna's dad, Carl. He's the one I consider my dad. They were married for about twelve years, then the course ran dry. Husband number three, David, lasted two years and the current husband, Luis, is a trophy husband."

"Trophy?"

"Yup, he's five years older than me," he replied dryly. *Oh.*

Sensing he didn't want to talk more about Luis, I moved to ask about his dad. "How about your dad? Do you have any relationship?"

"Yeah. I see him when he's not globetrotting. He's made a name for himself in the tech world. I think he's on wife number five or something. I lost count. No kids, though. I think he had a vasectomy to skirt anyone trying to get knocked up."

"That's hardcore."

"Yeah. He's an ass." He shrugged. "Carl was a great father to me." His face brightened and the corners of his mouth turned up, mentioning Carl. "We still have a relationship. He never made me feel like I wasn't his. He was the reason I found baseball. Mom wanted us kids to have some normalcy and not just become spoiled brats. Carl suggested baseball because he saw I had a natural talent. When they divorced, he demanded the same rights as Jenna." He paused and cast his eyes down, closing them for a brief second. When he opened them, they were the deepest shade of blue I'd ever seen. "When we broke up, I went to him for advice. He told me being a step-parent wasn't DNA, it was a privilege. A choice to love and raise a child, not out of obligation, but from sheer desire."

I choked up, squeezing his hand. "He sounds like an amazing role model."

He sighed. "Babe, I need to come clean about something." He rubbed his chin, his brows furrowing and his muscles tensing. *Oh, this can't be good.* "I wish you searched about me sometimes. Things would be easier."

"I told you... I don't need tabloid crap. If it was important, then you would tell me."

"Baseball isn't the only reason my name holds fame. My family are the owners of Parsall International Investments."

"Okay? I don't know who they are."

He smiled. "It's an elite investment company. It deals in a bit of everything, including stocks and real estate globally."

"Why are you so nervous about telling me?"

"We're engaged now. When we marry, then you become part of this world, access to an elite lifestyle." His voice drifted off.

"Like how elite, Jake? Are we talking like old, oil-rich money, or have we won the lottery, and have a few million to burn?"

He sucked in a breath of air. "More like billions..." His voice drifted off.

"Are you ducking, kidding me?"

He reached for me. "You're mad, I get it."

I threw my hands up. "I'm upset you hid this until now. I don't care about the money, I have money. Sure, it's nowhere near as deep as yours. We're only millionaires, not billionaires, but you should have warned me. I feel like an idiot."

"Wait, what? Your family are millionaires?" *Seriously?*

I snorted. "Jake, my parents own the biggest construction company in the entire region. It's not only luxury vacation homes they build, but they also do commercial and subdivision developments... My great-grandparents founded Beachers Bay and built it from the ground up."

"Why the hell were you driving that old car for so long?"

This is what he focuses on? "After I left home, I was determined to do it all on my own. Choosing Nick meant giving it up. It's part of the reason we fought so much. He thought I would still take my parents' support. Even when everything fell apart, I refused their help. I was ashamed and wanted to prove I was capable on my own."

He held onto me. "I love how independent you are and that you love me for me without knowing who I was. I'm sorry I held it back. It wasn't for another reason than making sure you didn't bolt. I felt like it was another reason you would have used to convince yourself to walk away from me."

As upset as I was, he made a point. I would have walked away. Told myself there was no way I could live in the world of the rich and famous. *The rich and famous. Like ultra-rich. I'm so not prepared for this!* "I need more clothes."

Jake's brows shot up with my outburst. "I'm sure what you brought is fine."

"Jake, you're introducing me as your fiancée to some of the richest people in the world. I doubt my yoga pants are sufficient."

A smirk tugged at his lips. "But your ass looks so great in them." I swatted at him.

"Ouch. Okay, okay. Shopping it is," he said, still grinning.

Aubree was fast asleep on the couch. Her earphones were still on. Jake scooped her up and carried her into the bed, propping the door open in case she woke up. I wanted to be mad at him. Why did he have to be so damn great?

Chapter Thirty-One

Jake

After our whirlwind shopping spree, we pulled up to my mother's beach house estate.

"Holy crap. This is your mom's house? It's a mansion."

I pursed my lips. "Well, this is the beach house."

She stared out at the modern white three-story stucco house with a four-car garage in the center of a perfectly mani-cured lawn, with lush gardens filled with palm trees. Every-thing shouted luxury.

Her expression faded as she muttered, "What does the regular one look like?"

I shook my head and took her hand, leading her through the wide double doors. Millie noticed the neutral décor with lavish cream furnishings. She clutched Aubree's hand. "Touch nothing," she warned, giving her the *mom eye*. Aubree nodded in fear.

"Babe, it's fine. If she gets something dirty, Mom will just buy a new one." I shrugged. Millie scoffed.

"Mom?" I called out toward the kitchen, while Millie stood frozen, taking everything in.

"How many bedrooms is this?" she asked.

"Only seven and eight and a half bathrooms."

"Eight bathrooms? That's a lot of toilets to clean," she grumbled under her breath.

"C'mon." I smirked, pulling her through the kitchen and out to the backyard. We stood on the second terrace overlooking the spacious grounds, complete with a two-level infinity edge pool and spa.

"A pool. Mommy, they have a pool!" Aubree squealed.

"No going near it unless an adult is with you," Millie sternly directed.

"Okay," Aubree said, with a hint of disappointment.

"Well, hello there." My mother's perky voice floated down off the terrace from her bedroom.

"Hi," I replied dryly. I glimpsed at Number Four pulling up his pants. I pinched the bridge of my nose and my cheeks heated. *Seriously gross.*

"Wow, that's your mom?" Millie asked in shock. "She looks like she stepped off the runway. No wonder she doesn't stay single."

"Ha. Don't worry about making a good impression. I'll tell her what you said. She'll love you."

A minute later, my mom appeared and immediately wrapped her arms around Millie, then held out her arms for Aubree to jump in. My mother wasn't big into hugs, so I nearly fell over at the sight of such a warm welcome. I did the formal introductions.

"Millie, this is my mom, Juliette Parsons. Mom, Millie and Aubree."

"You two are gorgeous," she cooed, winking proudly.

We sat and talked for almost an hour while Aubree played on her tablet and with some toys my mom had purchased. I didn't doubt that she bought out the toy store.

"Now, I know you want your space. I assume you will stay at Jake's, but I have a room ready for you. It is in the west wing, and there's plenty of privacy."

"No, thanks."

She shrugged. "If you change your mind, I re-decorated the spare room for Aubree. Jake mentioned she loved princesses."

"Oh, you really didn't need to do that," Millie politely objected.

"Can I see, Mama?" Aubree asked, jumping up and down.

"Sure, you can. Greta can take you up," my mom answered.

I stared at my mom, confused. "Who's Greta?"

"Her nanny, of course."

"Wait, what? What nanny?" *This is absurd*. I gawked at Millie, who was trying to hide her shock, but failing miserably.

"We don't need a nanny, Mom. We watch Aubree," I huffed.

My mother rolled her eyes. "Listen, don't be so damn dramatic. It's for the week. You have some events in the evenings. I doubt Millie is comfortable leaving her. She won't want to go to boring adult functions. Consider her a babysitter."

I blew out a frustrated breath. Millie tapped my leg as if to say it was okay. *Realistically, it wasn't a bad idea.*

Just as we were about to leave my mom's, we heard a deep booming voice calling from the foyer. My face scrunched up. *For fuck's sake.*

"Are you fluffing, kidding me?" I grumbled, clenching my jaw. "We don't swear in front of Aubree," I clarified when my mom wrinkled her nose.

My mom called for Greta, asking her to take Aubree upstairs for a few minutes as my uncle entered the room. I stiffened when I noticed the two suits behind him. He greeted us, sounding slightly friendlier than he did from the hall.

"I'm Julian, Jake's uncle. They," he motioned toward the suits, "are our lawyers, Adam Carlings and Robert Davine."

"Julian, don't be an ass. Why did you show up *here*?" my mom asked, sounding very bored with her brother.

Out of nowhere, Millie turned to them. "Where do I sign?"

My head whipped around. "Millie, we're not signing a prenup."

"Why not?" She didn't seem bothered. "That's what this is about, right? Why the hesitation about telling me about your family?"

I hung my head, not knowing what to say. She took a moment to examine everyone in the room. It felt like my stomach was knotting.

Millie folded her arms, grounding herself. "Can I make amendments?" She turned to my uncle.

"She already wants more money?" Everyone's head spun to Mr. Carlings when he tried to whisper. My uncle clenched his teeth, but it was Millie's voice that distracted us.

"No, you ass. I won't sign it because I know Jake, and whatever he put is too much." Millie glared at him before continuing. "If you want me to sign it, give me nothing."

My uncle cleared his throat. "Excuse me?"

"I want nothing. No houses, no cars, no fancy lifestyle. I can provide for myself, but if we have any children, he can leave whatever he wants in a trust that they can access when they are twenty-five." She spun on her heel to me and pointed her finger. "Jake, I mean it. If there's anything else in there, I won't marry you."

Her confidence was incredible. I tangled my arms around

her, kissing her forehead. "Not marrying me isn't an option." I glanced around at my family and our legal team. "We're not signing anything. I don't give a fuck what anyone in this room thinks."

"Oh, yes, we are." Millie placed her hand on my chest, gazing up at me.

I groaned out of frustration. "Amelia, I told you I would never let you go, and I meant it, so it doesn't need to be signed. We're never breaking up." My mother and my sister clutched their chests as wide smiles beamed on their faces. I tightened my hold around her waist, snugging her against me, feeling her body soften within my grasp.

* * *

Millie

It was a Thanksgiving charity event like I'd never seen before. The hotel was filled with some of the most beautiful people I'd ever met in my life. When Jake mentioned all his events and charities, it never really sunk in until I was standing in a room full of famous people. I had a conversation with a pop star five minutes ago, and I totally fangirled and embarrassed myself.

Jake was in protective mode, barely letting go of my hand as we worked the room, until someone I didn't know summoned him. Jake told me to mingle, and that he'd be back as fast as he could. Honestly, I didn't mind. I loved watching him. He was charming and funny, not to mention the way his suit was tailored to showcase his muscular physique. I never knew suits were a thing until Jake stepped out of the bedroom. Christ, I almost dragged him back into it.

"I almost didn't recognize you," Mitch teased, coming around the corner with Lisa, snapping me out of my trance.

"You made it!" I immediately hugged Lisa. It was comforting to have someone else there with me.

"Close call," Mitch replied. "We had a plane delay and de-icing, or some shit."

I shrugged my shoulders. "That's what happens when you fly out of Toronto."

Lisa scoffed and nudged him. "I told him that!"

I recognized a familiar face from the crowd as he approached. Seeing Jax brought back memories of the cruise. A blush crept up my cheeks. He greeted Mitch with a quick handshake. Jax took a minute to eye me, his deep eyes lighting up.

"Mitch, man. Long time no see."

"Jax. It's literally been like three weeks." He deadpanned.

"I know, but you missed out on the last poker night and my wallet missed yah." Jax laughed.

"I bet it did." Mitch rolled his eyes.

"I didn't realize you guys had kept in touch after JJ's bachelor party," Jax said, pointing to Lisa and Mitch.

"Yeah, man, as if I could stay away from her." Mitch pulled Lisa close.

Jax gave him a playful swing on the shoulder. "Aw, shit, man. That's so cute."

"Yeah, yeah. Jax, play nice," he warned, nodding toward Lisa and I. "I need to go over and say hi to Charlie Ecklestop."

"Tell him to re-negotiate himself," Jax ordered. "He lost me a shit ton of money in the playoffs."

Mitch flipped him off as he walked over to some big, burly guys who must have been linebackers. Jake was on the other side of the room with a group of people who had adhered to him. I noticed his face scrunch when he saw us talking with Jax.

"Happy to see you locked him down," Jax told Lisa before turning his smoldering gaze to me. "Millie?" He scanned my body, grinning. "Damn, you're prettier than I remember."

I blushed, even though I tried not to. I'm certain he'd used that line on every woman in here.

"I didn't think I'd see you again," he continued. "Reid was pretty sad you never reached out to him but, seeing at the massive rock on your finger, someone else got you." I fiddled with my ring. "Who's the lucky guy?"

Instinctively, I searched the room, my gaze landing on Jake. Jax followed my stare.

"Wait. My cousin? You're the snow bunny?"

How do I take that? I held out my hands and stared at Lisa, silently asking for support, but a woman interrupted our conversation.

"I'm sorry, but did you say you're *with* Jake?"

I turned around to see a stunning woman with a perfectly cropped blonde bob. Nothing was out of place, from her flawless features to her dress. Her light brown eyes were wide as she gazed at us expectantly. I shifted on my feet, suddenly feeling out of place next to her. A little warning bell went off in my head.

Before I could speak, Jax pulled her in for a hug that lingered a little too long.

"Haley, you're still smoking hot!"

"Oh, Jax. Still the same old man whore," she taunted, giving him a playful push.

"Hey, I'm not that bad." He laughed when the blonde, Lisa, and I shared the same skeptical expression. "What are you doing here? You're like the last person I'd expect here, after..." His stare quickly moved to mine, a flash of reservation crossing his features.

She flicked her wrist to wave him off. "Jenna asked me to donate some stuff for the auction tonight. You know how she is about the vintage stuff I carry." Lisa and I shot each other a glance and started to back away when Haley grabbed my arm.

"You're with Jake?" she repeated.

I didn't know what to make of the situation. Was she an ex? A friend? Family? A knot formed in my stomach. Something didn't feel right. I flashed back to the way women watched me when I was out with Nick, like they were surprised he had a girlfriend. It read the same way.

She smiled at me approvingly. "I wondered if he ever found you."

"I'm sorry." I cleared my throat. "What?" Lisa spit out her champagne in shock.

"You met Jake at his bachelor party. On the ship, right?" I blinked. *What the fuck did she just say?* She caught my deer in headlights gaze. "Oh, shit. I'm so sorry. Wrong girl?" Her gaze shifted to Jax as she bit her lip.

I wanted to tell Haley I was who she thought, but my throat went dry. My brain was processing the words, *His bachelor party.* My heartbeat thumped in my ears as I searched around the room for Jake, finally finding him talking to his uncle. It seemed heated. He tore his gaze away and turned toward me like he sensed my stare. When our eyes connected, he saw me standing next to Haley, and a grave look washed over his face. It sucked the air out of my lungs. My head spun and my stomach lurched. I needed to escape. I bolted for the exit, pushing past the patio filled with people. Lisa was hot on my heels.

"Breathe, Millie," she tried to soothe me while chasing me. When I made it out, I hunched over, trying to catch my breath. Every moment of our first night flooded me. *He was engaged?!*

The sounds of heavy footsteps coming fast snapped my attention back to reality.

"Don't even think about it!" Lisa yelled as they approached.

Jake called out for me, but I couldn't function. Lisa continued to warn him not to move, but I had one question I needed him to answer.

I whipped around to face him. He stood in front of Lisa, who acted like a shield, protecting me. His chest was heaving and his breath was ragged. His eyes were wild and searching mine.

"Is it true?" I finally asked.

Jake sucked in a gulp of air and dropped his head while catching his breath. "Yes."

I walked away without a word. Jake tried to follow me, but Lisa held him off. Haley's words replayed in my mind as I left. *Jake's bachelor party.*

For the second time in my life, I was blindsided, and my pounding heart shattered.

Chapter Thirty-Two

Jake

I escaped Lisa and made it back to the room. Millie was curled up on the bed next to Aubree, crying. She said nothing, not even to ask me to leave.

Not wanting to wake Aubree, I knelt on the floor next to them, resisting the urge to scoop Millie into my arms where she belonged. But I fucked up and now she might never come back into them. I ran my hands through my hair. *It was now or never*. I had to tell her everything. I owed it to her, to us.

"I won't make excuses about why I didn't tell you it was my bachelor party on the ship." My voice shook. "I knew exactly what I was doing when you came to my room." *And exactly why I said nothing.*

I watched her shoulders move with her sobs, wishing I could fix everything.

"She and I were over before we boarded that cruise," I explained, my throat tightening at her silence. "It's not a redeeming fact, but it's the truth. When you walked into my life, it changed me. I wish I could say how, but I can't. How do you tell a perfect stranger that you feel drawn to them, that you feel like they are meant to be in your life? You'd have called security on me." I steadied my breath. "Baby, I'm so sorry for not telling you," I continued. "But I'm not sorry for what happened. We were meant to meet, meant to have that night. You were more than one night. I refuse to believe that's all it was. Even if I could go back, I'd do it all over again. You would be my choice. Every. Single. Time." My voice cracked with emotion, and tears slid down my face, praying that she believed me.

She never uttered a word. I hung my head in my hands. My heart shattered with every whimper and tear she wiped away because of me, but I endured every minute. It was my fault.

The sun hadn't even come up, and I heard the soft tiptoeing of Aubree as she crept out of bed to find me.

"Morning," she whispered, holding onto her new doll that we bought for her the day before.

I cradled her in my arms, afraid to let go. Millie's phone vibrated against the nightstand. She mumbled as she grabbed it, our eyes meeting briefly, showing me her devastation, before she turned away from me.

"We're leaving, sweetie," Millie told Aubree.

"I don't want to go." Aubree pouted, clutching onto me. I felt breathless.

Millie left the bed and grabbed their suitcases from the closet. I watched her shove their clothes inside, feeling the gravity of my mistake.

I couldn't take the silence anymore. "Say something. Anything. Hit me or punch me. I don't care, but please talk to me."

She opened her mouth, but a soft knock at the door interrupted us. I scrubbed my hand down my face. *Fuck.* Aubree ran to open it. Lisa was in the doorway in sweats and her sunglasses on, sneering at me.

"What the hell are you doing here?" she demanded.

"It's my room, my relationship. I'm going to do what I can to save it," I rebuked. Lisa glanced over at Millie, who was hastily dressing Aubree and ignoring the interaction between us.

"I'm hungry," Aubree said as she patted her tummy.

"Auntie Lisa can go with you to get breakfast. Mommy needs to finish here." It was a statement that even Lisa didn't seem to argue with as she took Aubree leaving us alone. Now was my chance.

"Millie, please. Listen for one second," I groaned. When Lisa and Aubree left. I planted myself in front of her. "You saved me, Millie. You made me feel a love I was powerless to resist. I can't regret what happened because I would never have met you. And, Jesus, baby, you and Aubree are everything to me." I dropped to my knees, hugging her legs like a child.

She froze. "A cheater is a cheater, regardless of the reasons." Her words cut like a knife. Her hand trembled as she swiped tears from her cheeks. Millie stepped out of my embrace and bit her lip, before sliding the ring off her finger and placing it on the nightstand. My chest tightened, and my brain screamed to put it back on, but no words came out. She walked out the door with me behind her, begging her to stay, but she wouldn't even glance at me.

Aubree and Lisa were waiting in the hotel's foyer when we got downstairs. Millie carried on like I wasn't there, desperate to get away.

"C'mon. We fly home," Aubree told me.

"No, sweetie. Jake has to stay here for a while," Millie answered weakly.

Aubree frowned and freed herself from Lisa's grip, coming

over to me, flinging her tiny arms around my neck. "Bye, Daddy Jake."

I held on to her a little tighter, unable to stop my tears. *Daddy* Jake repeated in my head. A deep ache formed in my chest as it suffocated me. It was hard to let her go, but Millie came and took her hand.

"Time to go, sweetie." Her voice was strained.

I tugged on Millie's arm, pleading with her silently. Lisa took Aubree out to the airport limo, waiting outside.

"I get it, I fucked up. Hugely fucked up, but I swear on my life I'm going to spend every day winning you back. I don't care how long it takes or how much you push back, our love is too epic to let it go like this."

Tears streamed down her face as she walked out. The limo left and I couldn't stop them. *What have I done?* I was ready to put my fist through a wall.

There was no way around it. There were at least a thousand times I wanted to tell her and twice as many opportunities. I was a chickenshit.

The night we met, I had absolutely no right to touch or kiss her, but I couldn't stop myself either. Millie was different. *We* were different. I felt it the second our eyes met and my entire body responded to it. I was inexplicably drawn to her. It was more than her eyes that I could drown in, or the smile that brought me to my knees. The second her hands landed on me, it was a lightning bolt to my heart. Something stirred like never before and I wanted to know why. What was it about *this* woman that had me in a frenzy and willing to risk it all for? She was like a drug I needed and when I found her again, under my nose, through Mitch and Lisa, it was meant to be. Everything had fallen into place. My entire chest felt like it collapsed in one fell swoop.

* * *

It took less than an hour before Mitch showed up at my door, looking like I felt. He swung and hit me square in the jaw. I stumbled backward, knowing I deserved it.

"You'd better fucking have a plan to fix this," he barked at me. "I'm not about to lose my woman over shit I had nothing to do with."

Fuck, that hurt. I grabbed a cloth to wipe my bleeding lip. Mitch was still on a rant. He followed me into the apartment and went straight to the bar. "Lisa won't even talk to me. Her phone goes straight to voicemail. She stayed at the hotel last night instead of my place. Fuck, she even told security to throw me out." He poured out two shots of whiskey, which I downed.

The thought of Mitch being thrown out of the hotel by security was a visual. I almost laughed, but I knew enough not to. "Why the hell didn't you tell her?" he growled.

"You're kidding me, right?"

He poured out two more shots as I sat across from him. "What happened? What did Millie say?"

I hand ran down my face, the silence of last night hanging in my ears. I may not know a lot of things, but a silent woman is the scariest type of woman. I shook my head. "Nothing."

"What do you mean?"

"Silent treatment. Except for telling me that a cheater is a cheater, regardless of the reasons."

Mitch's eyes widened. "Shit, that's bad." He slid his glass across to me.

We sat in silence for a long time, lost in our thoughts about last night. The sound of Millie's sobs haunting me.

I pinched the bridge of my nose, pulling the ring from my pocket and slamming it on the bar top. "I don't think I can fix it."

Mitch's lips twisted up, and he took a swig from the other glass he just overfilled.

We spent the afternoon calling them. Every time it went to voicemail, we took a shot, creating a game out of our misery. Two hours later, I held the empty bottle, crying like a goddamn baby.

"Okay, we need a plan. It's not like you cheated on Millie, you cheated *with* her." He shook my leg.

"Dude. Not helping."

"There's nothing in a million years that would make you cheat on Millie, right?"

"Like you need to ask."

"We have to do something. It can't end like this. Not after what I've seen between you two." Mitch spoke like the true romantic fucker he was.

"Why the hell are you still here and not groveling on her doorstep?"

Excellent question.

Mitch smacked me. "Sober up buddy, we got some groveling to do."

Chapter Thirty-Three

Millie

When we landed, I remembered I didn't have a ride. We drove Jake's car to the airport. I cursed to myself until I saw Brody standing in the arrivals area with a sign for us. Lisa was just as shocked as I was.

"I—what are you doing here?" I stammered.

"Jake asked me to come get you," he explained. Brody's worried expression told me he knew what happened.

"I can drive you home," Lisa suggested. As much as I loved her, I needed to be alone. I already felt bad that she was pissed at Mitch. I tried to reason with her for Mitch's sake. After all, it wasn't his place to tell me. She figured in all the conversations they had and knowing whose bachelor party it was, he would have said something, but he didn't. *That was hard to argue against.* I hoped she would at least go easy on the poor guy.

When I got home, the house seemed hollow without Jake. I could barely keep it together for Aubree. Even at bedtime, she felt it.

"Don't be sad, Mommy. Jake will come home soon, he promised," Aubree said, kissing my cheek. My heart tore even more. *How could he make that promise?* Everything Jake said last night made sense. I didn't want to understand how he could keep it from me. My head and heart were battling whether he should've come clean. The thought of never having him was worse than anything else. But how could I consider someone who wasn't faithful? Was that even what happened? He told me they were over before getting on the cruise, but was it the truth?

A deep, dark feeling of shame enveloped me, remembering how it felt when I found out about Nick and Misha. The fact that I caused someone else that pain was unbearable. How could I forgive myself?

My phone rang again, and I silenced it without looking. The flood of texts and calls from Jake ripped my chest open.

Jake: I'm sorry.

Jake: I was a fool.

Jake: I won't ask for forgiveness. I'm going to earn it.

I sobbed hysterically into my pillow, moving to sleep in the guest room instead after Jake's lingering scent on the sheets broke me. I had the worst night of sleep since finding out about Nick and Misha.

I was barely functioning when dropping Aubree off at school. Nick was in the parking lot, and it felt like his eyes could bore through me. I didn't have the capacity to deal with him. I pretended to get on my phone so he would turn and walk away. It worked. I sat in the car for a minute, figuring out what to do. I wasn't due at work since we came home early, and I didn't think I could stand a day at home.

My feelings were all over the place, and I couldn't control

which side was winning. Memories of the weekend I met Jake flooded me. How he made me feel with just a look was more than I had ever felt before. He was protective, sweet, and genuine. Nothing I expected and everything I never knew I needed. He was right. Something pulled us together. I was ready to be with him the second his arms wrapped around me on day one. I had thought about that night for months and I was ecstatic to see him again, despite my awkwardness. He was more than I could have imagined, and now it was all over.

My thoughts paused when I got home to see Nick parked in the driveway. I sighed, not wanting to deal with his crap today. He gave me a once over, eyeing my sweats and messy hair.

"Your fiancé here?" he asked in an icy tone.

"Not yet. He had things to finish in Florida." He didn't need to know the truth, and just his tone sent chills up my spine enough that I backed up onto the front step of the porch.

"I've thought about what you said." He gave me a sinister grin. Every hair on the back of my neck stood up. "You're right. Aubree shouldn't feel unloved by me or worry about what happens when the baby comes. I should show her." The way his lips curled suggested there was more. "We decided she should live with us full time."

Holy shit. Did I hear him wrong? My knees wobbled. "What?"

"Like you said, she should have a full family. Be with her siblings and loved equally. Your words, Mils."

I wanted to punch the smug grin right off his face. I balled my hands, staring at him. "No."

"Why not? Weren't you spouting about not hurting our daughter? Don't you think it would be nice for her to have what she wants?"

As if this prick is using my own words against me. I blinked,

281

not believing what I was hearing. Nick was an ass, but this was a new level. Tears formed in my eyes.

"I will not lose my daughter, Nick. You want to involve the courts? Fine. But you never wanted her full time before. I don't really believe you want her now. You're being spiteful."

"Maybe I just want my kids together," he said and jumped back into his truck, peeling out of my driveway.

Panic consumed me, clueless about what to do and, for the first time, I was truly terrified of Nick. How could he threaten to take her away from me? Because of Jake? What a petulant asshole. He achieved exactly what he wanted. It finally hit me. I had no way out from him, bound for life through Aubree.

My instinct was to call Jake. My hands trembled as I tried to dial, but then stopped halfway through. He can't help, and it's not his problem. I re-dialed Lisa instead, in full-blown panic mode. She could barely understand what I said through my sobs.

"He'll get custody of Aubree over my dead body. Jesus, Millie. The girls and I are on our way."

"Okay," I whimpered, my breath slowing. What a fucking couple of days! First, Jake, and now Nick. I was done with men.

I went inside and grabbed my computer, because I needed a lawyer. Someone knocked on the door ten minutes later. It was too soon for the girls, unless they flew here. *Right, Millie. Like what? On the broom express?* I rubbed my hands over my face, making sure I had no snot or anything from crying.

Jake stood on the other side of the door, all disheveled; his hair wild and dark circles under his eyes. I crumbled to the floor into a blubbering heap at the sight of him.

He crouched down next to me, cradling me in his arms. "Babe, I'll make this better, but I couldn't stay away. I never meant for any of this."

"Not you," I sobbed. "He wants Aubree."

He moved back, his brows furrowed. "What?"

"He wants Aubree full time. Nick is going to take her from me." Nothing I said was coming out clear.

He tilted my face up. "I don't understand."

I told him what Nick said through broken words and gasps for air. "I can't lose her Jake."

"He's a vindictive prick. That's never fucking happening," he finally said. "What does your custody agreement say? Can he just change it?"

Jake cupped my face, our eyes meeting. "Amelia, please tell me you have an official court document that states the rules of custody and child support?"

"No."

"Why the fuck not?" he shouted, running his hands through his hair, tugging at the strands.

"We never needed it. He barely saw her. We managed without involving the courts."

He jumped up, pacing the entryway. His anger was palpable as he loudly exhaled and something incomprehensible.

My sobs came more quickly when I considered if this was all my fault, since I thought if I played nicely, an arrangement wouldn't matter.

Jake kneeled at my side again, whispering in my ear that everything would be okay. He kissed my temple, and I wanted to believe him.

"How do you know? What if he takes me to court and wins?" I argued.

Jake scoffed. "Not if he's smart."

I stared at him. "What do you mean?"

"Babe, listen to me, it won't ever happen. My lawyers will look into it immediately." He grabbed his phone. I didn't know who he shouted orders to, but it sounded like he lit a fire under someone's ass. While he finished his call, I went inside and crashed onto the sofa, the weight of the day wearing on me. People that really loved me warned me about how he treated me, and I blew them off like it was nothing, thinking I knew what I wanted. People didn't exaggerate and, once the rose-colored glasses came off, I was ashamed of myself.

I called Lisa to let her know Jake showed up. She was less than thrilled. She insisted on coming, anyway. I wasn't sure if I was more afraid of what she would do to Nick or to Jake.

* * *

Jake

Within five minutes of my call, Brody had contacted my lawyers and sent me the email file on Nick, but I told Brody not to show it to me because I wasn't sure I could trust myself. I only meant it to be a backup plan in case of an emergency, and Nick pushed the alarm today.

I filtered through it, relieved to have more on him. Nick was a bigger piece of shit than I realized. Concocting my plan, I told Millie I was going to grab lunch. I hopped in the car, readying myself to pay a visit to Mr. Nicholas Patrick Maclean.

I refuse to have him hold Aubree for ransom as if she was a pawn in his game. Nick should be a warning sign to women, to be careful who they have kids with.

I plugged the address into the GPS. I learned he ran a small music store in the next town over, funded by his in-laws. They already owned a chain of boutique kitchen housewares stores. I guess they didn't want their new son-in-law in the rock and roll life, especially since his gig record wasn't anything spectacular. Most of it was small clubs around Toronto or a few of the neighboring towns. A particular interest I held in the report was that Nick was still celebrating each gig with a different woman each night. *The balls on this guy.* What would his pregnant wife think if this should come out?

I spotted him through the store window displays, strumming an acoustic guitar. He looked up when the door chime went off.

"What the fuck do you want?" he barked when he noticed me.

"What do you think?"

"Hey, I let you guys take Aubree to Florida." I wanted to punch the smirk off his face.

"Yup, it was a great family trip for us. It was incredible watching Aubree meet all her favorite characters and the smile on her face from the rides. Game changer, man." I smirked, watching him squirm as his face contorted with anger. "Millie mentioned you want full custody of Aubree now?"

"Oh, she told you," he scoffed. "Let me guess, you came to threaten me, tell me it won't happen, right?" A cocky smile plastered his thin face. "There are cameras all over the place. Go ahead, take a swing."

There was nothing I wanted more than to punch the everloving shit out of him, but I knew the game he was playing. If I was a loose cannon, it could jeopardize Millie's custody, but that would not stop me from teaching that asshole a lesson.

"First, I don't give a shit about the cameras." I pointed around at each of them. "Second, I don't need to threaten you. I did some thorough research on you, you know, to find out exactly what kind of guy you were." He stood up abruptly while I reached for my phone.

"Let's see here... How's business? Not this one." I swirled

my fingers around the place. "No, I mean the less-than-legal pot shop you run out of the back of this place? I mean, your in-laws can't really believe you sell that many music lessons. If it's not enough, how about we break the news to your pregnant wife that you use the vacant upstairs apartment to fuck your way through your groupies? Oh, you try to be careful, but no one is that careful, Nick." I slammed a picture of him and a woman half-dressed in the shop's window, right next to the advertisements for music lessons.

"Fuck you!"

"Ha! I'm not even done yet. I bet it would be easy for the courts to pull up your criminal record. Do Millie or Misha know about your armed robbery stunt and the assault charges from your high school girlfriend, Sara?" The color drained from his face.

Exactly where I needed him to be. Fucked. Just like he had done to Millie. I laughed in his face, knowing he had something to lose now.

"Listen here, you piece of shit." I inched closer, gripping the counter. "You'd be lucky to ever see your kids again if this got out. But, if you're a good boy, I'll work with you. I'll have my lawyers draw up a custody agreement that still lets you see Aubree with a few fucking conditions. You won't ever hold Aubree against Millie again, you'll have an arranged drop off and pick up spot *not* at our house, and you'll be fucking respectful to Millie from now on."

"What if I don't agree?" He said through gritted teeth, despite knowing I had him by the balls.

"I may not know the Canadian system too well, but I have a hard time believing they'd award custody of a small child to a violent criminal with documented abuse, who is also a drug dealer, over a stable, loving mother with no vices. It's your choice, Nick, and you should probably pick the right one for once," I ordered, walking away and slamming the door behind me.

My nerves shook with how badly I wanted to lunge over the counter at him, but my revenge was going to be sweeter than physical pain. He and I both knew he had no choice but to agree. He was a fucking moron, but I'd bet my career he wasn't willing to risk it. I went and picked up Thai food, whistling the entire time. No matter what happened between Millie and me, I knew I could do this for them.

* * *

Amelia sat on the couch with her laptop perched on her knees, like a woman on a mission, when I greeted her and placed the food in front of her. I didn't know how she'd take what I had done, but I was going to tell her, anyway.

"What are you doing?" I asked.

"Plotting murder." She deadpanned.

I exhaled nervously, hoping she wouldn't be mad at what I had done. I took the computer from her and grabbed her hands. Her gaze lifted to mine, her eyes still red and puffy from crying.

"I wouldn't worry too much about Nick's threats," I began, squeezing her hands.

"Oh, God, do you need an alibi?"

I should probably be worried that she was confident in asking me that. I shook my head. "Don't be mad, but... I had him looked into and there's enough to keep him away."

Her eyes widened. "You what?"

"Amelia, it was for your safety, for Aubree's safety." I held my ground. "Did you know about his past?"

"In what way? His ex? His troubles in school?"

Well, this was interesting. It seems he confessed something, but I was curious about what Nick would say.

"He said his ex-girlfriend spread lies because she thought he was cheating, and she claimed he hit her," Millie explained. "He started having a hard time at school, failing his classes. It was causing a strain on his family. They moved here to get away from her."

Frustration coursed through me. I pulled my hands down my face, trying to compose myself. She needed to know how deep that fucker's lies were.

"Everything he told you was a lie."

"What?"

I pulled out my phone, handing it to her. She paused nervously, but I knew the only way she could believe it was to see it. She read the information Brody sent me, as she paced around the room, her hand on her forehead. A gasp here or there.

"Oh my God, oh my God. Everything was a lie. Son of a bitch, I trusted him. Armed robbery? Assault? He said she made it up. She was spiteful. He always said I would do the same to him. Jesus, Jake, I begged him to stay with me so many times.

Desperately, I tried to prove I loved him and wouldn't turn against him. He made me believe she lied. Fuck, I was so stupid."

I clutched her shoulders, grounding her. "Amelia, he manipulated and abused you. It is *not* your fault. He brainwashed you, hoping you would fall for his shit." I pulled her against my chest, my chin resting on her head. "I confronted him. He is going to back off, I guarantee it. I already have my lawyers drawing up a custody agreement and, before you get upset, I swear it's only what's best for you and Aubree."

Tears filled her eyes, and she tightly wrapped her arms around me. "Thank you," she cried. When she moved away, she flashed me one of her signature Millie smiles. My heart pounded at the sight of it. I missed that smile.

"Anything to see you smile," I whispered to her.

She turned to me. "I'm sorry."

"Why?"

"Since we started dating, my life has been nothing but baby daddy drama and it hasn't been fair to you. Nick had zero interest in Aubree, which is why I moved back here. To force him to have a better relationship with her. Never did I expect this."

"Listen to me," I tried to reassure her. "You and Aubree are everything to me. We can handle what Nick the Prick throws at us. He was stupid enough to believe you wouldn't move on from him. He thought he had pinned you down. What the fucking idiot failed to recognize is how absolutely incredible you are, and that you'd find a love like ours." I wiped a tear from her cheek. "I love nothing more than when I come home and you're dressed in a costume for no reason other than it was princess day, or when you read Aubree's bedtime stories with funny voices to match the characters. You're the sexiest when you're being an incredible mom, which is always."

The emotion in her eyes was conflicted as her gaze flicked between my mouth and my eyes.

"Jake, I can't take any more heartbreaks. You've saved me again today, but I can't forget what happened. I don't know if I can trust you."

I shook my head. "I swear I'm going to show you every fucking day that you've been it for me since the minute I saw you. For better or worse, right? This is the worst it will ever get, and I'll die trying before I give up on us." I took her hands in mine.

"I need some time."

"Take all the time you need. I am not going anywhere." Time kills a relationship when waiting for forgiveness, and I held my breath, hoping for strength. "I'll show you I'm not him and I will never be him. Please, baby." I held her to my chest. "I can't erase the past, and I already told you I wouldn't. I don't want to imagine a life without you."

"I don't know," she whispered.

Three words brought my world crashing down, but I refused to give up.

Chapter Thirty-Four

Millie

It had been a week since Florida. Jake had slept in the guest bedroom, and it was tough. Him helping with dinner and playing with Aubree like nothing has changed was confusing. I might have taken off the ring, but it didn't feel like we're over. What's worse was I was okay with being in limbo, afraid to let go and wanting to keep him.

He came into the kitchen, his earbuds in, and grabbed a glass of water. I watched his sweaty body glisten from working out as he gulped down the glass. Gaping, I was ready to forgive him right there on the counter. Why couldn't he put on a shirt? It was like he strutted around shirtless, showing off that delicious line from his low-riding shorts from working out. Hell, his frigging muscles were about to explode off of him.

Thank God, I was going to Lisa's on the weekend. They summoned me for a girls' night since I called them off when

Jake showed up. I had a feeling they were going to intervene again.

As much as the girls hated how Jake hadn't told me, they were equally mad that I didn't do my research. It was public knowledge he had been engaged and I never once asked him about his past relationships because, as usual, I wanted to stick my head in the sand. He was Jake Parsons. Playboy billionaire and a baseball player. Why would I want to torture myself with pictures of beautiful women hanging off him? *No, thanks.*

He stood against the counter and smiled at me. I blushed, knowing he caught me ogling him. "When do you leave for Lisa's?"

"As soon as I drop Aubree at my parents'. Nick is picking her up from there."

"Message when you get to Lisa's. I want to make sure you're safe." I nodded because, even though he didn't need to worry, he would.

As I drove to Lisa's, I got ready to hear it all from them. When I got to Lisa's, I felt the tension in the room before I even had my coat off. The girls were all quiet, sitting around the kitchen island.

Something wasn't right. Lisa's greeting would have been something like, "take your margarita and shut up while we lecture you on the idiot decision you made." My skin tingled.

"Who are you? What did you do with Lisa?"

She rolled her eyes at me. "Ha. Ha. Funny."

Sam and Gia sat on the other side, both with worried expressions. Sam grabbed a bottle of vodka and poured me a shot glass, placing it in front of me.

"Here. Drink this," she directed. *Well, that's not freaking suspicious.* Before I could ask any question, someone cleared their throat behind me. When I turned around, I nearly fell over. Haley, Jake's ex, stood there staring at me. *Yup. I'll be taking that shot now.* I grabbed onto the glass and poured it down the hatch to gain some liquid courage to face the woman I had screwed over without knowing.

I don't know what came over me, but I hugged her. "This was all my fault."

"Oh, no it isn't," she replied, returning my hug.

Stepping away from her, I dried my eyes and turned to Lisa, and mouthed, "What the hell?"

"The only way we would ever get the truth would be straight from the horse's mouth," Lisa said. "No offense or anything."

Haley shrugged. "Mild offense. But I agree. When Lisa called me, I thought it was absurd, but here I am. Mostly because she scares me." She winked.

I laughed. "Yeah, she can be a lot."

She clasped her hand over my forearm and her eyes cast down. "I'm sorry. I didn't know, you didn't know."

"Why are you apologizing to me? I was the one who ruined your relationship. You were engaged."

"There wouldn't have been a wedding, anyway," she declared. *At least that confirms what Jake had told me, but then why was he celebrating his bachelor party?*

We sat down around the island while Lisa poured out drinks, listening to Haley explain another part of their story. "I knew Jake was going through a rough patch after his last break up, and he was a bit of a playboy, but I could see it was all just a front for his heartbreak. I had met him through a charity event, and I was nervous at first, but we took things slow and kept it casual. His ex-did a real number on him. One of those princess types, landing herself a big baseball player. She used him for everything, then trampled on his heart when she left him for someone richer, so she thought. She tried to come crawling back once she found out who Jake was."

I stared blankly. My heart tightened for him. Not knowing

if someone truly loved you or just wanted to use you was an awful experience.

"Jake was amazing. We became friends with benefits more than a relationship. We lived separately, despite him asking me to move in, because I didn't feel the need to. He was gone so much for baseball, so we barely saw each other. In fact, his old PA and I had a better relationship. There were days we would go without talking or texting. It was weird. I'm not blaming Jake for that. It was me as well. I was busy running my store, and he had his career. That's how things went."

The man she talked about wasn't *my* Jake. He was persistent, and he wouldn't have accepted not communicating, no matter the distance. He couldn't keep his eyes or hands off me.

Her eyes softened. "You should know, he told me the minute he got home from the cruise. I was so damned relieved I cried. It felt like a weight had lifted. I already had cold feet with the wedding, and I was planning on calling it off, anyway. But I didn't want to hurt him after knowing his past. My friends and family thought I was nuts. Who didn't want a rich, famous, nice guy? It was a dream for everyone but me. I felt like an asshole."

In shock, everything we'd gone through crashed against my heart, and I glanced around at my friends, not sure what to do. Haley put her hand on my shoulder tentatively, getting my attention as she continued.

"I was in love with someone else."

Gia dropped a spoon, getting my attention. I think we were all on the edge of our seats. All that was missing was the popcorn.

"Sorry. I was just... Wow," Gia uttered as sat back down with wide eyes.

"I had already met Luca two months before. He was a photographer assigned to the magazine featuring my store. It was an instant connection. The minute I talked to him, I had a smile that wouldn't go away. It started harmlessly over work stuff, but the more time I spent with Luca, the less I wanted to go through with the wedding. I fought it. I told myself to ignore my growing feelings, but I craved to be around Luca. Every time my phone went off, I hoped it was him. It was like nothing I'd felt with Jake. He felt the same and told me right before our bachelor parties. It was only then I told myself I had to end things with Jake, so when he came home and told me what happened, I was so fucking happy."

"It still doesn't excuse his behavior. He didn't know all of that."

"True. He's a moron, but let me say this... for him to act on his feelings, you must have flipped his world upside down. Jake is one of the most loyal guys I've ever met. The one thing I learned was that love comes at the most inopportune time. What you do with it matters. From what I hear about you two, Jake made the right choice. I loved him, but he wasn't the guy for me. He is the right guy for you. Don't let me be the reason it doesn't work."

Was she right? If Jake told me he was engaged, I would have bolted and never taken a chance. There would never have been an *us*. I'm not sure I would have felt the love that I have since he came into my life, and I probably wouldn't have learned that I wanted and deserved that all-encompassing love.

"Thank you for coming to talk to me. It takes a lot for you to come help your ex-fiancé," I laughed nervously.

She grinned. "I know. They should give me an award or something." She flipped her hair and winked. "Come on, let's get drunk and become totally awkward friends before you go back and forgive him," she smiled. "And you will. I can see you really love him. One day, this will all be a funny story of you sweeping him out from under me, and we'll all laugh. But you should totally make him sweat it out a bit more. He needs to grovel."

We were in awe of her. It kind of sucked that she was so damn awesome because she gave me a lot to think about. Most of it wasn't about how Jake and I met and the surrounding circumstances. I threw myself at him, wanting nothing but a good time. What I got was a lifetime. It wasn't our past I was concerned about, but our future and what it looked like if he wasn't in it. An overwhelming pit formed in my stomach, because I couldn't imagine not being together.

* * *

Jake

My nerves were on fire standing outside Lisa's bar, but I needed to win back my girl. Lisa had called shortly after Millie left and demanded I come to meet them at her bar, but she wouldn't say why. I paced for a good ten minutes outside in the snow before I grew a pair and walked in.

She scoffed at me when I made it inside, forcefully pulling my arm as she guided me down a long corridor and into an office.

"Took you long enough," Lisa taunted. "I bet twenty bucks it was another ten minutes." Closing the door behind us, Lisa folded her arms and narrowed her eyes at me. "I rooted for you. I did everything I could to push you together." Her sharp fingernail poked me in the chest.

I threw my hands in the air in retreat. "I fucked up, but I swear on my life I love her with everything I have."

Lisa sighed and moved to the door, telling me to stay there. I didn't know what she was plotting, but my nerves were fucking fried. I heard Millie's voice a few minutes later, as Lisa pushed open the door.

"Ow! Easy, Lis. What the hell?" Millie tumbled in, freezing in her tracks. "Wh-what are you doing here?"

Straightening my shoulders, I swallowed the lump in my throat. "Everything I can to win you back."

Lisa closed the door, leaving us alone, to Millie's surprise. *If Lisa and the girls were with me, then this might be my only chance to win her back.* I was ready to lay it all on the line. I dropped to my knees and held Millie's waist.

"I can't breathe without you."

"I know," she whispered, running her hands through my hair. Millie kneeled down in front of me and kissed me, her lips trembling against mine. It felt like I came back to life when I wrapped my arms around her.

I fished her ring out of my pocket. Her warm hand fit perfectly in mine as I slid the ring back on her finger. "I love you,"

My thumbs ran over then large stone. "This never comes off again." she simply leaned up and cupped my jaw, holding me as she kissed me again.

A thunderous clap and flash of streamers met us when we walked from the office into the bar, where our friends greeted us in celebration. I paused when I met Haley's gaze as she approached us. Millie released my hand as Lisa pulled her into a hug.

"What are you doing here?" I asked Haley as we stepped to the side.

She nudged my ribs and winked. "Saving your relationship... I'm sorry... I..."

"That's on me." I held up my hand to stop her. "I should have told her, and I'm sorry for hurting you. I truly never meant to."

"I know. I'm sorry, too. I let things get too far without being honest with you. But look where we are now. It might be the one and only time two wrongs made a right."

I chuckled, agreeing with her. Millie hugged Haley like they were old friends. It was weird to see them get along, but I was grateful for whatever brought them together.

Sam knocked me on the shoulder, getting my attention before she handed me a drink. "Jake," she warned. "I love you to death, but if you ever hurt her, I'll bury your body where they won't find you. This is Canada, and we have a lot of forests."

I swallowed hard. "I'd buy you the shovel."

She smiled appreciatively as we clinked glasses, toasting to our deal.

Chapter Thirty-Five

Millie
New Year's Eve
One Year Later

Snow blanketed the mountains beyond the Blue Mountain Resort as I stared out of the picturesque window, waiting to be called into the room. Lisa fluffed out the kick skirt of my strapless all-lace mermaid wedding gown that shimmered in the lights while Luca, our photographer, snapped pictures.

"Oh, Millie. You are breath-taking," Lisa cooed.

I fanned my eyes, willing the tears not to come. "Don't do that. You're going to make my make-up run."

My parents entered the room with Aubree, Sam, and Gia, all pausing when they saw me. My mother gasped and hugged me, and my dad's eyes welled up with tears.

"Mommy, you're a princess!" Aubree's eyes were wide with amazement.

Aubree was precious in her miniature version of my dress and tiara, like a genuine princess.

"You too, Sweetie." I embraced her in a hug.

The double French doors opened wide behind us, and we took our places.

"Here we go, kiddo," my dad whispered in my ear as we linked arms.

The guests stood, and I smiled softly, with one person was on my mind. *Jake.* He stood with his back to the crowd, waiting for me to walk down the aisle.

The wedding march played and the anticipation of meeting my soon-to-be husband was overwhelming. The day was finally here. Jax and my brothers were beside Mitch, who was next to Jake. They were styled perfectly in their tailored suits, cleanly shaved and with fresh haircuts. They could have been featured in a wedding magazine. Their eyes lit up when I came down the aisle. Mitch leaned over to whisper something in Jake's ear, and I smiled.

Mitch clapped Jake on the back, telling him it was time to turn around. He slowly spun, and my heart exploded from the way he took in the long lace gown with the fit and flare hugging me in all the right places. He brought his gaze to mine, his eyes filled with tears, and for once, he was speechless.

Jake took a shaky breath and mouthed, "Hi, Blondie."

The minister started his speech, but I could only focus on Jake, and how one night turned into forever with him.

Jake held my hand in his, intertwining our fingers when it was his turn to say his vows. "Amelia Rosalie Harte, I never knew a love could consume one so much that without it I would seize to exist. Our paths crossed when we least expected and, like all really great love stories, it has a past, present and future that is only beginning. You have shown me what unconditional love is." His voice was thick with emotion as he struggled to get through the last of his vows without crying. "I promise to love you and Aubree every minute of every day. I vow to hold on to this love for a thousand minutes, hours, days and years."

He turned to Aubree. "My little princess, can I be your stepdad? I promise you will always be my number one little girl."

She eagerly nodded at him and jumped in his arms, giving him a big hug and a kiss on his cheek.

"I love you," he whispered to her.

"I love you too, Daddy," she quietly replied.

The tears I had been fighting gushed out. How did I deserve him? I grabbed hold of his hand and held it tight.

"Jakob Jenson Parsons, you are the epitome of what the perfect partner in life should be. You devote yourself to us every day. Since meeting you, I have truly learned what a soulmate is. I know without a doubt our love led us to each other. There's nothing I would change because I love us. The good, the bad and the messy. You are the love of my life and I only hope that I can make you as happy as you've made me."

Jake moved closer, our noses grazing as he tugged me tight against him. The gleam in his denim eyes made my heart race. "Baby, I live and breathe for you, and I won't stop living for you until my last breath."

I softly kissed him on the lips, and only a second later, he deepened it, dipping me back as a loud cheer from the guests filled the space.

"Of all the wild ideas about a bachelor party on a cruise ship, it turned out to be the best decision I ever made. I met the love of my life."

"There was no stopping falling for you, even though I tried. You have given me everything I ever wanted."

"We're just getting started." He kissed me softly on the lips.

* * *

My parents took Aubree for the rest of the weekend while we honeymooned. A horse and carriage waited to pull us through the snowy night to our private ski chalet.

Jake swept me off my feet and carried me over the threshold.

"You better not drop me."

He snorted. "Yeah, that would ensure I wasn't getting laid tonight. I'll make sure you're safe."

I swatted him. "Is that all you think about?"

He winked. "Just ninety percent of the time."

When we entered the cabin, rose petals covered the four-poster bed, the oversized fireplace was lit, and champagne was on ice waiting for us. Everything was beyond what I imagined.

"Wow, Jake. This is beautiful,"

He snaked his arm around my waist as we overlooked the magnificent view. "Better than you hoped?"

"Beyond my wildest dreams."

"Speaking off..." He wiggled his eyebrows and lifted me up, making me squeal. "In case I hadn't mentioned it for the billionth time, you are beautiful," he softly whispered in my ear. He squeezed my ass. "But this dress is nothing but trouble."

"You should do something about it," I said, as he gently dropped me on the bed.

We stared at each other like the first time we met. His eyes darkened with desire, making me want nothing more than to tear off his shirt. My finger coiled, telling him to come closer and, once he was within reach, I undid each button until his sculpted chest was exposed. I licked my lips.

"That wedding work out of yours paid off." I gaped at his rock-hard abs and perfect pecs.

He hissed when my nails ran across his nipple. His lips smashed into mine in a kiss so deep and passionate that my toes curled. Jake's hands slid along my breasts, down my rib cage, and to my center. His tender touch had me begging for more. He flipped me over and unzipped my dress in a way that was more erotic than sex itself. *Jesus*. I exhaled sharply as my body thrummed with anticipation. He tugged at the lace panties, giving my ass a smack. The sting was an extra layer of pleasure as he ran his fingers over the folds, already soaked and begging for him.

"You are so fucking beautiful," he groaned, before assaulting my clit with his mouth. I gripped the sheets when he licked and sucked, plunging his fingers in and out until I was screaming his name into the pillows.

He gripped my hips and thrust himself into me. My body had barely recovered from my orgasm, and the sensitivity had me ready to burst again. "Oh, God, Jake! I am going to come again."

"You feel so good, Amelia," he panted, grinding my hips further down. I exploded above him. He was right there with me. He tensed and rocked within me.

Lying next to each other, I smiled to myself. *This for life? Yeah*. It was about damn time I had everything I ever wanted, and it was because of him.

Epilogue

The entire gang joined us to celebrate Aubree's birthday. Sam and Gia came, even though Gia was expecting a baby boy any day. Lisa and Mitch showed off her fabulous engagement ring to my brothers. My parents talked with Jenna, Juliette, and Carl, who cooed over our newborn twin daughters. Ava let out a little cry, and Aubree immediately grabbed her pacifier and put it in Ava's mouth while Aria slept soundly.

Placing a kiss on Ava's head, Aubree shushed her. "It's okay, little baby. I will take care of you."

She was already such a good big sister.

"I guess you were destined to be a girl dad," I teased Jake. He watched our girls fondly, his smile wide and bright.

"Maybe the next one will be a boy," he chuckled.

I playfully smacked his leg and shook my head. A hush fell over the room as Misha, Nick, and Gracie came in, and everyone's gaze fell to the stroller that carried their little guy, who was almost one.

"You're too damn nice," Jake whispered to me, gripping my hand as they approached.

Aubree ran to Gracie, the girls nearly tackling each other. They were so happy.

I was better than Nick and Misha, and I wasn't going to disappoint Aubree by not letting her sister come to her birthday party. They were sisters, and there wasn't a way around it.

"Thanks for coming," I told Nick and Misha. "It means a lot to Aubree."

Nick simply tipped his head. Misha had become our go-between, and it wasn't as horrible as before. There had been a mutual peace offering, but I heard rumors about the leash she had put on Nick.

"Thanks for inviting Gracie," Misha replied. "We won't stay long, but we would like to take Aubree for the night after. We want to celebrate with her."

I turned to watch the girls head over to a bouncy castle, hand-in-hand.

"I'm sure Aubree would love that," I agreed.

Misha nodded and gave me a small smile before she dropped a present off at the table. Nick lifted Axel from the stroller and headed to the toddler play zone, mostly avoiding us. I was relieved he hadn't caused any trouble.

Jake laced our fingers together and sighed. "You're amazing."

"If nothing else comes out of this mess, I hope maybe we could be civil. I'm exhausted from all of it and, thanks to you, I'm not afraid anymore."

"It was all you, baby. You are a force to be reckoned with," he murmured, kissing my temple.

I felt surrounded by love, watching our friends and family. Jake let go of my hand and wrapped his arms around me from behind.

"You okay?" he asked, nuzzling his face against my neck.

"I am," I replied, smiling. "Because of you."

He was the best thing that happened to me. If everything I went through meant that it would lead me to Jake, I would do it all again.

Acknowledgments

Holy cow, I wrote a book! Honestly, this was such a pipe dream that I never thought would become a reality. When I set out to write this, I had a story in mind, but as the story went on, it became something more than I ever imagined it could be.

I did not do this alone. I had so much help as a newbie and every single one of them is what led me here to this moment of being able to thank all the readers. Seriously, thank you to anyone who reads my first book baby. I hope this story finds a place in your heart as it does mine.

I would like to thank my publisher Parcel & Page for taking a chance on a debut author, and for loving this story and wanting it to be told. Their enthusiasm for Millie's story was everything I hoped for. Without Parcel & Page, this wouldn't be my reality.

My Parcel & Page editor, your patience with my umpteen million fixes despite being 'edited' is truly appreciated. Thank you for making Millie and Jake shine and for helping polish this story beyond my expectations.

Holly Bourque at Red Door Editing, for giving me my first-ever developmental review even when it was far too early, and I'd lost my way in the storylines. Micheal Dolson at Winding Road Stories, you were the first editor who took a moment to help me out and for that, I will be forever grateful.

And I would still be in the drafting stages if it wasn't for my beta readers who answered the plea of a stranger. Karoline,

Gunvor, Karelin, and Kate, each of you helped me craft this story into something that resembled a book.

To Alyssa Pedrick and her critique giveaway, you helped me hone the hook, which landed me Parcel & Page.

I have to thank the entire writing community for the support and for teaching me how to go from the "I'm going to write a book" to getting it out into readers' hands! Without this special community, I would never have known about pitch events, writing groups, or beta readers.

And I cannot forget my true partner, my husband Hugo. My number one supporter, my alpha reader. You didn't even bat an eye when I laughed and cried with my characters. I love how you encouraged me to "smut it up more," but mostly because you truly believed I could do this when I came to you and said, "I'm writing a book." I love you. Thank you for all of it. And to my three amazing boys, anything is possible. Just believe.

To my parents, Mom, thank you for being incredibly supportive and for being an inspiration. I know things weren't easy, but I am me because of you. I can't imagine what being a young single mom was like, but I am glad you took a chance and found Dad, whom I thank endlessly. You have never been my stepfather, you've always been my dad.

And I wouldn't be anywhere without my absolute besties, Tammy, Karen, and Holly. All of you have been amazing sounding boards who listened to me tirelessly about this book and everything that came along with it without complaint. Without fail, all of you believed in me even though I did not know what would become of this idea I had to write.

About the Author

Madyn is a debut author writing contemporary romance with heat inspired by love, laughs, and Ladywood. But love's never easy, right? Although her characters may find their happy endings, they're going to have to work to get them, just like everyone else.

Madyn is Canadian, eh! Living in Ontario, Madyn and her husband are outnumbered by their three boys and an overly spoiled Cockapoo. Madyn is a coffee junkie with an unhealthy love of tacos and late night snacking with the hubs while watching TV. She loves to travel and you can often find her on a lido deck somewhere in the Caribbean (or at least dreaming of it).

Milton Keynes UK
Ingram Content Group UK Ltd.
UKHW020634081123
432193UK00019B/835

9 798989 194902